STREET LIFE

Ben stared at the screen, watching two teenage lads in a bedroom talking in what sounded like German. Suddenly the conversation stopped, the boys started to kiss and Ben realised he was watching a pornographic film. The boys, one with floppy blond hair and the other, who looked older, with short dark hair, had their hands all over each other. The dark-haired one was taking off the other's clothes and moving his lips down his naked chest.

Ben's cock began to stiffen in his underwear as he watched the figures on the screen pleasuring one another. He'd never seen one of these films before, but it certainly was exciting to watch. The fair-haired lad was now getting his cock sucked by the other one. It was such a beautiful scene. All the while, Ben's penis ached in his pants and he longed to be able to touch it and relieve himself. However, the rope prevented him from doing anything and all he could do was watch and imagine. Even though it was agony not to be able to touch his prick, he could not resist watching the boys having sex. By this point Ben could feel a sticky patch forming at the front of his boxer shorts. His cock was straining to be set free, but with his hands so firmly tied there was nothing he could do about it.

There was once again footsteps on the ladder, and his kidnapper came into view. 'Enjoying the film?' he asked.

STREET LIFE

Rupert Thomas

First published in Great Britain in 2000 by
Idol
an imprint of Virgin Publishing Ltd
Thames Wharf Studios,
Rainville Road, London W6 9HA

ISBN 0 352 33374 X

Cover photograph by Colin Clarke Photography

Typeset by SetSystems Ltd, Saffron Walden, Essex
Printed and bound in Great Britain by
Mackays of Chatham PLC

This book is dedicated to
Ian Blake

SAFER SEX GUIDELINES

We include safer sex guidelines in every Idol book. However, while our policy is always to show safer sex in contemporary stories, we don't insist on safer sex practices in stories with historical settings – as this would be anachronistic. These books are sexual fantasies – in real life, everyone needs to think about safe sex.

While there have been major advances in the drug treatments for people with HIV and AIDS, there is still no cure for AIDS or a vaccine against HIV. Safe sex is still the only way of being sure of avoiding HIV sexually.

HIV can only be transmitted through blood, come and vaginal fluids (but no other body fluids) passing from one person (with HIV) into another person's bloodstream. It cannot get through healthy, undamaged skin. The only real risk of HIV is through anal sex without a condom – this accounts for almost all HIV transmissions between men.

Being safe
Even if you don't come inside someone, there is still a risk to both partners from blood (tiny cuts in the arse) and pre-come. Using strong condoms and water-based lubricant greatly reduces the risk of HIV. However, condoms can break or slip off, so:
* Make sure that condoms are stored away from hot or damp places.
* Check the expiry date – condoms have a limited life.
* Gently squeeze the air out of the tip.
* Check the condom is put on the right way up and unroll it down the erect cock.
* Use plenty of water-based lubricant (lube), up the arse and on the condom.
* While fucking, check occasionally to see the condom is still in one piece (you could also add more lube).

* When you withdraw, hold the condom tight to your cock as you pull out.
* Never re-use a condom or use the same condom with more than one person.
* If you're not used to condoms you might practise putting them on.
* Sex toys like dildos and plugs are safe. But if you're sharing them use a new condom each time or wash the toys well.

For the safest sex, make sure you use the strongest condoms, such as Durex Ultra Strong, Mates Super Strong, HT Specials and Rubberstuffers packs. Condoms are free in many STD (Sexually Transmitted Disease) clinics (sometimes called GUM clinics) and from many gay bars. It's also essential to use lots of water-based lube such as KY, Wet Stuff, Slik or Liquid Silk. Never use come as a lubricant.

Oral sex
Compared with fucking, sucking someone's cock is far safer. Swallowing come does not necessarily mean that HIV gets absorbed into the bloodstream. While a tiny fraction of cases of HIV infection have been linked to sucking, we know the risk is minimal. But certain factors increase the risk:
* Letting someone come in your mouth
* Throat infections such as gonorrhoea
* If you have cuts, sores or infections in your mouth and throat

So what is safe?
There are so many things you can do which are absolutely safe: wanking each other; rubbing your cocks against one another; kissing, sucking and licking all over the body; rimming – to name but a few.

If you're finding safe sex difficult, call a helpline or speak to someone you feel you can trust for support. The Terrence Higgins Trust Helpline, which is open from noon to 10pm every day, can be reached on 0171 242 1010.

Or, if you're in the United States, you can ring the Center for Disease Control toll free on 1 800 458 5231.

One

———

B en opened his eyes to the usual display of posters and records that lined his bedroom walls and floor. It was another day closer to his exams and the longer he spent in bed the less time he would have to revise in. His mum had already yelled from the bottom of the stairs so he knew that it wouldn't be long before she would enter the room, offer tea and force him to get up and study.

He leaned out of the bed and pressed play on his CD player. The Velvet Underground started up – the same album he had fallen asleep to the previous night. He turned up the volume and turned over in the bed, enjoying the sound and the relaxation. It was a bright May morning and the light that streamed in through his yellow bedroom curtains, together with Lou Reed's singing, was enough to prevent him from falling back to sleep.

'Ben.' His mother's inevitable call came from outside the door. 'You awake, love?' The door opened before he had a chance to reply. 'I've brought you a cup of tea.'

'Thanks,' said Ben, turning over in the bed in order to smile at her as best he could first thing in the morning. He did not hate her as most other kids of his age did their parents, but just resented being forced to study when all he wanted to do was lounge in bed, listen to music and soak up the atmosphere.

'You know what I'm going to say, don't you?' his mother asked.

'Yeah. I'll get down to it in a minute.' Ben sipped the tea and, as he suspected, it was too hot. He preferred it warm and milky, but his mother always forgot.

He knew that after a shower and some breakfast he would have to revise. The A level exams were coming up next month and he still had so much work to do before he would be able to walk into the school hall with confidence. It was the same school hall that he'd seen every weekday morning since he was thirteen and had first been sent there. It was an independent school that his parents — when they were still together — had agreed would give him the best possible education and thus the best start in life. Ben had wanted to go to the local high school, but his opinion didn't count at the age of thirteen. So, here he was five years later: still there, and thoroughly sick of it. The end of the exams couldn't come soon enough for him and many a time he'd contemplated running away somewhere more exciting and forgetting the whole A level business.

His mother left the room, having made him promise to be out of bed in five minutes. The Velvet Underground were singing about how they were set free and Ben wished he was too. He lay under the covers, a hard-on distracting his thoughts from study or exams. As usual his best friend, Paul, came instantly to mind. He reached down below the covers, slipped his hands under the waistband of his boxer shorts and began to stroke his stiff cock, a picture of Paul at the front of his mind. He always felt horny in the mornings, but this time was even worse than usual. Ben had not made himself come for several days and the urge to wank the shaft of his erect prick was so acute that he automatically closed his eyes, fixed his attention on the image of Paul's arse — which he had memorised from the changing rooms and running behind him on cross-country runs — and pulled the loose foreskin backwards and forwards over the swollen head. Ben felt waves of pleasure swelling from the base of his cock and let his other hand take hold of his balls and softly rub them. He began to feel the aching sensation you get as your body becomes aware of your mental desire to ejaculate.

Ben straightened his legs, pointed his toes and arched his back slightly. He imagined Paul slowly undressing in front of him and wondered what his cock might look like. He pictured it as huge and pendulous and hanging within his reach. As Ben turned these thoughts over in his mind he stroked, with ever-increasing energy, his straining penis. A trickle of pre-come eased its way out of the head of his cock and he rubbed the liquid about until it made the head slippery. The feeling caused his whole body to shudder.

'Ben? Are you up yet?' His mother's voice drifted up the stairs.

'Kind of,' he muttered under his breath and released his member so that it flapped back against his stomach and left a sticky patch there. 'In a minute.' Ben jumped out of bed, his cock still hard, and, grabbing his dressing gown, headed towards the bathroom.

He stood in front of the mirror over the sink and eyed himself with careful consideration. He could not decide whether he thought himself attractive or not. He had floppy brown hair cut short at the sides and back that fell with a central parting across his forehead. His eyes were large and sad and dark brown. His lips were thick and clearly defined along their perimeter. Ben didn't like his nose. He thought it was small and a little too turned up at the end. He pushed the bangs of hair back from his eyes, pouted into the mirror and decided that he was quite sexy. He'd screw him, even if no one else would!

Ben took off his dressing gown, slipped down his underwear and turned on the shower. The water felt warm and calming on his skin and he once again began to stroke his cock. It immediately stiffened back into its earlier position and thoughts filled his mind. Firstly there came Paul and how cute he looked. Then Ben thought about escaping from his home, his mother, the exams, the dull suburbs. He thought about how exciting it would be to live in London, where he knew how easy it was to find boys who liked boys. There was no one he knew of in his home town who felt the same as him. He couldn't share his feelings with his friends – they wouldn't understand. The only place he could meet other boys would be in a public toilet and he didn't want to get into that. The few brief dabblings he'd had with other lads had been in his early teens and tainted by the fact they had been usually one-off moments of childish curiosity. However, Ben took more enjoyment out of them than he knew he should.

The sensation from the jets of water hitting his cock and balls, together with his repeated rhythmic stroking, made Ben want to shoot his load. Reaching for the soap, he lathered his left hand and allowed it to stray over his arse-cheeks and then between them. With the other hand he continued to stimulate his penis. Ben's forefinger slipped with ease deep inside himself and he began to move it about, probing his own cavity. This made the feeling at the base of his cock grow all the more intense and he felt his orgasm swell up from within. His balls ached and the warm water that caressed them added to the sensation.

All of a sudden, with the thought of Paul naked in his mind, Ben could not stop himself letting a thick spurt of semen shoot from the tip of his prick. The feeling was overwhelming. Another jet came out, followed by another and another. Ben closed his eyes and let the feeling of the orgasm spread all across his body, while the water continued to fall steadily from above.

'What are you doing tonight?' his mum asked as she poured milk over Ben's cornflakes.

'I thought I told you. I'm going over to Paul's.'

'Oh, yes. That's right. You did say. You're camping in his garden for the night.'

'Um. Yeah, I think so. Just as long as it doesn't rain or anything.' Ben shovelled the cereal into his mouth. The wank had taken it out of him and he felt hungry.

'You'll be all right,' said his mum. 'Don't be such a big girl!'

'What?'

'You heard.'

Ben finished his tea and toast and sat at the kitchen table looking out of the window at the street and the parked cars. It was a small town in Surrey that he lived in, close enough to London to make Ben wish that he lived in the city, but too far away to make that dream possible. A train to East Croydon took twenty-five minutes and from there one could travel on to Victoria or King's Cross. Ben could not cope with how small-minded and insular his home town was, considering the fact that it wasn't really that far away from London – home of the brash, outrageous and free.

'Isn't it time you started studying?' asked his mother. Ben nodded and left the table for the confines of his bedroom and his books.

He switched on his stereo and changed the CD. The Sex Pistols this time. Ben liked the whole notion of punk, he felt it spoke to him, reflected his own urge to escape the humdrum suburban setting that he seemed obliged to put up with. He stretched out on the bed and looked up at the ceiling. If only he could find the nerve to leave it all behind.

Ben put some stuff into his bag: a T-shirt, a clean pair of pants and socks, cigarettes, lighter, his personal stereo and some tapes, toothbrush and toothpaste, deodorant and the tin that contained his dope and papers. He tried hard to think whether there was anything else he'd need to take to Paul's house. A condom perhaps? He chuckled to himself and thought, if only.

Ben shut the door of his room, said goodbye to his mother and left the house. The walk was short and pleasant: through streets filled with detached houses with garages and driveways, through the recreation ground where he had played football as a kid and out past the back gardens of some more elegant houses that put him in mind of Kensington and Chelsea. Ben was looking forward to seeing Paul's cheerful face, and as he walked he wondered what the evening would bring. He looked at his watch and noticed that it was six-thirty.

He knocked on the door. Mrs Jennings answered and invited him in, calling up the stairs for her son as she did so.

Paul came running down. 'Hi, Ben,' he said.

'Hi. How's it going?'

'Yeah, OK. Come upstairs.'

Ben followed his friend to his room and sat down on the edge of the bed. He was thinking how great Paul looked. He was wearing a sleeveless T-shirt that Ben had never seen him in before, with SURF BOY written across it, light cotton beige-coloured trousers and trainers. Paul sat down on the floor next to his stereo and turned up the volume on some dance tune. The two boys had very different tastes in music, but Ben didn't mind humouring his friend as they had lots of other things in common besides pop.

'So, what have you been up to?' asked Ben, reaching into his bag and taking out his cigarettes. He moved across to the open window in his friend's attic room and stuck his head out.

'Trying to revise and stuff.'

'Me too.' Ben lit a cigarette and inhaled the smoke. 'D'you want one?' he said, offering the pack to Paul.

'Thanks.'

'I can't wait till it's all over and we can get on with having some fun,' said Ben. 'I'm sick to the back teeth of school.'

'Don't worry. You're not alone.' Paul lit his cigarette. 'My mum's so bothered about me getting good grades. It's probably because she wants to get me off to university as soon as possible. Have some time to herself.'

'Are you still set on going to Bristol?' asked Ben.

'Yeah. It's a really good course.' There was a moment of silence. 'What are you going to do?'

'Don't know,' said Ben. 'I don't want to go straight to university. I've just done thirteen years of education, so I'm not ready for another three.'

'I know what you mean, but as far as I'm concerned the sooner I get away from home the better.' Paul took a drag of his cigarette.

'There are other ways to get away from here, you know.'

Paul nodded an agreement. 'I guess so.'

The two boys crowded near the window and smoked. Paul was looking out over the back garden and at the tent that was set up down there. Ben glanced at his profile from time to time. He loved to watch his friend smoke a cigarette, especially one of his. It was as if Paul were touching a part of him with his lips.

'Did you bring any gear?' Paul broke the silence.

'Yep. It's in my bag.'

'Cool. I've got some vodka that I stole from that party, so we can have that too.'

'Do you want a joint now?' asked Ben, a little too zealously.

'No. Let's wait till we get into the tent.'

Ben could not stop his imagination from running wild. He had fantasised so many times about what might happen if they were alone together in a tent. He wondered whether Paul might be feeling horny tonight.

Ben watched as Paul unscrewed the vodka bottle and poured them a large measure each. He filled the rest of the glass up with orange juice he'd taken earlier from the fridge. Paul sipped his drink in silence while Ben rolled a joint. He had plenty of gear as he'd only just scored the night before, so being over-generous was not a problem. They were at liberty to get thoroughly stoned.

'I really don't want to carry on with these A levels,' said Ben.

'No?'

'No.' Ben lit the joint and inhaled. 'What's the point?'

'The point is that we'll be able to get a place at university and get the hell out of here,' said Paul.

'Well, there is that. But then what? You have to go some place and get a job eventually, so we might as well get on with it now.'

'Yeah, I suppose you're right.' Paul took the joint that was being offered and put it to his lips. It gave Ben a thrill to see his friend getting stoned – to watch him relax under the drug's influence.

Ben thought for a moment. 'I might just chuck it all in and go somewhere more exciting.'

'What would your mum say?'

'I don't know. I probably wouldn't tell her.'

'Yeah?'

'I've got a friend in London. I could stay with him.' Ben took back the joint and sucked on it. He told Paul that he'd met a man at a party once whom he'd hit it off with, and had got himself invited to visit whenever he wanted. Somewhere among his stuff Ben had this bloke's address. He could always turn up on his

7

doorstep and hope to crash there for a few days until he found a place of his own. Paul agreed that this was an option, but Ben would have to be careful.

'Have you got his phone number?' Paul asked.

'No. But I'm sure he would be in.'

The two boys carried on smoking and drinking into the small hours. All the lights in the house had been turned off and they were alone with one Calor gas lamp and their sleeping bags in the tent in the garden of Paul Jennings's house.

'So what's been happening with Laura?' asked Ben.

'Oh, I don't think she's really very interested.' Paul poured the last of the vodka into their glasses. The orange juice was already finished, so they drank it neat. 'She wouldn't let me screw her or anything.'

'Not even a swift finger?' giggled Ben.

Paul shook his head and lit a cigarette. 'God! I feel so horny. Must be something to do with the summer.'

Ben's ears pricked up. 'Really?'

'I need a shag soon, I'm telling you, or I think I'll explode.' He let out a low chuckle. Ben laughed with him and began to skin-up again. Perhaps his friend was feeling pent-up enough to consider messing about with him tonight. Ben could not stop the idea from filling his mind to the point where he knew that he would sooner or later have to find out.

'You ought to try wanking,' Ben offered. 'I do.'

'Oh yeah, so do I. But that's not enough. I need the real thing.'

Ben's cock began to twitch at the thought of this. He imagined what Paul must look like stretched out on his bed pleasuring himself. 'There's no reason why you shouldn't be able to get it as often as you like.'

'What do you mean?'

'There are loads of people who'd do it with you. I'm sure,' Ben added.

'Like who?'

'Just . . .' Ben floundered, 'lots of people.' He drew in a breath and looked up at his friend who was lying on the outside of his sleeping bag, hands behind his head. He had dark blond hair that looked thick and slightly unruly, blue eyes, full red lips and soft cheeks. His body was slim, pale and hairless, from what Ben had observed in the changing rooms at school.

Paul dragged on the joint that Ben handed him. He looked stoned. His eyes had a distant, misted gaze and his body seemed relaxed. Ben wondered whether he could risk making a pass at his friend. He felt pissed and stoned himself and wondered how far gone Paul was. He looked at his watch. It was eleven-thirty.

'How are you feeling?' Ben asked.

'Pleasantly stoned,' Paul replied.

Ben stepped outside the tent and looked up into the night sky. The moon was almost full, with just the slightest amount still covered in the Earth's shadow. The sky was not as dark as usual. The fullness of the moon lit it up and made the stars seem dimmer, or further away. Ben drank in the still air and his head swam.

'What are you doing out there?' Paul's voice drifted from inside the tent.

'Just looking at the stars.'

'Why?'

'I don't know,' said Ben. 'Because they're there?'

'Right.' Paul's head poked out from the flap at the front of the tent and he looked up to where Ben was looking. 'Oh, yeah. Very nice.' His head disappeared back inside. 'Come in here and finish this for me.' Ben obeyed.

While he smoked the joint Paul lay stretched out with his eyes half closed. He looked tired, but maybe that was just the effects of the smoke. Ben's imagination was running away with itself. The moment was so vivid. He could virtually taste Paul's body as it lay before him, and he racked his brains for an excuse to touch him.

'God! I wish I had a girl tonight.' Paul broke the silence. 'I'm gagging for a shag.' He turned to Ben. 'Aren't you?'

'Oh, yeah. Definitely.'

'It's been almost six months since the last time. I'm just trying to remember the exact sensation of feeling her cunt around my prick.' Paul let out a sigh and swallowed the last of his vodka.

Ben had screwed girls before – he knew what it was like. Perhaps he didn't feel as strongly as Paul did, but he remembered that it hadn't been an unpleasant experience. 'Tell me about it,' he said.

'It was really cool. The first thing I did was to get her tits out and play with them.'

'Who are we talking about here?' asked Ben.

'Louise, of course.'

'Oh, right.'

'They felt really nice,' Paul continued. 'Next I took down her knickers and licked her out. She tasted amazing. Just the way a girl's supposed to.' He took the joint off Ben and began to smoke it. 'She was really getting wet and I knew it wouldn't be long before she'd let me fuck her. So I pulled my pants down and let her see my dick, which was totally hard by this point.'

'Of course,' Ben agreed.

'So, she was on her back on the bed and I started to slip it inside her. She parted her legs and let me in.' Paul closed his eyes and inhaled the joint. 'Amazing.'

Ben looked his friend up and down. He was lying on his back with one arm behind his head. His cock was visible through his flimsy trousers, and Ben could tell that it was hard. Paul was getting turned on and this made his own prick stiffen. 'Carry on,' said Ben, adding, 'if you want.' He wanted to hear the story, but he also wanted his friend to get as horny as possible.

As Paul spoke and recounted the tale of his sexual experience with Louise, Ben watched the stiffness in his trousers grow and his own cock mirror it. Paul described the feeling of sliding in and out of the girl, and how every movement brought him closer to climax. Ben leaned closer to his friend who seemed totally absorbed in his fantasy. There was a moment of silence.

'Ben?'

'Yes.'

'I know this sounds really pervy or whatever.' He paused and Ben hoped he knew what Paul was going to ask.

'What?'

'No. It's stupid,' said Paul. 'You'll think I'm a fag or something.'

'No, I won't. What were you going to say?'

Paul took in a deep breath. 'Would you mind if I got my cock out and wanked for a bit?'

'Sure.' Ben couldn't believe what he was hearing. 'No problem.'

'I'm just feeling totally turned on and I need a bit of relief, that's all.'

'Fine by me,' said Ben, his cock growing stiffer by the second.

He watched as his friend slowly unbuttoned his trousers and slid them down a couple of inches. Paul was wearing skimpy white briefs that fitted him tightly and gave away a clear outline of his cock. Paul glanced up a little sheepishly and then looked back down at his bulge.

'Go ahead,' said Ben, and he swallowed with excitement. 'Don't mind me.' Paul lifted his T-shirt slightly, revealing his smooth, flat stomach. Ben was thrilled to see a faint line of hair that ran around his navel and down into his pants. Then, looking down at his crotch, the lad carefully eased his underwear down and slipped his penis out.

Ben could not stop himself from letting out a gentle sigh. The sight of Paul's genitals was breathtaking. His cock was much longer than Ben had imagined, yet slender and soft-looking. It was not circumcised and the foreskin still covered most of the head. His balls hung down below, small and tightly arranged with only a light covering of hair.

Immediately they were exposed, Paul took hold of his member and began to stroke it. He started at the base and drew his fingers along its length until they delicately caressed the tip, which still lay concealed. Every now and again he would let his other hand engulf his tight sac.

Ben stared in disbelief. He'd never seen such a pleasant sight. His best friend, whom he had lusted after so long, was about to perform the most intimate act upon himself. Ben drank in the view.

Paul continued to stimulate himself. He seemed to have become accustomed to his friend's presence and relaxed his hands more eagerly around his solid member. Ben watched as the boy moved his foreskin back to reveal the swollen purple head of his prick. He could tell that Paul was turned on – both from the heaviness of his breathing and the clear fluid that had started to seep from his cock. With a slow, full movement of his hand Ben's friend masturbated himself, pulling the foreskin back and forth over the shining head. His other hand cupped his balls and gently massaged them.

Ben's own cock ached and pushed itself hard against his underwear. He noticed that the both of them could not take their eyes off Paul's prick. The sight of the lad's exposed member was all too much for Ben. He needed more than just the view – he needed to touch.

'Paul?' he said.

'Yeah?'

'Let me.' Without waiting for a reply Ben reached forwards and took hold of his friend's cock. Paul moved his hand away and Ben caressed the stiff pole, gently beginning to wank the shaft.

He felt nervous, terrified, not wanting his friend to push his hand away or cry out in objection. Paul had once again closed his eyes. Ben took this as a submissive gesture – a sign for him to continue. Just as long as nothing was said, he knew everything would be all right; he would be allowed to carry on.

Paul let out a quiet little moan and Ben took a firmer grip on his cock. He cupped his friend's balls in his other hand and squeezed them. They felt warm and solid. He wanked the cock as thoroughly as he knew how, making each stroke extend as fully as the foreskin would allow. A steady trickle of pre-come seeped from the opening at the tip.

Paul was now lying with his arms behind his head and his eyes half closed. Ben continued to wank him, delighted by his friend's unspoken consent. He ventured a hand on to Paul's exposed stomach. It felt soft and firm.

Ben's own prick throbbed angrily in his trousers and he felt desperate to release the tension that was building up there. This and his insatiable desire to taste his friend made him instinctively bend closer to the cock he was masturbating – so close that he could smell the musky aroma of Paul's crotch. Without thinking twice he opened his mouth and engulfed the head of it with his lips.

His friend voiced no objection.

Gently Ben moved his mouth up and down the head, using his tongue to tease it and every once in a while dip into the slit, from which pre-come seemed to flow rapidly. The liquid was virtually tasteless, but still somehow lovely to consume.

Ben worked away on his friend's cock, using both his hands and his mouth. He rubbed the shaft just like he did to his own member when he was alone in his room, and at the same time sucked at the firm tip. Paul began to pant and for the first time Ben felt the lad's hand on his leg. He couldn't understand what this meant, but hoped that his friend wanted to reciprocate the act.

Ben moved himself so that his groin was level with Paul's face; the two of them were now lying side by side, facing in different directions. Ben's cock was throbbing with anticipation. He sucked frantically on his friend and, as he did so, he felt his trousers being wrenched open, his pants pulled down and Paul's cold hands take hold of his cock and balls.

Ben, too shocked to know what to do, glanced down and saw his friend put his cock in his mouth. The sensation was overwhelming. He could feel Paul's tongue and lips moving furiously over his prick. It seemed like they were so intimately locked together – each had the other's cock in his mouth, giving pleasure to a friend.

Paul looked so angelic with his mouth full and his eyes half closed. Ben could hardly believe his luck. He sucked and wanked Paul knowing that at any moment they might both come. It didn't take Ben long to reach his climax and having his friend's prick in his mouth only shortened that time. He could feel how tight Paul's balls were and how hard the head was becoming.

Ben could no longer stop himself coming. It was the inevitable product of his friend's sucking. The semen rushed along his prick and out of the end. At that very moment, Paul too started to tremble, and Ben knew that he was also climaxing. A warm spurt of salty liquid shot out of the tip of the lad's cock and into his mouth. More semen exploded out after this, filling Ben's mouth with the heavenly taste of Paul's most private fluid. He swallowed it down, not wanting to miss a drop. His own release into his friend felt strong and relieving, and he hoped his semen was being consumed too.

Ben licked the boy's cock clean, taking the last drops of come from the tip and savouring them. He felt his penis slip from Paul's mouth and he heard a long sigh of pleasure issue in reply to his own.

The two lads lay motionless, and all that could be heard was the sound of wind in the trees and their heavy breathing.

'That shouldn't have happened,' said Paul. 'I'm not queer.'

'No. I know,' Ben said, not daring to look at his friend. 'But it did happen, and there's not a lot we can do about it now, is there?'

For a moment Paul was silent and then he said, 'No.'

Two

————————

'Hi. It's me.'
'Ben?' Paul's voice came from the other end of the telephone line. 'You all right?'

'Yes. But I've decided to get out of this place once and for all.'
'What do you mean?'

'Well, it was like I was saying the other night. I'm sick of living here and doing these bloody A levels. I've decided to go to London.' There was a silence at the end of the line. 'What do you think?'

'It's a good idea in theory, Ben. But what about the exams?' asked Paul.

'Fuck the exams. I can do those any time.'

'Yeah. But you can go to London any time.'

Ben was becoming frustrated. If he couldn't rely on Paul's support then who could he rely on? 'Look. I've made my mind up. I'm going. I don't care what you think.'

'I don't want to fall out with you over this,' said Paul. 'All I'm saying is don't do something that you're going to regret in a couple of months' time. Be rational about it.'

'I've been rational for eighteen years and now it's about time I did something that I actually *feel*.' Ben fell silent.

'OK. Fine. You know best. I don't think you're making the

15

right decision, but I'm still your friend and I'll be here if you need anything.'

'Like what?'

'Like advice or money or whatever.'

'Thanks,' said Ben.

Ben's alarm went off at six on Friday morning. He woke and quickly switched it off, not wanting to disturb his mother. He went to the bathroom and hastily washed and cleaned his teeth.

The first light of the new day shone in through the misted window. Even though it was the beginning of summer it still felt cold first thing in the morning. Ben shivered as he stepped into his underpants and pulled on a shirt. He'd packed a bag the night before so there was little to do.

He went downstairs and into the kitchen. The fridge was stocked up as usual. His mother thought of everything. A sudden sadness took hold of Ben as he gazed into the lit interior and selected some snacks for the journey. He was going to have to look after himself from now on. He closed the fridge door and took a last look at the house.

On a scrap of paper he tore from his notebook Ben wrote a message for his mother. It read: *Mum. Gone away for a while. Don't worry – I'll be fine. Will phone you at some point. Love, Ben.*

The train clattered out of the station and down the tracks towards East Croydon. Ben sat with his feet up on the seat in front looking out of the window. It was seven o'clock. He wanted to arrive in London early so that he'd have the whole day to locate his friend, persuade him to let him stay and take a look around the city. He planned to visit some of the renowned bars that night and find himself some excitement.

The train seemed to stop at every station on its journey north – places that Ben had heard mentioned in conversations from time to time but had never really placed. The towns looked tatty and depressing; insignificant uglinesses on the Surrey landscape. He was glad to see them pass by his window and disappear into suburban anonymity.

In his bag he had decided only to bring the bare essentials. Hopefully after a while he might find a job in a bar or something and get himself a room and have some money of his own. He felt determined to make a success of things; show everyone back home that he was quite capable of looking after himself.

It was not long before the train pulled into East Croydon station. He'd often been there as a boy when his mother had wanted to go shopping. It was a modern, functional station and Ben waited on the platform for his train into London. The place was crowded with office workers waiting for their transport to the city. He looked up at their tired, impatient faces and wondered what each was thinking. This must be a journey they made every day, but for him it was the first time – well, the first time under these circumstances.

As the train arrived in King's Cross, Ben put on his jacket and took down his bag from the overhead racks. It was a quarter past eight and for the first time he felt a little tired. There was, however, no time to rest – things were just beginning to get hectic and Ben could not afford to relax.

He got down from the train and stood in the Thameslink terminal, a little lost and uncertain what to do first. Here was London and he didn't really know anything about it.

Outside it was bright and warm and Ben breathed in a lungful of traffic fumes. People pushed past him and it seemed as if they were saying, 'We know where we're going, but do you?' This made him feel even more lost. Everyone had a destination but he was a wanderer, a stranger in a strange city.

Ben sat down in a cafe and ordered a cup of tea. He hadn't had one yet that morning and when it arrived he lit a cigarette and left the tea to cool down. He looked through the addresses in his diary until he came to Phil, the man he was planning to stay with: 129 St Peter's Road, Hammersmith, W6. Ben got out his tube map and saw that it was an easy journey. All he had to do was sit on the Hammersmith and City line until it ended and then ask someone where the road was.

★

He rang the bell again and waited for an answer. Nothing. He could hear it chime inside the house but there was no other noise than that. In desperation, he rang for a third time. There must be someone in, he thought.

'You looking for Mr Jameson?' A woman poked her head out of the upstairs window of the house next door.

'Er, I think so,' replied Ben.

'Well, he's gone away.'

'Oh.' Ben started to panic. 'Are you sure?'

'Yes, I'm sure,' said the woman. 'I'm looking after his cat.'

'Right. Thanks.'

The woman remained where she was for a moment, as if she expected Ben to say something else, and then she put her head back inside the house and closed the window.

Ben did not know what to do. He had nowhere to stay. This had been his only plan. Perhaps he should give up and go home. No, that would be defeatist. He felt determined not to let a minor setback ruin his new life.

Ben turned around, took a last hopeless look at the house and headed back in the direction of Hammersmith tube station.

The signs he was gazing up at said LIVE SEX SHOW and GIRLS, GIRLS, GIRLS. Their glaring neon bulbs were lit up even though it was still the daytime. Soho seemed sleazy and corrupt, just like on television. When he'd visited London with his mother, they had never ventured here. Bored women stood outside the sex shops and porno cinemas, occasionally inviting him in or just staring. Ben walked quickly past, trying not to catch their eyes or even be seen at all.

On Berwick Street he looked in the new and second-hand record shops. He knew that he couldn't actually buy anything. He had hardly any money and nowhere to play the records anyway. All the music he'd wanted but couldn't get at home was there. For a moment the city seemed the only place in the world to live – how could anyone survive anywhere else?

Ben carried on down the road until it came to Oxford Street. He knew where he was now. He had been shopping here with his mum before. It didn't seem so crowded today. Everyone was probably at work and only the tourists and the dispossessed hovered around claiming the city as their own. Ben didn't feel part of either category.

He passed by the shops, looking into their windows at the clothes and jewellery and all the things you could buy if you had the money and the desire. Ben still didn't know what he would do that night, where he would sleep, whom he could talk to.

Dusk settled over London as Ben sat alone on a bench in Soho Square. It was a warm evening and his jacket was enough to keep him warm. Suspicious-looking people scurried past, some of them looking down at Ben as he sat smoking a cigarette. He knew that he must look odd, just hanging around not doing anything. A few men eyed him up. Ben was flattered but at the same time unnerved. It was nice to be looked at, though, and perhaps even lusted after.

Ben had enough money to get a drink, so he walked back into Soho in search of a gay bar. They were not hard to distinguish from the others. You could see the clientele through the window. Their smart clothing and attention to detail singled them out as different to the rest. Ben was a little disappointed at their clean-cut looks and their exaggerated gestures.

He chose a bar that looked a little smaller and quieter than most and pushed open the door. This was the first time he'd ever been into a place like this. He knew nothing of the world of homosexuality and felt very scared to be standing alone at the bar, ordering himself a drink.

Ben took his beer and sat down at an empty table near the wall. It was only when he had lit a cigarette and taken several sips of his drink that he dared to look around the place and take in the scene.

It was still quite early so there were few people about. A lot of the drinkers seemed to be alone. There were, however, a few couples chatting quietly at tables or leaning against the bar. Every now and then laughter could be heard rising above the hush of their conversation. In the corner was a table at which sat four people – three men and one woman. They looked intimate and at ease with one another. The woman spoke with the twang of a foreign accent.

Ben sat with his drink and watched the other people. Those who stood alone occasionally glanced in his direction. When their eyes caught his, Ben looked away, not wanting to make them think he was interested. Some of the men were wearing suits as if they had just left their offices, while others were dressed casually – clothes that said an evening on the town.

One man in particular seemed to be staring at Ben. He wore a grey suit and looked about thirty-five. He was smoking a cigarette and sipping a drink that Ben guessed was gin or vodka and tonic. He could not help making eye contact with the man, even though he did not intend to. However, every time Ben looked up, the man was looking at him.

Ben lit another cigarette – he was practically chain-smoking – so that he had something to do with his hands. As he did so the man who had been looking at him came over.

'Do you mind if I join you?' he said.

Ben was rather startled to see him so close up. 'No.'

'You looked lonely sat all by yourself.' The man had dark hair and dark eyes and Ben thought that he was quite handsome. He was well spoken and clean-looking – someone you might find behind the counter in a bank.

'I wasn't really,' stammered Ben. 'I was just thinking.'

'I see,' said the man. He held out his hand. 'My name's Mark.'

Ben took his hand and shook it lightly as he presumed he was expected to. 'Right.'

'What's *your* name?'

'Oh, sorry. It's Ben.'

'Nice to meet you,' said Mark.

Ben was not stupid – he knew that the bloke was trying it on with him, but he was willing to humour the situation and see what happened. He smiled shyly.

'So, Ben, what do you do?' asked Mark.

'Well, nothing, really.' Ben thought of his new life in London. What was he going to do? 'I'm kinda looking for a job.'

'As what?'

'I don't really know.' Ben thought for a moment. 'Anything that pays well, I suppose.'

'Do you want another drink?' Ben had not noticed, but in his nervousness the cigarette in his hand had burned down and he'd drained his bottle.

'Sure,' said Ben. 'That'd be very kind of you.'

Mark got up and went to the bar. Ben watched him order drinks for them, pay the barman and sit back down at the table. 'Thanks,' he said.

Mark clinked his bottle against Ben's. 'Here's to you finding a job.' Ben just smiled. 'So where do you live?'

Ben was at a loss for words. What should he tell him? 'Well, I don't really live anywhere, to be honest with you.'

'So, let me get this straight,' said Mark. 'You haven't got a job and you haven't got a home.' He looked into Ben's eyes for a moment. 'If you don't mind me saying, it seems like you're in a bit of a mess.'

Ben didn't like the idea of some stranger making him face up to the drastic nature of his situation. He informed the man that he could cope perfectly well as he was and that something was sure to come along sooner or later.

There was a long silence which eventually Mark disturbed by saying, 'Look, Ben. I don't really know how to say this . . .' He broke off momentarily. 'But would you like to come back with me tonight?' Ben was taken aback. 'I mean,' continued Mark, 'I'll pay you.'

'Pay me for what?' asked Ben, not quite sure he could believe what the man was suggesting.

'Do I have to spell it out?' Mark's voice dropped to a whisper. 'Pay you to have sex with me.'

'No, thanks,' said Ben, shocked. 'I think you've got the wrong impression.'

Mark looked embarrassed. He said, 'Sorry. I just presumed you needed some money. We could have done one another a favour.'

There was an awkward pause, then he said, 'I really ought to go. It was nice meeting you.' He smiled at Ben and left.

The sky was black and clear. It was hard at first to see the stars but as your eyes became accustomed to the darkness they seemed to appear one after the other, as if they hadn't been there all along.

Ben took a swig from the Coke can he was holding. He was sat alone on a bench in Green Park. It was nine o'clock. He felt lonely and slightly afraid. The thought of Mark's suggestion was still buzzing around his head. Perhaps he should have said yes. It was surely better than sitting out here all night.

Just then he saw a figure approaching across the grass. It was hard at first to see the face but as it got closer Ben could tell that the figure was male and not old.

'Got a spare ciggy, mate?' said the figure. As the man stepped closer, Ben could see that he was young, not much older than himself, tall with fair hair that was short and spiky on top. He was very slim and his face was cute and boyish. He spoke with a broad Scottish accent.

Ben could not resist getting out his cigarettes and offering one to the lad. He took one himself and offered a light before lighting his own.

'Can I join you for a sec?' he said. Ben replied that he didn't mind and the Scot sat down on the bench beside him. He told Ben that his name was Lee and he came from Glasgow. He'd only been down in London for a few months and was living on the streets.

'What's it like?' Ben asked.

'OK,' said Lee. 'So, what's your story?'

Ben was wary at first. The lad seemed harmless enough, but then you never could tell. He was rough and obviously destitute and perhaps had made it his mission to rip Ben off, steal his money, beat him up. You never can be too cautious these days, that's what his mother had always told him – and for once Ben thought it wise to take her advice. He said, 'Oh, nothing very exciting, I'm afraid.'

'You must have a story,' insisted Lee. Ben hesitated. 'Look, pal, you're OK with me. I'm not trying to get information out of you to tell MI5 or your parents or whoever it is you're running away from -'

'Who says I'm running away?' interrupted Ben.

'We're all running away from something. I know I am. We wouldn't be sat here at nine-thirty at night if we weren't trying to escape something. We'd be at home in front of the telly, wouldn't we?'

Ben felt obliged to agree. There was something very reassuring about the soft lilt of Lee's accent and his bright blue eyes. Ben felt like he could instinctively trust him, but then perhaps that was just because he found him very attractive.

'So, what are *you* running away from?' Ben asked.

'Ah, that'd be telling. We all have our secrets.'

Ben knew that it was best not to press him any further. He changed the subject. 'Do you smoke dope?'

'Of course. D'you know someone who doesn't?'

'Yes,' said Ben.

'Who?'

'My mother.' They both laughed.

'You never know,' said Lee. 'Maybe you're out of the house when she does it.'

'I don't think so, somehow.' Ben got out his tin and started to roll them a joint. There was no one around so it didn't seem to matter that he was skinning up in public.

'Where are you staying tonight?' Lee asked.

'I don't really know.' Ben felt at ease enough to reveal the details of his situation. 'Where are *you* staying?'

'Where I usually do,' replied Lee.

'Where's that?'

'Anywhere that takes my fancy. You know, Knightsbridge, Holland Park, Hampstead, Mayfair.'

Ben laughed and handed him the joint he'd rolled. 'You mean, in the poshest doorway you can find.'

'Aye. You're starting to get the idea.'

Ben watched his new friend take a drag off the joint and inhale it deeply. His eyes were so startlingly blue and his face so angelic that Ben wanted to lean across and kiss him. But instead he asked, 'Lee, how old are you?'

'Twenty-two. How old are you?'

'Eighteen.'

'Same age as my little brother.' Lee smiled warmly.

'What's his name?' asked Ben.

'Joe. I haven't seen him in ages.'

'Tell me about him.'

'No. I'd rather not, if you don't mind.' Lee looked a little sad as he said this. 'Are you hungry?'

Ben said he was, but didn't have very much money. He wondered whether Lee knew of anywhere cheap they could eat. Lee was confident that they could get something virtually free. 'Where's that?' he wondered.

'Oh, anywhere you choose.' Ben was puzzled but was sure that his friend would sort it all out; he seemed terribly streetwise. 'How much money have you got?'

Ben put his hand into his pocket. 'About ten pounds,' he said, counting the money he found there. 'I've got some more in the bank, but that's kind of for an emergency.'

'No problem,' said Lee. 'We can use some of what you've got on you for a little pre-dinner drink and some more cigs.' Lee paused and smiled. 'That's if you don't mind.'

'No, not at all,' said Ben. 'But how are you planning to pay for dinner?'

'I'm not.' Ben looked confused. 'Trust me,' Lee reassured him.

Ben sat quite still on the bench in the park, waiting for Lee to come back. He'd given him almost nine pounds to buy cheap cans of lager and some tobacco. He was told to wait there until the lad returned. That was more than a quarter of an hour ago. The first seeds of doubt were entering Ben's mind. Had he been stupid and gullible? He lit his last cigarette and looked up into the night sky.

Ben knew that he was too young and naive to deal with something as difficult as London and wondered whether he'd be better off at home with his mum, continuing his studies for the A levels that loomed like a desperate reminder of his own failure to cope with life.

'Ben? Is that you?' Lee's voice drifted through the blackness and Ben sighed with relief. He could clearly be trusted and that made Ben feel a little better about being in London.

They sat and talked and drank the cans of lager, punctuating the drinking experience with joints that Ben rolled. Lee looked beautiful, he thought, in the light from the distant street lamps and the moon which was virtually full in the night sky. He wondered as to the nature of the lad's sexuality – he hadn't mentioned either girls or boys.

Lee talked of his life in Glasgow. He'd had a tough childhood. His father was a violent womaniser who cared more about fixing up and selling dodgy cars than he did about his wife or children. His mother was a drinker and Lee recalled her frequent drunken rows with his father. He was too embarassed to have friends over. The house he lived in only had one bedroom. He and his brother had had to sleep on a mattress on the floor in the front room, while his parents had the bedroom. These night times, he said, were his only times of peace. Alone in the room with his little brother they were able to talk in hushed voices about their parents and their plans for the future. Joe dreamed of making it big as an actor. He wanted to go to drama school, but thought he'd never be able to raise the money. Lee said he wanted to make sure Joe got where he wanted. He was good. The amateur plays he'd been in proved this.

Lee knew that nothing was ever going to happen if he stayed where he was, working in poorly paid jobs, waiting on other people and cleaning up after them. His brother was still at school and that didn't give him much opportunity to save up money for college. If Lee got a good job he'd be able to help Joe out. So, firstly he went to Edinburgh then Leeds and then Manchester. Finally, after having had little luck finding work, he came down to London. That was four months ago.

'That's the trouble with London,' said Lee, 'if you don't have a

job you can't get a place to live. And if you don't have anywhere
to live you can't get a job.'

'The chicken and the egg theory.'

'What do you mean?'

'Well,' explained Ben, 'each needs the other in order to begin
existing.'

'I see,' said Lee. 'But what's that got to do with being
homeless?'

'Oh, forget it.' Ben chuckled to himself. He felt drunk and
stoned and happy to be with a new friend on a summer's night.

The restaurant that Lee had decided they would eat at was in
Victoria, not far from the station. Even though it was late – almost
eleven – the place was still crowded and people were arriving all
the time. Lee explained that it stayed open later on a Friday night.

The waiters were kept busy with constant orders, tables to
clean and drinks to replenish. They buzzed about the place barely
noticing the customers coming and going. It reminded Ben of
dinners he used to have with his parents before they divorced,
usually when they had something to celebrate or else just couldn't
be bothered to cook. He'd never expected to be eating in such
style now.

Lee caught the waiter's attention and ordered them an expensive bottle of wine.

'How are you going to pay for that?' Ben asked.

'Don't you get it?' Lee sighed. 'Christ, you're so naive. We're
not going to pay for it.' His voice had dropped to a low murmur.
'When we've finished we're gonna do a runner.'

Ben was lost for words. Although he wasn't the most law-
abiding citizen that there'd ever been, he'd never done anything
as bad as this before. 'What happens if we get caught?'

'We're not going to get caught.'

Ben didn't say anything, he just looked at the menu.

After they had eaten three courses and finished off the second
bottle of wine, Ben felt full and drunk. Lee explained that they'd
have to make a run for it soon or otherwise the waiters would be
suspicious that they were taking so long to ask for the bill. He

told Ben that he was to get up in a moment, shake his hand, wish him goodnight and casually leave the restaurant. He would follow in a few minutes. Ben was to wait for him round the corner.

Ben did as he was told and left without being noticed by the staff. He walked down the road a little and waited for Lee. The door flew open and Lee came running towards him.

'Come on,' he shouted as he passed.

Ben ran after him.

When they reached the station Lee stopped. 'Easy, eh?'

'Yeah,' Ben agreed, a little out of breath. He looked at his watch. It was getting on for midnight. 'It's late, Lee. Where am I going to sleep?'

'With me, of course.'

A smile lit up Ben's face which he could not conceal, even though he wanted to. Lee's words, together with the way he said them and his Scottish accent, turned Ben on. He wondered whether something exciting was going to happen tonight. He certainly found Lee incredibly attractive. 'Where are we sleeping?' he asked.

'I thought we'd stay in this deserted warehouse I know of.'

'Where's that?'

'Under the train lines near Loughborough Junction.' Lee began to walk towards the station.

'Where are you going now?' asked Ben.

'I left my sleeping bag and stuff in a locker.'

'Oh, right.'

Ben followed him and helped collect his belongings, which consisted of a canvas satchel, two carrier bags and a huge sleeping bag. 'Are these all your worldly possessions?' he asked.

'Yes. I used to have more stuff but either I was forced to sell it or else it got pinched.' Lee was silent for a moment as if deep in thought, then he said, 'Shall we go?'

'OK.'

They took a bus that dropped them in Elephant and Castle and went the rest of the way on foot. A long, dark road lined with parked cars led the way towards the arches under the rail tracks that people used as workshops and garages.

Lee walked along the outside looking at the numbers above the doors. He stopped when he reached one that had nothing written over it. 'Here we go,' he said, more to himself than Ben. He extended an arm and pushed at the door. Nothing happened, so he gave the thing a shove and it creaked open.

Inside it was almost totally dark. The only light came in through a few gaps in the ceiling and far wall – streams of man-made light from the surrounding street lamps. There were some boxes in one corner and what looked like a sofa and armchairs in the other.

'So, what do you think?' asked Lee.

'Er . . .'

'Well, it's not the Savoy by a long shot, but it'll do fine.'

'How did you know about it?' Ben cautiously entered.

'A friend told me,' said Lee, dumping his belongings on the floor. 'At least we've got the place to ourselves. None of your usual homeless riff-raff to compete with.'

Lee busied himself with preparing a bed for them. He took the cushions off the sofa and chairs and laid them in an oblong on the floor close to the back wall. Then he spread his sleeping bag across them, folded up his jacket into a pillow and placed it at one end of the makeshift bed.

'That's a big sleeping bag,' commented Ben.

'I suppose it is. Keeps me warmer than a normal one, though.' Lee reached into one of the plastic bags and produced a candle which he lit and placed next to the bed. 'Shall we go to bed, then?'

'What, with the door open?' asked Ben.

'Oh, yeah, I forgot about that. Close it for me, will you?' Ben did so and when he came back over to the far side he could see that Lee was already in the bed. Ben stood still for a moment, not knowing quite what to do. 'You gonna get in or what?' said Lee. 'It's cold so I'd keep your clothes on if I were you.'

'OK,' said Ben and climbed under the sleeping bag. He turned his head so that he was looking at Lee's profile. The lad looked slender and beautiful lying beside him and Ben wished for the courage to say something, make a move on him.

'So, do you have a girlfriend?' asked Lee.

'No. Do you?'

'No. Not at the moment.' There was a silence during which a train slowly pulled itself across the tracks above them. Then Lee said, 'Can I ask you something a bit personal?'

'Yes.'

'Do you go with boys?'

Ben could barely believe what he was hearing. 'Why?' he asked.

'Because I think you're very beautiful, that's all.' And with that he leaned across in the bed and kissed Ben on the mouth. After a second Lee pulled away and just looked at him, his face still so close that Ben could feel his breath against his cheek. Then it was Ben's turn and he put his hand on the side of the lad's face and brought him closer. He moved his lips on to Lee's and gently kissed him in return. At the same moment they both opened their mouths and Ben felt Lee's tongue slide over his own.

It seemed to Ben that they had been kissing for hours, their mouths colliding, tasting each other's saliva. He held his hands around Lee's neck and softly rubbed the hair at the back of his head. It felt lovely to be so close.

Ben could feel the lad's hands running over his back and down the inside of his legs and he longed for their kiss to end in sex. He pulled away, too out of breath to continue.

Lee leaned forwards again and kissed his neck. Ben could feel the soft touch of the lad's lips on him, and every now and again Lee would lick him like a puppy would his owner's face. His breath felt hot and pleasant against his skin and the sensation of Lee's stubble sent shivers through his body, causing his cock to stiffen in his underwear.

Ben put his arms around the lad and caressed his back and arse. Lee's arse felt firm and rounded and he squeezed the cheeks and let his hands run between them, pushing the fabric of his trousers into the crack as he did so.

Lee once again kissed him full on the mouth, this time even more passionately than before. It was as if the lad wanted to consume him, taste every part of his mouth. Their tongues crashed into each other and they shared one another's saliva.

Lee stopped for a moment and looked into Ben's eyes. 'You're very sexy,' he said in his slurred accent. 'D'you know that?'

Ben just smiled and said, 'So are you.' He could feel Lee's hand rubbing his chest and legs. Then the hand slipped under his shirt and over his naked flesh. It felt cold but heavenly. Lee continued kissing him throughout.

Ben stayed motionless, not wanting to do a thing, but let Lee take the lead and give pleasure to them both. He could now feel the lad's hands stroking his hard-on through his trousers. It felt great, he thought. For once somebody was interested in him sexually. It wasn't one-sided like before. He could tell that Lee really wanted him.

The lad's hands started to unbutton his trousers and slide over his cotton boxer shorts. Ben could feel a hand wrap itself around his cock and massage it back and forth.

All of a sudden, Lee stopped kissing him and disappeared beneath the covers. Only the shape of his head through the sleeping bag showed his whereabouts. Ben felt his friend lift his shirt and kiss his stomach. The lad's tongue ran across his smooth skin and into his navel. Then his underwear was pulled down and Lee's hands took hold of his cock and balls.

Ben moved back the covers from them both and was just in time to see Lee's head move down and then feel the lad's mouth engulf his hard prick. It felt amazing to have his lips and tongue around the sensitive, swollen head.

At the same time Lee was rubbing his balls and gently wanking him. The rhythm of his hands coincided with the movements he was making with his mouth. Ben felt his whole body tremble as he was sucked so intensely towards the inevitable.

Lee moved his hand off Ben's balls and let it wander down between his legs. His trousers and boxer shorts were pushed even lower until they lay below his knees, and Lee stroked his perineum gently with the tips of his fingers. Ben parted his legs a little to allow the lad as much access to him as possible.

All the while, Lee continued to suck on his penis, moving his head back and forth over the shaft with ever-increasing speed and energy. And as he did so, Ben felt the lad's fingers push between his arse-cheeks and rest on his sensitive opening. Then he felt the incredible sensation of a finger being gradually eased inside him.

The combination of Lee's finger working its way in and out of his arsehole, together with his sucking, made Ben feel desperate to come. He didn't need to do anything himself, but just lay there and let the lad bring him to a climax.

Lee himself sounded like he was having a fantastic time too. His breathing was heavy and laboured and he was sucking so frantically, enjoying every moment of giving head, that Ben wondered who was getting the most pleasure from the act.

All of a sudden the teasing, stimulating movement of the lad's finger inside him became too intense and he could not stop this triggering off his orgasm. Ben let out a groan and thrust his hips further into Lee's face, which seemed to make him suck all the more zealously, and he felt himself begin to ejaculate. The first spurt was the most pleasurable and, as it shot out of his cock and into his friend's mouth, Ben took hold of Lee's face and pushed it firmly down on himself, holding him there, forcing him to swallow his semen.

The sensation of Lee's hot, wet mouth around the head of his pulsating, discharging cock was truly amazing. Ben could barely breathe. He wanted to shout out but felt too self-conscious. Lee continued to suck on his prick until every last drop of come had been drawn from it and Ben panted with exhaustion.

The feeling of lips around his cock stopped and Lee's face reappeared in front of his own. The lad leaned forwards and kissed him hard on the mouth. Ben could taste his own fluid on his friend's tongue and around his lips. It felt great to share that with Lee. And in this tired, spent state he felt that, for the first time in a long time, he really had a very special friend.

Three

———

Ben awoke to the sound of a train passing overhead. The building now seemed to be filled with shards of light and tiny specks of dust floating in them. Lee was sitting on the edge of their makeshift bed smoking a roll-up. As Ben opened his eyes the lad smiled at him.

'Morning,' he said.

'Hi.'

'Did you sleep OK?'

'Yeah, it wasn't too bad,' said Ben, trying as he did to suppress a yawn. 'It was warmer being cuddled up to you though. Come back to bed.' Ben stretched out his arm and stroked Lee's back.

'OK,' he said, smiling. 'You've persuaded me.' He pulled back the sleeping bag and slipped under it and into Ben's arms. They cuddled and kissed for a while, laughing.

It had been a great night, Ben thought, spending it in his friend's arms. He had woken up several times and just looked at Lee's sleeping face, marvelling at the luck he'd had in meeting him.

Ben put his head on the lad's chest and kissed him there. 'What shall we do today?' he asked.

'Funnily enough, that's just what I was thinking about.'

'And what did you decide?'

'Well, there's this bloke I met a few weeks ago that I thought we might go and visit him. He's nice enough. A bit on the dodgy side, but very generous.'

'What's his name?' said Ben.

'Eddie. He said that he'd be able to find me some work and a place to stay. Perhaps he can help you out, too.' He kissed Ben on the head and gently stroked his hair. 'Even if nothing comes of it, we might at least get some free drugs.'

'How come?' asked Ben.

'He's a dealer.'

As they walked down to Elephant and Castle tube, Lee told him that Eddie lived in Stockwell. Ben had never heard of the place. They took the Northern Line three stops south. Lee had wanted to jump the barriers, but Ben had insisted that he pay, not wanting them to get into any trouble.

'You'll never get anywhere with that honest attitude of yours,' Lee had commented.

They arrived in Stockwell at one o'clock in the afternoon, found a shop and bought a packet of crisps each. That was about all they could afford. The drinks of last night had used up most of Ben's cash.

Lee led the way. At first he had trouble remembering which road it was, but as soon as he'd found that, finding the actual house proved less problematic. He rang the bell and waited.

Ben looked up at the massive mansion block before him. 'Which floor is his flat on?' he asked.

'The very top floor.'

The intercom buzzed, as if someone had turned a vacuum cleaner on at the other end, and Lee was able to push open the door. They were let into a long narrow hallway with no doors on either side. At the end was a flight of stairs that led to a landing and another flight. This was followed by three more sets of stairs and then they were on the top floor. At the end of the hallway was the door to Eddie's flat. It was wide open and the sound of someone cleaning the kitchen came drifting out.

Lee stepped inside and gestured for Ben to follow. The first thing Ben could see as he entered was the toilet, which seemed to be the only room in the flat. However, as he turned the corner, four other doors became visible.

'Hello,' said a voice from one of the rooms.

'Hi. It's Lee.'

They walked into the kitchen which was the first door on the right.

'Do you want coffee?' said the voice.

'Have you got anything stronger?'

'There's vodka in the freezer.' Eddie appeared from around a corner and began to pour hot water from the kettle into a cafetiere on the table. He was not a particularly tall man and looked to be in his late thirties. His hair was dark with the first touches of grey apparent at the sides and his face was angular and attractive. Surprisingly, Ben thought, Eddie spoke with a refined, almost posh voice. 'There are glasses in the top cupboard on the left.'

Ben sat down at the table and watched as Eddie moved slowly about the kitchen, performing each part of the coffee-making process with precision and grace. He hardly seemed to have noticed their arrival. He had obviously been in deep conversation with the boy that, for the first time, Ben noticed sitting at the far side of the kitchen table.

Lee had pulled a frost-covered bottle of Smirnoff from the freezer and was pouring them some. 'Is this all right for you?' he said turning to Ben.

'Great.'

'Oh, sorry, I never introduced you.' Lee turned to Eddie and said, 'This is Ben, by the way.'

Eddie swivelled around in his chair and smiled at Ben. 'Hi,' he said. There was something very charming and absorbing about his manner. Even though he might not be talking to you, you still somehow felt you had his attention.

Ben smiled back and said, 'Hello.'

Lee sat down beside him and handed him a glass of vodka and tonic which Ben sipped occasionally. He lit a cigarette and just listened to the conversation that was going on.

The youth in the corner had long, dark hair that looked as if it hadn't been washed or combed for days, and a cute face. He was smoking a roll-up and nodding slowly at everything that Eddie said. Ben couldn't understand what was being said, but he was sure that it must be terribly important, from the looks on their faces.

After he'd poured out coffee for himself and the boy in the corner, Eddie left the room and came back with an ornate wooden box in his hands. This held a huge array of what Ben assumed to be drugs. Eddie took out some cannabis buds and began to make a joint.

Suddenly his attention turned to Ben. 'Do you want a line of speed?' he said.

Ben was surprised. It seemed a little too early in the day to move on to hard drugs. 'No. Why?'

'You look tired.'

'No. I'm fine. I just had a bit of a restless night,' said Ben.

'Oh, yeah?'

Ben just smiled and looked over at Lee who didn't seem to be paying much attention to what was being said.

When he looked back, Eddie was once again talking to the boy. He had lit the joint and was casually smoking it and sipping his coffee. Ben sat in silence listening to them and wondering what the day would bring. Eddie didn't really seem bothered by their presence. It was as if they'd always been there, unnoticed onlookers.

Occasionally Eddie would turn to Ben and ask him whether he agreed with some particular point in their discussion and Ben would just nod or shake his head, not really knowing what he was agreeing or disagreeing with.

Eventually, after the joint was smoked and the next one had been started, the boy in the corner mumbled something about needing to get to his Reintroduction to Society class and he stood up. 'Eddie,' he said. 'Can I take an eighth off you now and give you the money next time?'

Eddie nodded an OK and weighed up the grass for him. 'But

make sure you don't forget, because I never do.' The boy took the eighth and left. 'Shall we go into the lounge?' asked Eddie.

Lee went first. It was the room directly opposite the kitchen and quite different in style. The kitchen was light and spacious, and even though there were piles of papers and ornaments covering the table and shelves, it still appeared clean and what one might term respectable. The lounge, however, was smaller and darker. The one small window in the room was half covered with some decorated fabric. There were two dark green sofas and a patterned rug on the floor. In the corner was a record player and lots of records propped up on the floor and against the wall. Music was pouring loudly from the speakers.

Lee sat down on the sofa that faced the door and Ben on the one opposite the window.

'You all right?' asked Lee.

'Yes, I'm fine. It's just that I don't always know what to say to strangers.'

'Oh, don't worry. There's no such thing as strangers here.'

Eddie entered the room with his drugs box, the bottle of vodka and a glass, presumably for himself. He turned down the music a little and sat on the floor in the centre of the room. 'More vodka, anyone?' he asked. Ben and Lee held out their glasses to be filled. 'If you want some orange juice or tonic, then you'll have to get it from the kitchen. I prefer mine like this. You can taste the stuff better.'

Ben took a sip of his drink and realised that it wasn't too bad by itself. After you've drunk a few you hardly notice that it's neat. He watched as Eddie poured himself a large one, then opened his box and pulled out a bag of white powder. 'You sure you boys don't want some?' he asked. They shook their heads and Eddie proceeded to cut a line and sniff it with the aid of a ten-pound note.

Ben had hardly any experience with anything more serious than pot. He'd once tried an E, which was OK, but he didn't really know anyone to score off, so his experiments with Class A drugs ended there. It was shocking and at the same time exciting to see someone snorting speed as if it were nothing. It stole away the glamour that accompanies the act, but then again it showed that taking drugs is a reality and an everyday event for some people, just like eating or sleeping is for the majority of the population.

The music stopped and Eddie moved to turn over the record. 'Who's this?' asked Ben.

'Auntie Horrorfilms.'

Ben pulled a confused expression, which he hoped suggested he was trying to recall their name, even though he'd never heard of the band.

'You must know them,' Eddie said. 'They're one of the top new groups.'

'Yeah. I'm sure I've seen them on *Top of the Pops*.'

'So, Lee,' said Eddie, swiftly changing the subject, 'where did you find Ben?'

'I met him in Green Park, as a matter of fact.'

'Really?' said Eddie, not sounding at all surprised. 'That's cool.' He turned his eyes on Ben in a way that made him feel embarrassed, as if he were being mentally violated, scrutinised. 'So, Ben, do you have a trade?'

'What do you mean?'

'Well, where does your skill, your talent lie?'

'I don't know,' said Ben.

'Oh, there must be something you excel at.'

Ben shrugged.

'You're very well spoken. You must have had a good education. I expect your parents are rich.'

'They're comfortable,' said Ben. 'But that doesn't mean I am.'

Eddie smiled and lit a cigarette. 'You're twenty-two, aren't you, Lee?' Lee nodded. 'How old are you?'

'Eighteen,' said Ben.

'Perfect,' he said. 'Look. I've got a proposal for you – something that will make us both some money. This goes for you, too.' He glanced across at Lee. 'I run a little enterprise in providing services to respectable gentlemen who are unable, for whatever reason, to get any.'

'Get any what?' asked Ben.

'Sex.' Eddie dragged on his cigarette. 'Therefore I'm always on the lookout for new boys to join my team. What do you say?'

Ben looked over at Lee who held his eye contact for several seconds and then said, 'Wait a minute. Are you asking us to become rent boys?'

'Well, I wouldn't put it quite as bluntly as that,' said Eddie. 'But you're on the right track.'

'I see,' said Lee, for the first time seeming shocked and speechless.

The man in the bar the previous night flashed through Ben's mind. This was the second time in as many days that someone had suggested he sell his body. Perhaps it wasn't such a bad idea. 'What exactly would we have to do?' he asked.

'Ben!' Lee blurted out, exasperated. 'You're not seriously considering –'

'Let's just hear what it's all about first,' interrupted Ben. 'I'm not considering anything at the moment.'

Eddie took a swig of his vodka and said, 'All that happens is you –' he was choosing his words carefully '– service a few male clients that I arrange for you. You don't have to do anything that you don't want to. However, the closer you come to meeting their sexual requirements, the more they're going to pay. Obviously. I take a small cut of the payment and you get to keep the rest.' Eddie paused to pour himself another drink. 'There's a house,' he continued, 'where the rest of the boys live. You can stay there. You won't have to pay any rent, so everything you make is profit. Of course, the more clients you do, the more money you make.'

Lee looked across at Ben, a sweet, confused expression on his face. Ben smiled at him.

'Think about it,' said Eddie after a pause. He looked at his watch and stood up. 'Look, I've got some business to take care of. Why don't you stay here till I get back? It'll give you some time to make your minds up.' Without waiting for a reply, he left the room and went into the kitchen, where he busied himself moving papers around as if he was searching for something. 'Help yourself to anything. Treat the place as your own,' said Eddie's voice. 'The bedroom's next door.' He chuckled as he said this.

Lee raised his eyebrows in disbelief as they heard the door to the flat open and then slam shut. 'Bit of a character, isn't he?' said Lee.

'Certainly is.'

Immediately, Lee moved from his sofa to Ben's and put his arms around him. 'Are you all right?' he asked.

'Of course. I'm fine.'

'You're not going to start charging me for sexual favours, are you?' asked Lee with a chuckle.

'Well, I would if you had some money,' joked Ben.

Lee leaned forwards and kissed him. Ben tingled with excitement at the touch of the lad's warm lips and allowed him to push his tongue deeply into his mouth.

'I know it's stupid,' said Lee pulling away for a moment, 'but why don't we take advantage of Eddie going out and use his bedroom, like he said?'

Ben smiled and ran his hand through Lee's hair. 'OK,' he said.

The two boys left the lounge and opened the door at the end of the hall. It was a large room with heavy curtains covering the windows so that light was only able to enter at the edges. The double bed was pushed into a corner next to a desk that was piled high with paperwork and letters. Lee closed the door and pushed Ben backwards on to the bed. He straddled him and shoved his hands up the front of his shirt.

'God, your hands are freezing,' yelled Ben.

'Don't be such a wuss.' Lee smiled, lifted his shirt and kissed his smooth stomach, making Ben's cock immediately spring to life. 'Um,' he said. 'You have a lovely tummy.' With his hands still on Ben's bare flesh, Lee moved his face towards Ben's and kissed him deep and long on the mouth. Ben put his arms around the lad's neck and pulled him as close as possible. He wanted to make the most of every second of their time together.

After several minutes, Lee pulled away and started to take Ben's clothes off. Firstly he unbuttoned his shirt and pulled his body free of it. Then, with the grace of an expert, he began to undo his jeans and slide them down. As he did so, he gently ran his lips and tongue across Ben's taut stomach and bit at the waistband of his boxer shorts. Ben tingled all over and hoped that the lad would soon move down and give him the same treatment as he had the night before.

He took off Ben's shoes and socks and slid the trousers down until they dropped to the floor. He was lying on the bed now with only his underwear covering him.

Ben watched as his friend positioned himself between his legs, parting them a little in order to gain full access, and started to touch and kiss the area surrounding his underwear. Ben's prick was already as hard as it could be and he trembled a little at the tickling sensation as Lee explored his stomach and thighs.

He could feel the lad getting closer to his cock and the excitement had caused him to make his shorts wet with pre-come. Through his underwear, he felt Lee's hands roaming across his cock and balls. The lad's mouth was brushing against them too and in the same second his penis was slipped out of the gap at the front of the shorts and into Lee's warm mouth.

Ben looked down and watched his friend using his mouth to excite him. He felt Lee's lips and tongue move around the head of his cock and down the length of the shaft. All of a sudden he pulled the pants down so that Ben was lying there completely naked. Lee returned to the sight of interest and began furiously to lick and suck his balls and at the same time wank the erect member. He lapped at the skin beside the penis and all down the inside of Ben's legs, straining as he did so to reach between them and tongue his tight hole.

Ben parted his legs a little more and raised his knees a few inches. Almost immediately, Lee dived between them and began to rim him. Ben could feel the lad's tongue working away at the edges of his hole and then, quite taking his breath away, it slipped inside and he felt himself open a little to receive it. No one had ever done this to him before and it felt strange and rude.

After a while, Lee returned to Ben's prick and carried on sucking it, his hands either gripping firmly on to his balls or sliding between his arse-cheeks, exploring his hole as they did so.

Ben felt as if he might faint with the intensity of the feelings that now rushed through his body like a drug. He wanted to touch and play with Lee – to do, not just lie back and be done to.

Ben sat upright on the bed and pulled Lee up to face him. With his hands frantically undoing the lad's shirt, he let his lips explore Lee's face and neck, kissing and gently biting him with the greatest passion. When he'd taken off Lee's top, Ben started to move his attention downwards. Lee was standing against the edge of the bed and Ben sucked on his nipples. Firstly the left one, taking it into his mouth as a baby hungry for milk would, and ever so carefully using his teeth to bite and nibble at it. All the while, his hand played with and pinched Lee's other nipple. Then he swapped over and gave the right nipple some attention from his mouth. He could hear the lad letting out yelps of pleasure and felt a hand grab hold of his hair at the back and push his face closer to Lee's chest.

Next Ben moved down the torso and licked at the lad's slender stomach. The skin tasted salty and he gently bit at it. His hands were now running over Lee's trouser-clad buttocks and between his legs. He was desperate to take his pants down and suck on the lad's cock, just as he had been sucked.

Ben began to undo his friend's trousers and soon they fell to the floor. Lee stood in front of him in just his cotton briefs, which clung tightly around his genitals. Last night Ben had not felt as if he was able to do to the lad what he was now about to do.

He could see the outline of Lee's cock and balls through the material and could not resist leaning close and taking a sniff at them. He knew that Lee lived on the streets and probably didn't wash very often, so he was pleasantly surprised by the stale, musky odour that filled his nostrils. It smelt strong and masculine, like the smell that used to waft from the changing rooms at school every time there was a rugby match. Ben inhaled deeply and let his hands run over the bulge in the front of the briefs. He could tell that Lee was erect and could not help kissing the stiff member.

Barely able to contain his excitement, Ben pulled the lad's pants down at the front and for the first time was confronted with Lee's penis. He reached out for Lee's balls and squeezed them in the

41

palm of his hand. With his other hand he grasped the erect shaft and angled it down towards his lips. Ever so gently, he drew back the lad's foreskin to expose the shiny, purple head and licked the tip of it with his tongue. There was a tiny droplet of pre-come there which Ben eagerly drank down.

He looked up at Lee's face and smiled sweetly before taking as much of his cock into the cavity of his mouth as was possible. The penis was not exactly long, but it was certainly thick. Ben found it difficult to stretch his lips around its circumference. However, as soon as it was in his mouth, it seemed to fit and he started to move his lips up and down the length, caressing Lee's balls as he did.

Lee let out a grunt of pleasure and Ben pulled his pants down completely, exposing the lad's buttocks. He squeezed and caressed them, and every now and again, while he sucked away, let his hand slip between them and rest on Lee's arsehole.

The lad's prick felt so hard in his mouth and he enjoyed every second of sucking it. Ben pushed him forwards so as to take in as much of it as he could. Soon he found his fingers slowly slipping into Lee's bottom. His arsehole felt warm and tight around the two digits that it engulfed and Ben sank them inside as deeply as he could without hurting his friend.

This was obviously too much for Lee and he let out several groans of pleasure, as if he were bursting with uncontrollable excitement. Ben sucked away furiously and clenched his free hand firmly around the lad's balls.

All of a sudden Lee went silent and then, to Ben's surprise and delight, a spurt of semen shot out of the cock in his mouth and he swallowed it down immediately. More come came flooding out and he savoured the flavour of it.

When Lee finally stopped ejaculating, Ben let the cock slip from his mouth and licked the head, just in case there was a trace of semen he'd missed before. Lee fell gently forwards and kissed him on the lips. Ben hoped that Lee would still be able to taste himself on Ben's tongue.

'You're fantastic,' said Lee, looking him straight in the eye.

'Thank you. So are you.'

The two boys dressed and went back into the lounge.

Ben and Lee sat in the lounge drinking Eddie's vodka. They had the stereo up loud and were wondering whether becoming rent boys was a good idea.

'I can't see what's wrong with giving it a go,' said Ben. 'If we don't like it then we can always get up and leave.'

'I know. But I just don't feel comfortable with the idea of selling my body to some sleazy old man.'

'Well,' said Ben, 'it can't be any worse than having to sleep on the streets every night. At least this way we'll have a roof over our heads.'

Lee was silent for a moment, then he smiled and said, 'I guess you're right. I suppose we could give it a go.'

'It'll be an adventure.'

As he said this, Ben heard the door to the flat open and then close again. There was a muffled rustling of paper or perhaps a coat and Eddie walked into the lounge with a bottle of vodka in one hand and an envelope in the other.

'Hi, boys,' he said, sitting down on the arm of one of the sofas. 'Brought us something for this evening.' He put the Smirnoff down on the floor.

'What's in the envelope?' Lee asked.

'Oh, it's nothing.'

'Must be something. It looks important.'

'It's money, if you must know. But not for me to spend, unfortunately. I've got a little debt to pay off.' He left the room and went into the kitchen. 'What have you two been doing while I was out?' he asked from the other room.

'Not much,' Lee replied, smiling at Ben as he did so. 'Just chatting and stuff.'

'Really?' said Eddie. 'Are you sure you weren't screwing?' He walked back into the room with his box of drugs and sat down on the floor where he'd sat before. 'Put some music on if you want,' he said, looking up at Ben.

'What do you want to listen to?'

'Whatever you like.'

Ben looked through the pile of records that rested against each other and the wall. Most of them were by bands he'd never heard of, but after a while he chose a Nico album and put it on to the turntable.

Eddie did not comment, nor even seem to notice when the music began. He was sitting on the floor cutting a line of speed on the cover of a book. 'Do you want some?' he asked.

Ben looked at Lee, who raised his eyebrows in question. 'What do you think?' Ben asked him.

'Oh, make your *own* mind up, Ben,' Eddie interrupted. 'You're a big boy now.'

'OK,' he said.

'Lee?' asked Eddie.

'What?'

'Do you want a line, too?'

'Yeah,' Lee said, adding, 'thanks.'

Ben watched as Eddie cut two more lines next to the one he'd already laid out and held out the book and a rolled up ten-pound note. 'Help yourself,' he said.

'Thanks.' Ben took the book and held it close to his face. With the other hand he held the note to one nostril and squeezed the other shut. Then he inhaled one of the lines. He had to stop halfway because the sensation of the amphetamine kicked in immediately and made him feel light-headed and dizzy. When the initial rush had passed, Ben snorted the rest of the line and passed the book on to Lee.

Ben leaned back on the sofa and closed his eyes. The speed had made his nose tingle and feel as if it was running or he was about to sneeze. He let it wash across him and relaxed into the sensation. He felt great – calm and yet at the same time full of energy. His body was in a heavenly state.

By the time he opened his eyes, Eddie was hoovering up the last of his line and the three of them sat there in silence for a moment until Eddie broke the silence by asking, 'So, have you boys thought about my offer?' He poured them all more vodka and lit a cigarette.

'Yes,' said Ben.

'And?'

'We've decided to give it a go. But –' Ben tried to sound firm '– if we don't like it and want to get out at any point, then we will.'

'That's fine,' said Eddie. 'But I can assure you that as soon as you try it you'll never want to get out.' He paused to drag on his cigarette. 'Oh, there's one thing I need to do before you're on the team.'

'What's that?' Lee asked.

'Well, you wouldn't buy a car, for example, without test-driving it first, would you?'

Ben knew immediately what he was getting at. In fact he was surprised that the subject hadn't been broached before. Eddie obviously wanted to be the one to do the test-driving, try them out, see what they were like in bed. 'Oh, I can assure you that Lee's engine is running just fine,' said Ben.

'Really?' said Eddie, his voice tinged with sarcasm. 'And what's Ben's bodywork like?' he said, turning to Lee.

'Very nice,' the lad replied.

'All the same, I'd still need to try you both out myself, because it's no good taking other people's word.'

Eddie was not an unattractive man, thought Ben. In fact there was something really rather sexy about him. 'So, what do we have to do?' he asked.

'I just want to test you out, that's all. Make sure you both –' Eddie searched for the words '– *work* properly.'

The speed was affecting Ben hugely and the vodka they'd drunk throughout the day enhanced the feeling and made him feel bold and horny. 'All right,' he said. 'Let's get on with it. Lee, are you up for it?'

Lee nodded and they both stood up.

'Oh, one at a time, please.'

'I'll go first,' said Ben.

Eddie stubbed out his cigarette and walked out of the room. Ben followed. The door to the bedroom was open and he went inside and closed it behind him. Eddie was sat in a chair facing the bed. 'Right,' he said. 'Come a bit closer.' Ben stood in front of him. 'Take off your shirt and your shoes and socks.' He did as he was told. Eddie stood up and ran an admiring hand across Ben's smooth chest. 'Put your hands behind your head.' Once again Ben obeyed the command. Eddie explored the whole of Ben's torso, like a doctor checking out his patient. His hands travelled up Ben's back, around his arms, under them, running his fingers through the hair, over his pectorals and down towards his abdomen.

Ben felt as if he were powerless against the older man's exploring hands. Eddie unbuttoned his jeans and slowly slipped them down to the floor. Then he lowered the front of Ben's boxer shorts enough so as to reveal the top of his pubic hair. He stroked the hair and then began to manipulate his cock through the material of the underwear. This caused Ben to become semi-erect. Anyone playing with your penis will naturally cause a reaction and this pair of hands was no exception. Ben's front was facing Eddie and his cock now hung, half-hard, to the left.

Eddie turned him around and caressed his back. The hands soon reached his bottom and Ben felt them squeeze and rub the cheeks. The next thing Ben knew was that his shorts were slowly being pulled down at the back and he could feel the cold air in the room touch them, shortly followed by Eddie, who ran his fingers over them and between the cheeks, virtually touching Ben's arsehole as he did so. The hand went so far between his legs that he felt it brush against the long muscle that joined the base of his balls to his anus. Ben felt violated and soiled, as if he were being trespassed upon by the man's touch.

'Turn to the side,' instructed Eddie. Ben did so, now facing the wall, his pants still revealing his buttocks and his hands behind his head. Eddie, continuing to stroke Ben's arse, reached forwards and pulled down the shorts so that Ben's cock and balls became exposed. Immediately, he wrapped a hand around the length of the cock and slowly pulled back the foreskin. Ben was by now fully erect, not able to resist Eddie's touch.

He watched as the man ran his hands freely over Ben's cock, gently wanking it, around his balls and between his buttocks. The

exploration felt rude and that turned him on. The whole experience had also made him ready to come.

'Right,' said Eddie, taking his hands away, 'I want you to lie
on the bed, on your back.'

Ben stepped out of his trousers and pants and got up on to the
bed. He propped a pillow behind him and lay back. Eddie stepped
up to the edge of the bed and sat down. 'Part your legs,' he said,
and once again he took hold of Ben's prick and manipulated it.
'That's great. But could you raise your legs in the air too?' Ben
did so, allowing access to his genitals as well as his arse.

With one hand, Eddie wanked Ben's cock and occasionally
stroked his balls, and with the other he was gently introducing a
finger to Ben's arsehole. Ben raised his legs higher in the air at
Eddie's command and let the man take complete control of his
orgasm. Eddie pushed first one and then a second finger inside
Ben's bottom and masturbated his cock more vigorously, angling
it down so that it would shoot over the sheets.

Ben found the movement of the man's hand and the stimulation
from his fingers made him feel as if he was about to come, and all
of a sudden the first pleasurable moments of climax ran through
his body. He let out a little gasp and watched as a long stream of
semen shot from the end of his prick. This was followed by other
spurts, each one becoming less and less violent, until only a trickle
of Ben's sticky fluid eased out from the tip of his penis. Eddie
wiped the semen that had hit his hand on to the bed-sheets,
where the rest of it was.

Ben felt exhausted and drained. He breathed out a long sigh of
relief and relaxed his legs, which he'd supsended in the air for the
duration of the test.

'Very good,' said Eddie. 'You'd better dress and send in your
friend.'

Four

Ben woke just after eleven o'clock on a futon in Eddie's spare room. Lee was still asleep, so he carefully pulled back the covers, not wanting to disturb him.

They'd had a late night. More speed had been followed by more drinks and soon it was three in the morning. They'd hit the sack feeling high and drunk and hopeful about the future. Eddie had talked endless rubbish, most of it now condensed into a few phrases in the back of Ben's mind. The gist had been lost in the night.

Ben carefully shut the bedroom door behind him. He went into the kitchen where their host sat at the table drinking a cup of coffee. 'Morning,' he said.

'How are you today?' asked Eddie. He seemed amazingly awake, especially since he'd stayed up even later than they had. Then Ben spotted the rolled-up note and the drug box on the table. Eddie was addicted to speed, it seemed.

'Not bad. A bit hung over, I guess,' he replied.

'Where's Lee?'

'Still asleep.'

'Well, don't wake him,' said Eddie. 'We'll let him have his beauty sleep.' He paused to take a sip of coffee. 'Later we'll go round to the house and get you settled in.'

'What house?' Ben enquired.

'The house where the boys all stay. It's a bit crowded, but everyone just mucks in and gets on with it. At least it's better than sleeping on the streets. You should get on with them. They're all much the same age as you. They'll be able to give you some advice about how to be a good rent boy.'

In the cold light of morning Ben felt nervous at the thought of having to have sex with horrible, ugly strangers just to make some money and keep a roof over his head. Then again it was very flattering that these people would be willing to actually pay for the pleasure of a few moments with his body. It wasn't as if they wanted to take away a part of his personality or cause him physical harm. They only wanted to worship for a while at the altar of his skin.

When Lee was awake and dressed, Eddie said that they shouldn't waste any more time and they left the building and made their way towards his car, which was parked down a Stockwell side street. Ben sat in the back and looked out of the window.

'Where are we going?' asked Lee.

'New Cross Gate,' Eddie replied.

Ben had never heard of it. The areas they were driving through seemed very poor and depressing. There was something grim about them and it was hard to believe that people actually lived there day in, day out.

Finally Eddie announced that they were there and he parked the car in a long road of terraced houses. The sign at the bottom told Ben that this was Prospect Road. They got out of the car and followed Eddie up the road and down the path of number twenty-eight. It was much shabbier on the outside than the other houses, some of which were quite posh, their lack of net curtains revealing stripped pine floors and Habitat sofas. Number twenty-eight looked as if it had never been looked after, and almost as if no one had lived there in years.

'So, do you own this?' asked Ben.

'Of course not,' said Eddie. He opened the front door and they followed him inside.

'Who does, then?'

'I don't know, Ben. It's a squat. He who lives there is king for the day.'

The corridor was not carpeted, but not in the sense of stripped pine flooring: it was more the dirty floorboard look. Other than a few empty tea chests, there was nothing there. Eddie pushed open the door of the front room and they went inside.

There were two boys sitting on a tatty sofa watching a television set that seemed far too close to them. They didn't look much older than Ben. One was black and one was white.

'I want you to meet two new recruits,' said Eddie, addressing the lads. 'This is Ben and Lee.' The boys greeted them with a nod. 'That's Nathan.' Eddie gestured towards the black lad. Then, looking at the boy beside him, Eddie said, 'And this is Ringo.'

'Hello,' said Ringo, smiling at Ben. He was a tall lad with very short, dirty-blond hair and hazel eyes. He was skinny and spoke with a rough South London accent.

Nathan was smaller and more well built. He had jet-black eyes and short hair to match. He had a cute face and looked like a little boy boxer.

'Where are the other two?' asked Eddie.

'Upstairs, fucking, I expect,' replied Nathan. Ben was surprised at his frankness, but glad that he'd stumbled on such an exciting household. If they were half as attractive as the two boys on the sofa, he was surely in for a good time.

'Well, go up and get them down here. Besides, they ought to save their energy for work,' said Eddie. Reluctantly, Nathan got up and left the room. When he returned he was followed by two boys. They sat down on the rug that covered most of the floor in the front room. Eddie introduced them as Alex, a lad of about twenty, with long dark hair, and Luis, a South American-looking boy with spiky, sculpted hair. He looked younger than the other one and a little cuter. Ben greeted them and they smiled at him and Lee.

'Well,' said Eddie, 'I've introduced you. The boys will tell you what you have to do. But remember, I could call you at any time with a client. They might come here or you might have to go to them, but be ready at all times and don't pick up any bad habits from these lazy sods.' Eddie turned to leave the room. 'And always use a prophylactic.' The door closed behind him and he was gone.

'What's that, then?' asked Lee, looking very puzzled.

'He means a condom, you fool,' said Ben.

'Oh, right.'

Ben felt nervous to be alone with these four tough boys. He only had Lee to fall back on. At least they were both in the same boat. He hoped they'd not be treated with hostility.

'How old are you?' asked Ringo.

'I'm eighteen,' said Ben.

'Twenty-two,' said Lee.

'Bit old for all this, aren't you?' Ringo had a cruel sneer on his face.

'No,' retaliated Lee. 'Not everyone's into twelve-year-olds.'

'Thankfully. Or else Alex would be out of a job.'

'Fuck off,' said Alex, obviously sensitive about his age.

'Leave him alone,' Luis burst in. 'Lee is only three years older than you, Alex, anyway.' Luis spoke with a Spanish or Portuguese accent.

'Have you ever done this kind of thing before?' asked Ringo, turning to Ben, who got the impression he was the mouthiest of the gang.

'No,' he replied.

'Well, it's obvious we're going to have to show you the ropes.'

'Are you and him fucking?' Nathan interrupted, pointing at Lee.

'That's a bit personal, isn't it?' replied Ben.

The lads all laughed.

'There's no such thing,' said Ringo, 'as personal. Not in this house. If you don't know how to be frank now, then you've got a lot to learn.'

'Ignore him,' said Luis. 'He's just teasing. You're very welcome here. We all need to stick together.'

Ben and Lee sat down on the floor.

51

'So, what's it like?' said Ben to Luis, the only one who seemed really friendly.

'What's what like?' interrupted Ringo.

'Doing it for money,' said Ben, turning to the lad.

'OK,' he said. 'Most of the clients are married businessmen, with their wives safely tucked away behind the kitchen sink. They need a bit of attention and some sex, so they come to us. Sometimes they don't even want to do much. Just watch you wank or something. Or suck your dick. Some only come to talk. It's sad, really. But then I'm not complaining. It still means money for us.'

'Do they come here?' asked Ben.

'Sometimes,' said Ringo. 'But more often than not they've got a place to go to. Either their house when no one's in, or a hotel room, or a friend's place. If they haven't, then we do them here.'

'Is it dangerous?'

'No. Not really. Only as dangerous as it normally is to be alive.'

Ben and Lee chatted away for most of the afternoon with the boys – their initial hostility seemed to have fallen away. Ben was keen to find out exactly what he had to do, and his continual questioning seemed to amuse Ringo and the lads.

Later, Ringo said, 'Why don't we give you a little practical lesson in what to do?'

'What do you mean?' asked Ben.

'Well, let's have a practice run . . . at sex.'

Ben found all the lads pretty attractive, but Ringo was by far the most sexy, and he would certainly like to have a session with him. 'OK,' he said.

'Right,' said Ringo. 'Me and Nathan'll take Ben, and you two –' he looked over at Alex and Luis '– can have Lee.'

Everyone was agreed and there was a little buzz of excitement in the room. Ben could tell that the lads were pleased to have some new talent to take advantage of. They were probably bored with having one another and the paying clients.

Ben followed Nathan and Ringo up to a bedroom on the first floor. It looked more comfortable and lived-in than the lounge. There was an unmade double bed under the window, which faced out on to a messy backyard. There were also some comfort-able chairs, a wardrobe, a chest of drawers and even a sink in the corner. The floor was carpeted in a rather threadbare floral pattern.

Without a word, Ringo stepped close to where Ben was standing and started to kiss him. He immediately opened Ben's mouth and thrust his tongue deep inside. It felt great. Ringo was so forceful and animalistic. At the same time, from behind, Nathan ran his hands over Ben's back and arse. Soon he was unbuttoning his shirt – Ringo still stuck to his face – and letting his hands explore the bare chest beneath them.

Ben was in seventh heaven. The feeling of the sexy black boy's groping hands coupled with Ringo's aggressive kiss made him shudder. He was a little nervous but at the same time overcome by the physical sensation.

Nathan undid Ben's trousers and pushed them to the floor. Ben felt the lad fall to his knees behind him and begin to kiss his bottom through the fabric of his boxer shorts. His hands were around the front stroking Ben's cock, which was already as stiff as a board. Ringo continued to kiss him throughout.

Next Ben felt his boxers slide to the floor. Nathan's hands took hold of his balls and prick and started to jerk the stiff pole back and forth. At the same time, the lad let his lips travel from the small of Ben's back, over his arse-cheeks and down to his thighs. The sensation was breathtaking.

Suddenly Ringo stopped kissing him and took hold of his balls. He smiled and then sank to his knees and started sucking on Ben's cock. From behind Nathan had parted Ben's buttocks and was edging his lips along the gorge between them. Ben could feel how close Nathan was getting to his sensitive opening.

Ringo was clearly an expert at giving head. Ben swooned under the sensation of the lad's lips. He was loath to admit it, but this was the best blow job he'd ever received, although that wasn't saying much. His experience only amounted to Paul Jennings and Lee. Ringo held Ben's cock tightly around the base, while he let his tongue and lips move wildly up and down the stiff shaft, sucking hard as he did so. The feeling made Ben's balls tighten and the delightful pre-orgasmic feeling engulfed him.

Nathan had now parted Ben's arse-cheeks enough so as to gain access to his arsehole, and Ben sensed the tip of his tongue probing its perimeter. There was a warm, wet feeling slowly getting closer to his anus and this, together with Ringo's continued sucking, made Ben light-headed.

Suddenly Nathan stopped his rimming and moved around the front, positioning himself beside the other boy. Now they both competed for Ben's cock, both keen to lick or suck it. Sometimes Nathan would gain control of Ben's stiff member and suck on it with gusto, while Ringo feasted on Ben's balls and the area surrounding them. Then they would swap. Ben felt like all the attention in the world was being lavished upon him.

However, as suddenly as it all seemed to have begun, it stopped. The two lads stood up to face Ben and then pushed him down to his knees. He knew what they wanted and was more than willing to give it to them. Firstly, he undid Ringo's trousers and was confronted with the hard-on that hid in the lad's tight cotton boxer shorts. He pulled these down and the lad's stiff, neatly circumcised penis sprang out. He immediately caught a lovely whiff of its soapy fragrance. Without hesitation, he took it in his mouth and began to work away on it.

With Ringo in his mouth, he let his hands tackle the front of Nathan's trousers. Nathan wore loose tracksuit bottoms. Ben could feel the huge prick that lay stiffly beneath. He pulled his trousers down. The lad had no underwear on and his cock fell straight away into Ben's hands. Nathan's was long, thick and uncut – a great piece of meat. While Ben sucked on Ringo's cock, his hands were concentrated on masturbating Nathan. It felt such a pleasure to be allowed to handle two pricks at the same time.

Soon Ben swapped over. His mouth came, for the first time, into contact with Nathan's member. At first he had trouble getting it in, its dimensions were so great, but soon he became able to accommodate it and he happily sucked away. As he did so, he cupped the lad's ample balls in one hand and used the other to continue wanking Ringo.

'Hey, Ben,' said the white boy. 'Get on the bed.' Ben did as he was told and climbed, naked, on to the bed. He lay back. The two lads stripped off completely. Ringo's body was pale and skinny in comparison to Nathan's muscular black frame. They climbed on to the bed beside him. Nathan began to suck his cock while Ringo straddled his head and aimed his stiff member towards Ben's mouth. He had no choice but to take the thing in his mouth and once again stimulate it. All the while he gripped on to the lad's thighs, thus being able to control how much cock he was subjected to.

Ben sucked at the lad and in turn was himself sucked. Ringo's balls rubbed against his chin every time the lad's cock sank deeply into his mouth. Ben could not resist letting his fingers wander across his bottom and between the tensed cheeks until they came to rest on Ringo's tight hole.

The lad did not seem to object to having a finger placed on his most tender spot, so Ben took the opportunity to press the digit a little further. Ringo's sphincter dilated and allowed him to probe further inside. It felt great, Ben thought, having the lad's tight passage around his finger, and he pushed it in as deeply as he could.

This seemed to make Ringo even more sexually excited and, all the while he sucked, Ben could taste the trickles of salty pre-come that oozed out of the boy's prick and into his mouth. He swallowed these down with great enthusiasm, his finger still wedged inside Ringo's bottom and his own cock being licked and wanked.

Ben stopped sucking the lad and shifted him up a little so that his face was directly under his arse. With Ringo straddling him, it meant that his legs were spread wide enough for Ben to have clear access to his bottom. He parted the cheeks a little more and inhaled the stale, musky odour that pervaded. The smell was strong and boyish, and without hesitation Ben began to lick along the arse-crack, which was covered in fine blond hairs. When he got to the opening itself, he carefully dabbed at it with his tongue and saw it dilate and take his probe inside. He flicked his tongue around as much as possible, trying to push it as far as he could inside the lad's arse. Ben then inserted a finger, its passage made smooth by the dribble he had left there. He wriggled it about and pushed it roughly inside.

It was amazing to be rimming this lad who looked so hard and laddish, like any boy you might see in the street and desire. Ben had access to the most intimate of spots – a zone that he could usually only dream about. This, coupled with the thrill of having his cock sucked, made Ben feel very horny indeed, and he felt the strongest urge to discharge his load. However, he held himself back for a moment, wishing to have Ringo in his mouth when he did finally come.

He pushed the lad back again so that his prick was once more in his mouth and sucked with an energy that he never realised he had. One hand was put to work squeezing Ringo's balls and the other remained in the saliva-moistened passage.

He could hear the heavy breathing of both boys and he knew that they were enjoying themselves. Ringo seemed to be trembling in his mouth and he instinctively knew that he was nearing his climax. Ben, too, felt ready to let his out, and all of a sudden the first waves of pleasure passed through his body. He sucked even harder and thrust his hips into Nathan's face. A jet of cream shot out of the end of his penis and he imagined how it must be gushing into the lad's mouth.

At the same time Ringo let out a yelp of excitement and clasped Ben's head close to his groin. A long spurt of semen issued from the tip of his prick and hit the back of Ben's throat. It tasted thick and salty. He drank it down and sucked on the stiff pole for another shot, as if he were milking the lad of his essence. All the while, his own penis continued to erupt in Nathan's mouth. All three boys had one thing in common: they were either delivering or receiving a dose of spunk, and in Ben's case it was both.

Soon Ringo's well seemed to run dry and so did Ben's. He felt the last trickles of liquid seep from the head of the lad's cock and his own prick stopped squirting, too. Ben took the thing out of his mouth and lapped the final droplets from the tip. He heard

Nathan breathe a sigh and the mouth was gone from around his penis.

Although Ben was relieved and exhausted, his prick was still hard and he was aware that he could easily carry on. He looked up at Ringo, who looked tired and hot. 'You OK?' he asked.

'Fine,' Ringo replied.

'We're not finished yet, are we?'

'Er . . . no,' said Ringo, a little hesitantly. He reached behind him and felt Ben's erection. 'Obviously you're not,' he added. 'Nathan?'

'Yeah?'

'Can you get me a johnny out of the drawer, please?'

Ringo moved himself back so that he could get access to Ben's cock. He opened the condom wrapper and unrolled the piece of rubber down the length of the shaft. Next, he unscrewed a tube of lubricant that Nathan handed him and squeezed some out on to the tips of his fingers. This he firstly applied to Ben's rubber-clad penis, and then to his own bottom.

Ben had never actually fucked anyone before and he felt nervous about it. However, having Ringo as his partner was enough to keep him hard and excited – the lad was so sexy. He remained stretched out on his back, and Ringo straddled him, facing his face. All the while, Nathan remained at the side of the bed, naked, calmly viewing the proceedings.

Ringo positioned himself over Ben's groin and took hold of his cock. He carefully guided it towards his lubricated opening and then slowly moved his bottom down on to it. Ben did not have to do a thing; he just lay there and felt the tip of his prick make contact with the lad's arsehole. To start with, it was a tight feeling around the head of his cock, but gradually, as Ringo allowed him to slide inside, it became more general and engulfed the whole of his penis. Soon the lad had him completely inside and he looked at Ben with what can only be described as an uncomfortable look on his face.

Ben stroked Ringo's stomach, which was easily accessible from where he was, and then moved his hands down to the boy's cock, which was stiff and upright. Ringo had started moving up and down on Ben's prick and Ben could feel the tight passage sliding over him. It felt great. Ben continued to wank the lad and stroke his balls, hoping that they might both come at the same time, like before.

Ringo continued to move up and down on his cock, now more vigorously than before. The sensation sent shivers through Ben's body and made him ache to orgasm. He pulled Ringo's cock back and forth and felt his balls tighten and retract towards his body.

All of a sudden, Ben became aware that he would no longer be able to resist climaxing. 'I'm going to come,' he said in a whisper. Ringo moved himself up and down even more roughly and Ben felt himself come inside the lad. It was a more subtle orgasm than the one he'd had previously in Nathan's mouth, but in its own way intense and draining. Ringo continued to move up and down, even though a climax had been reached, and Ben carried on stroking the lad's cock with rhythmic movements of his hand. Ringo was clearly enjoying the stimulation inside him and it was helping him to come.

The boy let out an exhausted cry. Ben knew what was coming next. A lengthy spurt of seminal fluid shot out of the tip and over Ben's exposed chest. He continued to wank the shaft and encourage more, squeezing his balls as he did so. Sticky white liquid seeped out all the while and covered Ben. It felt nice having the warm liquid all over him. He revelled in the sordidness of the situation.

Soon Ringo stopped squirting and he let his head fall back, exhausted and spent. Ben's cock was still inside him and it was beginning to soften. Ben put a hand on the lad's stomach in an attempt to move him off. Ringo lifted himself up and Ben felt his penis slide out of the lad's passage and back into the open.

'My turn for some fun,' said Nathan, approaching the bed. 'Turn over.'

Ben was shocked by the boy assuming he could go ahead and screw him. However, the whole session had been so exciting and eye-opening that Ben felt at ease enough to try something he'd never done before. He turned on to his front and said, 'Go gently. This is my first time.'

'Really? How flattering to be your first.' Nathan climbed on to the bed and started rubbing his hands up and down the length of Ben's back. Then he moved on to Ben's legs, caressing them from ankle to thigh. Finally he worked away on Ben's buttocks, massaging each cheek with careful concentration, making sure that his hands touched every part of the fleshy globe.

Nathan knelt at the side of Ben's bottom and began to kiss the cheeks. He licked and nibbled at them in a playful way and soon had his mouth close to the deep slit where they joined. Ben tingled all over as the lad's tongue slipped between and traversed the length of his bottom. He felt hands parting his buttocks and Nathan's warm breath on his opening. Then the tip of his tongue started to probe the tight little hole, and Ben felt himself automatically dilate to accommodate him. The lad had made him slippery with his saliva and he felt lips encircling his anus and a tongue slide deeply inside. It felt rude and sexually exciting, and Ben pushed his bottom further into Nathan's face – in a gesture of encouragement and co-operation. The lad seemed to be rimming him as deeply as was possible, and now, at the same time, inserting a finger into him. Ben squirmed on the bed, a hard-on raging that he rubbed against the sheets. The tickling sensation of the lad's tongue was so pleasurable that Ben was unable to resist letting out a little whimper.

Nathan withdrew his tongue and finger, and Ben looked back just in time to observe him pulling a condom over his huge, erect black member and opening the tube of lubricant. Next thing he felt was the lad's fingers, slicked with the slippery grease, sliding deep inside him. He braced himself for the inevitable and closed his eyes.

The tip of Nathan's cock touched his exposed hole and Ben felt a cold shudder run through his body. A push and his bottom seemed to open a little, just enough to take in the head of the prick. This did not feel too unpleasant. The next movement, however, made Ben yelp.

'Try to relax,' Nathan whispered into his ear.

Ben did his best, but the thing still felt so painful that he didn't know whether he could let the lad continue. 'Can you go really slowly, please?' he said.

'OK.' Nathan pulled his cock out a little and started again, this time moving with snail-like slowness. Ben relaxed the muscles in his back, legs and bottom as much as he could and readied himself for the next assault.

This time it seemed easier. With every forward motion the boy's penis cut into him and he opened up a little more. It was painful, but not like before. The sensation could be better described as discomfort.

'There you go,' said Nathan after a minute or two. 'I'm right inside you now.'

Ben felt pleased with himself for managing to take such a huge thing. He relaxed his muscles around the lad's prick and for the first time the feeling was almost pleasant. It had certainly made his cock and balls ache and feel like they were capable of another ejaculation.

Nathan began to move his hips back and forth, each time forcing his penis in and out of the passage. All the while he held on to Ben's hips and used them as leverage. The feeling was uncomfortable but intense and Ben tried to relax into the rhythm of it. However, every time the lad drew his cock out again, Ben could not stop himself from letting out a quiet gasp. Nathan pumped away all the while, making Ben's bottom feel hot with all the friction.

Ringo sat on the edge of the bed looking at Ben's face and the pained expressions on it, and slowly masturbated himself. Ben tried to smile up at the lad, but found it hard with Nathan's repeated pounding.

Soon he had become used to the feeling of someone's cock up his arse and, in an obscure sense, it was almost a pleasure. He knew that a stimulation so intimately inside you could be enough to bring you to a climax.

It wasn't long before Nathan started panting and making excited noises. Ben felt him tremble and shudder and for a few seconds hold his cock still in Ben's bottom. Then he drew it right back out and with new energy shoved it deeply inside once more. After doing this three times, he stopped moving and laid his body across Ben's back and kissed his neck from behind. As he did so, his penis slid from its comfortable refuge and rested against Ben's buttocks, and Ben felt himself involuntarily ejaculate over the sheets that lay beneath him.

'Did you have a good time?' whispered Ben.

'Certainly did,' Lee replied, and a smile lit up his face.

All six boys were sitting in the front room, recovering from their earlier exertion. Ben didn't mind the fact that Lee had been with Alex and Luis. He wanted him to have as much fun as he could and do the same himself.

The telephone rang and Luis answered it. He listened for a moment and then said, 'Ringo. It's for you.'

'Who is it?' the lad asked.

'Eddie.'

Ringo walked over to the phone and put the receiver to his ear. 'What?' he said, in an aggressive voice. 'OK. If I must . . . Who? Yes, OK . . . Seven-thirty . . . All right, I'll bring him . . . Give me the address.' He scribbled something on to a piece of paper and then put the phone down.

'What was that about?' asked Nathan.

'Eddie wants me to do a job for him. He told me to take Ben. Thought it'd be a good introduction for him.'

'Really?' said Ben.

'Yes.'

'Do you mean I've got to take part in it?'

'No,' said Ringo. 'Just watch.'

'Won't the bloke object?' Ben couldn't understand how he'd be able to sit in on someone's private paid-for sex session.

'No. He's into that kind of thing. He wants to be watched.' Ben could not stop his face betraying his confusion. 'It's part of the deal,' Ringo continued. 'He's paying extra for you to sit in.'

'Oh, right,' said Ben. 'I see.'

'There's a lot of weirdos out there,' said Nathan. 'Remember

– the city's a funny place. Something like a circus or a sewer. Different people have peculiar tastes.'

Ben nodded his head in agreement.

'We don't have to be there until seven-thirty,' said Ringo, 'and it's not very far away, so there's no rush.'

The boys relaxed in the front room, watching television and chatting.

Ringo strode impatiently down the street. He had told Ben, who trailed behind, unable to keep up with the pace, that it wasn't far to walk. It was clear that Ben's idea of what was far was vastly different to Ringo's.

It was still light outside, although the sun was low in the sky and threw a golden glow across the tops of the houses. Ben looked up into the pale blue air and thought of home and Paul. He missed his friend and wondered what he was doing now.

'I think it's the next one on the right.' Ringo interrupted his train of thought.

'What?' asked Ben.

'The next road on the right is the one we want, I think.'

They turned down it and Ringo kept his eyes on the numbers above every front door. He stopped when he reached number seventy-four and Ben followed him up the path and waited beside him while he rang the bell to the top flat.

Footsteps could be heard almost at once. They became louder as they neared the door.

'Who is it?' a voice said through the closed door. Ben could see the blurred outline of a man through the textured glass.

'I'm from the agency,' said Ringo, and then, turning to Ben, added, 'that's what we always call Eddie's sex business.'

The door swung open and Ben saw his first client. He did not quite match up to the sordid, dirty-old-man image that Ben had pictured in his mind's eye. The person before him was younger than he had expected, in his early thirties, and was not unattractive. He had short black hair and a stocky build.

'Hello,' he said. 'Come up.'

They followed the man upstairs to the second floor, where he let them into a poky two-room garret. They went into the bedroom and the two boys sat down on the edge of his bed.

'What's your names?' he asked, looking them both up and down.

'I'm Ringo, and this is Ben. What's yours?'

'I'd rather not say.'

'Fair enough,' said Ringo.

'So, which one of you is watching and which one's participating?'

'Ben's watching.'

'OK. Shall we get on with it, then?' asked the client.

'Fine by me,' replied Ringo. 'But I need to have the money first.' The man counted out seventy pounds and handed it over. 'Thanks.' He put it into his jacket pocket which was hanging on the back of a chair. 'So, what do you want to do?'

'Well, first I want to rim you for a while, suck you off, *et cetera*. Then, I want you to give me a blow job. Deep throat. OK?' Ringo nodded and started to take off his shoes and socks. 'Ben? Can you sit in the chair, please?' Without a word Ben did as he was told. The client turned to Ringo and said, 'Take everything off, apart from your underwear.'

Ben watched as Ringo silently stripped down to his boxer shorts and lay face down on the bed.

'No. Not there,' said the client. 'I want you to bend over the chair.' He pointed to a plain wooden chair that had obviously been positioned in the centre of the room for just that purpose. Ringo leaned across the back of it and gripped on to either side of the seat, his head bowed right down. The client approached from behind and ran his hands over the lad's buttocks, and parted his legs as far as he could. Then he fell to his knees and started sniffing the back of the boxer shorts. He pushed his nose right into Ringo's crack and used his hands to slowly slip the pants down. From where Ben was seated he could see that the client had complete access to the boy's arsehole. The man pried Ringo's cheeks apart even more and buried his head between them. He stayed there for what seemed like an age, just frantically running his tongue up and down Ringo's open gorge and lingering intently upon his tight, puckered opening. He used his fingers, too, in order to further explore the mysterious interior. The lad's arse was wet with saliva, and Ben could see how much the client had opened him up with his tongue and fingers.

This went on for about twenty minutes, at the end of which the client stopped his rimming and sat back on the floor, breathless and panting. Ringo looked up and threw Ben a cheeky smile. It was all just a game to him, Ben thought. He was forever playing the part of rent boy.

Next, the client positioned him so that he was seated on the edge of the bed, with his torso reclined. Ringo now had a hard-on, and the man once again sank to his knees, and started to suck on it. Saliva ran down from the sides of his mouth as he gave the lad's cock a thorough going-over. He squeezed his balls and jammed a finger into the well-lubricated arsehole. Ben's own penis was as hard as it could be, so exciting was the spectacle.

Before long Ringo let out a little moan of pleasure – the signal that his climax was approaching – and the client sucked with even more enthusiasm. Ben could tell when the lad was actually coming, because the man had ceased to move his mouth along the whole length of the penis and was carefully concentrating on the swollen head.

After a while he pulled his mouth away from Ringo's cock and, still erect, it flopped back against his muscled stomach. The client, whose erection was obvious through his trousers, moved over to the chair that he'd bent Ringo over and sat down in it.

Ringo got up from the bed and positioned himself on his knees between the client's legs. Next, he unbuttoned the man's flies and pulled down his underwear enough to be able to take hold of his prick and pull it out into the open. Then he bent forwards and started to go down on it. He had his eyes closed, perhaps thinking of someone else, and he worked the client's cock with both his hand and his mouth. He seemed virtually able to swallow the whole length of the man's more-than-ample penis. All the while, the client stared intently at Ben, as if he was getting off on the fact that they were being watched.

Ben stared back, transfixed. However, he did not have much time left to watch in, as the client had already started to very pant loudly and was running his fingers through Ringo's hair, and at the same time forcing his mouth down even further on to his stiff member. With an aggressive grunt he held the lad's head in a fixed position and Ben could tell that he was ejaculating.

When he'd finished, Ringo got up and started putting his clothes on. The client didn't say anything, he just did up his trousers and waited for the lad to get dressed. Then he opened the door, and, without a word, escorted the two boys down the stairs and out into the open once again.

It was now dark outside and Ben walked beside his new friend and workmate in the direction of Prospect Road.

'That was weird to watch,' ventured Ben.

'That's nothing, I can assure you.' Ringo lit a cigarette and exhaled a cloud of smoke into the calm night air. 'Vanilla, as we say in the business. Some of them want *really* weird things.'

'What like?'

'Once some bloke asked me to piss on his face.'

'Er. Disgusting,' said Ben. There was a silence and then he asked, 'What do you think about while you're . . . doing it?'

'Anything. Apart from the client.'

'But you must need to think of something that turns you on, otherwise wouldn't you lose your erection?'

'Yeah, I suppose so.' Ringo dragged on his cigarette and then offered it to Ben. 'I usually think about boys I've seen in the street or on telly and pretend it's their dick I'm sucking.'

'Really?' said Ben. 'So what did you think about this time?'

'I'm not telling you.'

'Come on. You don't need to be shy about it. I've seen everything possible of you over the last twelve hours.'

'Yeah, I guess you're right,' said Ringo.

'Well, then?'

'I was thinking about you, if you must know,' he said, and then went totally silent.

Ben smiled to himself, pleased that Ringo was capable of actually feeling something – betraying the hard image he liked to manufacture. He handed back the cigarette and accidentally brushed the boy's hand as he did so.

Five

Ben sat with Lee on the tatty sofa. They were watching television. Ringo and Alex were out seeing clients and the other two boys were in their rooms. It was Tuesday and Ben had only been in London for four days.

They had slept in the spare room on a sofa-bed. Ben had found it hard to sleep because of all the excitement of the day, and had even woken up several times in the night with strange, distorted dreams still in his head about the other boys and potential clients.

'Wonder when we're going to get our first job,' Lee mused.

'Don't know. I'm kind of excited about it, though, aren't you?'

'No. Not really.'

'Come on, Lee. Show a little willing.'

'It's not *willing* that I'm worried about showing,' he retorted.

'You must be having fun, though?' asked Ben.

'Yeah, of course.' Lee put his arms around Ben and kissed him warmly on the lips. There was a moment of silence and then he asked, 'You're not falling for Ringo, are you?'

Ben betrayed his feelings by not answering immediately. He hesitated before saying, 'Of course not.'

'You do seem to have taken a liking to him, though.'

'He's nice,' said Ben.

'I know. Sorry. It's not like I own you or anything, or even like we're going out together. I'm just rather fond of you, that's all.'

Ben smiled at his friend, wanting to put him at ease. He did still like him, but things were different now. He felt spoilt for choice. Ringo was very sexy and casual when it came to feelings. Ben was attracted to his nonchalance. 'Look, Lee. I like you both,' he said. 'In different ways.'

This seemed to put the lad's mind at rest a little and he smiled. 'I don't mind sharing you. I just wouldn't like to not have you at all.'

Just at that moment the telephone rang. Ben picked it up. It was Eddie. He wanted to speak to Lee. Ben handed over the receiver and listened to Lee's responses.

When he'd put the phone down, Ben asked, 'What did he want?'

'He's got a job for me. They wanted someone a bit older, that's why he didn't ask you.'

'Where is it?'

'In Deptford.'

'Where's that?' asked Ben.

'Somewhere not very far away.'

'What have you got to do?'

'He didn't say.' Lee got up and walked towards the door. 'I'm going up to take a shower. Ought to be clean for the customer, I suppose.' He left the room. Ben sat in the lounge, turned on the television and flicked through the channels.

Lee had been gone twenty minutes when the telephone rang again.

'Hello?' said Ben.

'It's Eddie,' said the voice at the other end.

'Hi. How's it going?'

'OK. I've got a little job for you.'

Just the mention of it made Ben's heart pound with nervousness. 'Oh, yeah?' he said.

'In Clapham South.'

Ben wrote down the address and how to get there, and then asked, 'What kind of sex does he want?'

'I don't know. Nothing kinky. Well, he didn't mention anything, because I usually charge extra for that.' There was a momentary silence at the end of the line, then Eddie said, 'I'll come over later and collect the money. I'm really in need of it.'

'Why's that?'

'I just am, OK? I owe someone rather a lot of money, that's all.'

'Sounds serious,' said Ben.

'It is.'

'You ought to try kidnapping someone and holding them to ransom, or something.'

Eddie just laughed.

'OK,' said Ben. 'How much is he going to pay me?'

'A hundred quid. I agreed it over the phone. Make sure you get it in advance of the sex.'

'All right. What time does he want me?'

'As soon as you can get over there. I said you'd be with him in about an hour. His name's Michael, by the way.' Eddie hung up.

Ben went upstairs and took a shower. He had been lazy today, lying around in his underwear all morning and well into the afternoon. It felt good to have the warm water splash down on to his naked body. Ben had an idea. He took down the shower-head from its fixture on the tiled wall and aimed it at his body. The closer he positioned the nozzle, the nicer it felt. The water shot out at such a great pressure that it made his skin tingle. He aimed it at his balls and it felt so good that his cock immediately sprang into an erection.

All of a sudden there was a knock at the door, and Nathan yelled out for him to hurry up. Ben, quickly putting the shower-head back in its bracket, felt like a guilty schoolboy caught wanking by his mother.

He dried himself, put on clean underwear and opened the bathroom door. 'Sorry,' he said to the impatient Nathan.

'I've got an appointment to get to. You've been in there for ages.'

'I know. I said I was sorry.' Ben slipped into his bedroom, dressed himself in the sexiest T-shirt he had and pulled on his jeans. He put on some aftershave and looked himself up and down in the small mirror over the mantelpiece. Not bad, he thought.

Ben took the bus to Clapham and walked in the direction Eddie had told him to. He rang the bell of the flat and waited for an answer. It was a very expensive-looking mansion block, with a Georgian façade. He was a bit late, but it didn't really matter. A man's voice spoke over the intercom and the door was buzzed open. Ben pushed it and went up the stairs to the first floor. He knocked on the appropriate flat door.

A tall, fair-haired man in his early forties answered. 'Come in,' he said. 'You *are* Ben, aren't you?'

'Yes, that's right. You're Michael?' The man nodded. He looked rather tired and run down, as if the week had been stressful for him. He was moderately attractive, the kind of man you'd never look at with desire, but, if push came to shove, you'd probably have sex with.

Ben followed him into the lounge, which was large and comfortably furnished, and sat down on the sofa. There was a top-of-the-range stereo, television and video in the room and lots of modern art on the walls.

'Do you want a drink?' Michael asked.

'Yes, please,' said Ben, who was feeling very nervous and hoped that alcohol would put him more at ease.

'What do you want?'

'What have you got?'

'Vodka, gin, whisky, rum, some beer in the fridge,' said the man.

'Can I have a vodka, please?'

'Do you want Coke with it?' Ben nodded, and watched Michael pour drinks from a tray behind him. 'Here you go,' he said.

'Thanks.' Ben sipped at his drink and smiled at the man as he sat down on the sofa beside him.

'So, do you want the money now?' he asked.

'Please,' said Ben, and Michael took his wallet from off the coffee table and counted out a hundred pounds in twenty-pound notes. Ben put the money in his pocket and took another large sip from his glass. 'What do you want me to do?' he asked, trying to sound as professional and confident as he could.

'Can I ask you something?' said Michael, ignoring Ben's question.

'Yes.'

'Is this your first time?'

Ben couldn't believe how astute the man was. However, he didn't want to look like a novice, so he said, 'No.'

'Sorry, I didn't mean to be rude, but you just looked a bit nervous, that's all.'

'I'm fine,' Ben retorted, a little defensively. 'So, what do you do for a living?' he asked, trying to sound more friendly.

'I'm a freelance designer.'

'That's nice. You must make a lot of money.'

'I don't do badly,' said Michael sipping his drink.

'How come you're not at work now?'

'I am.' Ben was confused and probably looked it. 'I work from home.'

'Oh, I see.' Ben was impatient to get on with things, so he once again asked, 'What do you want me to do, then?' He wasn't looking forward to it particularly, but there was something rather exciting about someone older and uglier taking advantage of his body just because of money. He felt worshipped and sexually desired.

'Right. This is the bit I've been looking forward to,' said the man, sounding, for the first time, slightly sleazy. 'Shall we go into the bedroom?'

Ben led the way towards a closed door next to the kitchen. He opened it and was greeted with a large room, with a king-size bed in the centre. It was furnished with a few choice antiques and long blue velvet curtains at the window. The most notable thing in the room was a huge grandfather clock in the corner.

'What I want to do is suck your cock and then fuck you. Is that OK?' Ben nodded, sat down on the bed and took off his shoes and socks. He was about to remove his T-shirt when Michael stopped him and said, '*I'll* undress you, if you don't mind.'

'OK,' said Ben.

'Can you stand up, please?' Ben did so and Michael took off his top and ran his hands over his bare torso. 'Can you put your hands behind your head?' The man stroked the area under Ben's arms and ruffled the hair. He leaned forwards and inhaled the aroma that they gave off. Then he began to lick at Ben's exposed armpit, quite frantically, as if it were his mouth or cock. He bestowed the same treatment on Ben's side, lapping up all the sweat and bodily tastes that were to be found there. Ben hoped to himself that they didn't smell too sweaty and that his deodorant wasn't toxic. However, it rapidly dawned on him that his body odour was the main attraction.

Michael moved his hands on to the front of Ben's jeans and groped his cock and balls. He undid the buttons and let the jeans fall to the floor. Ben was not hard, but the man's fondling of him through the cotton boxer shorts that were now the only things he was dressed in, was enough to excite him, and his cock gradually stood to attention.

Michael kneeled down in front of him and sniffed at his crotch, running his nose up and down the length of Ben's penis as he did so. Then he guided the stiff member out of the slit at the front of the shorts and pulled back the foreskin. Ben looked down and saw how a droplet of pre-come had trickled out of the tip. Michael did not hesitate in putting his lips to the soft, swollen head and lapping up the sticky fluid. Ben quietly gasped at this; the feeling of the man's tongue licking his sensitive glans gave him quite a thrill.

Michael ventured further and took the whole head of Ben's cock between his lips and started to suck it. Although he was not particularly good-looking, it made Ben feel sexy to watch Michael stimulate his stiff member. He let his mouth engulf the whole penis and at the same time gently grasped Ben's balls and stroked them.

Soon he had gained confidence and was working his lips more

aggressively up and down the prick, and Ben started to feel an ache at the base. Michael's technique was very professional and caused him to relax into the act and let himself be taken.

He felt a hand stray around the back and take hold of his bottom. His arse-cheek was squeezed and his cock sucked even harder. Ben felt himself starting to come and he made this plain to Michael by letting out an excited whimper. The man put his lips to their best use and Ben started to squirt semen into his mouth. Michael lapped it down, sucking on the head of the cock so as not to lose a single drop. Ben continued to pour out his salty liquid and Michael drank it down.

When he'd finished ejaculating, the man did not let him go, but continued to suck at the now ultra-sensitive head of Ben's penis. The feeling was heavenly and yet at the same time acutely unbearable. The head had been made so sensitive with orgasm that the continued movement of Michael's tongue and lips made him squirm. Michael gripped on to Ben's arse and balls and kept the prick inside his mouth.

'Stop!' Ben found himself forced to shout. The man let go of his penis and fell back on his haunches, breathless from the act. Ben sat down on the bed. He could see Michael's erection and panicked about having it inside him. There was, however, nothing he could do. It was part of the job, and he prepared himself.

'Right. Can you lie face down, please?' Ben did as he was instructed and turned over on the bed. Immediately he felt hands on his bottom and warm breath on his skin. The man parted his buttocks and sniffed at his bottom. Ben was glad that he'd had a shower before he came out. He felt a slippery tongue probe his hole and slip into him. As ever, being rimmed was a pleasure, regardless of who was doing the rimming. Michael made his bottom wet with saliva and then inserted a finger into him. The digit was manoeuvred inside him and rammed in as deeply as it could be.

The man took his finger out and Ben saw him move across the room and open a drawer in the bedside cabinet. He produced a condom and a sachet of lubricant. In full view, Michael undid his trousers, slipped out his cock and put on the rubber. Then he disappeared out of Ben's line of vision and the hands were once again on his arse-cheeks. He felt a cold, slippery finger insert itself up his bottom, and when it came back out he was lubricated inside.

Next, the tip of Michael's cock touched Ben's sphincter, and Ben prepared himself for the painful insertion. Michael's prick, however, was smaller than Nathan's and seemed to glide inside Ben more easily, making his passage expand as it did so. It felt uncomfortable, but not intolerable. Ben relaxed his muscles around the penis and tried to imagine that it was Ringo who was fucking him.

Michael, still with all his clothes on, pushed himself in and out, without a care for Ben's bottom. Ben knew that the man wanted to get as much pleasure out of his hundred pounds, and, even though Michael had been civil and generous to him, Ben was still no more than an expensive one-night stand. Michael took out his aggression and pounded into Ben, grunting all the while and biting the back of his neck.

Ben tried to take a little pleasure from the act and found, to his own surprise, that his penis was once again stiff and secreting sticky fluid on to the duvet. He tried to picture Ringo's face and his beautiful prick, and imagine that it was the lad he had inside him and not some older stranger.

Thankfully the business did not take long. Soon Michael started to make moans of pleasure and Ben knew that the end was in sight. He felt the familiar movements of someone in the throes of orgasm, and soon the man had pulled out of him and was lying at his side. Taking him unawares, Michael moved close to his face and tried to kiss him.

'I'd rather you didn't,' said Ben, trying not to sound too stern.

'OK,' the man said and moved off the bed and into the en-suite bathroom. Ben dressed himself and went back in the lounge. Michael followed him in and thanked him, mentioning that he'd like to use his services again at some point if that was possible. Ben said it was, and then let himself out.

When he was back on the street once again, Ben thought about what had happened and felt pleased with himself. He was really a man of the world now. He'd made the best part of a hundred pounds for less than an hour's work. It was very flattering that someone was willing to pay him for sex. He did not feel dirty and cheap, as somehow he had expected to, but elated and confident.

'How did it go?' asked Lee as he walked into the front room.

'Fine,' said Ben. 'And yours?'

'Yeah. It was all right.' Lee did not seem as pleased with himself as Ben was. 'The client was pretty old and certainly no oil painting,' he said. 'But I thought of you, and it didn't seem so bad.'

'Did you? Oh, how sweet,' said Ben, feeling rather guilty that his own thoughts had been filled with Ringo. It wasn't that he didn't like Lee any more; he just felt more of a thrill thinking about the other lad, probably because Ringo seemed so much less obtainable.

'Did you think of me?' asked Lee.

'No. I thought of England,' said Ben, evading the real question.

There was a lull in the conversation and then Lee suddenly exclaimed, 'You'll never guess who I spoke to today.'

'Who?' Ben asked.

'My little brother, Joe.'

'Really?' said Ben. 'How did he get the number here?'

'I phoned him, you fool. And do you know what else?' Ben shook his head. 'He's going to come down and visit next week.'

'That's brilliant,' said Ben.

'Now I'm going to be making all this money, I can afford to give him some. I said I'd send him the train fare.'

'It'll be nice to meet him, especially after all you've said about him.' Ben was intrigued to find out what an eighteen-year-old version of Lee would look like. Surely he must be very beautiful.

'I'm really excited about it.'

'I'm sure you are,' Ben said. Lee smiled at him and they cuddled on the sofa together. Ben allowed the lad to kiss him full on the mouth, and they remained kissing for some time. Lee's tongue slid over his lips and wetted them with his saliva. Ben sucked on the slippery probe when it entered his mouth. It felt nice to be kissing Lee again, especially after having had the client's hands all over him earlier. Ben reached down and put his hand up the lad's T-shirt. Lee's stomach felt smooth and taut, and Ben accidentally brushed against Lee's erect penis as it jutted out against the fabric of his trousers.

'Shall we go up to the bedroom?' asked Lee.

'Yes,' said Ben, eager to wipe off the reminders of the client.

Just at that moment the telephone rang. Ben answered it. It was Eddie wanting to speak to Lee. He handed over the receiver and snuggled up to the lad as he spoke on the phone.

Eddie wanted him to do another job, Lee told him after he had hung up. He had to leave straight away. Ben was upset, especially as they were just getting comfortable together.

'Never mind,' said Lee. 'Save it till later.'

'All right. I'll see you in a couple of hours.'

After Lee had left the house, Ben wondered who was in, so he called up the stairs. Someone shouted back, but he couldn't tell who. After a few minutes he heard footsteps on the stairs and Luis entered the room.

'Hi,' he said. 'Did you call?'

'Yes. I just wondered who was in the house.'

'Only me and you, I think.' Luis sat down on the sofa beside him.

'I had my first proper client today,' said Ben.

'Yeah? How was it?'

'OK. Not as bad as I thought.' He looked into Luis's eyes, which were so dark that you couldn't tell the difference between the pupil and iris. His Spanish colouring and accent made him seem sexy and exotic. He had full, red lips and rounded cheeks. His nose was small and a little turned up, and Ben thought that his face still looked like a little boy's, even though he had heard Ringo say that Luis was eighteen. He had thick, dark hair, cut short and spiked on top. The lad was really very beautiful to behold. Ben felt horny just looking at him. Lee had got him going and then vanished. He had to relieve himself with someone. 'Can I kiss you?' he asked, feeling panicked by the possibility of a rejection.

'Sure,' said Luis. Ben leaned forwards and gently allowed their lips to meet. His tongue slid out and edged its way into the boy's mouth. Luis parted his lips and they kissed more passionately. This continued for several minutes, only pausing temporarily for them to draw breath.

Ben put his arms around the boy's neck and stroked the soft hair at the back of his head that was cut short and bristly. Then his hands moved down Luis's back and felt his sharply defined shoulder blades and muscular flanks. The boy returned the gesture by gripping on to Ben's waist. All the while, they kissed with passion, exchanging saliva and letting their tongues collide.

Ben was the first to pull back. 'Shall we go upstairs?' he asked.

'Yes. My room or yours?'

'Mine, I think.'

They climbed the stairs and entered Ben's humble room. It was so small that there was only enough room for one piece of furniture: a sofa-bed that slept two people. The boys kept their belongings piled in the corner or in bags under the bed.

Luis lay down on the bed, passive and available, and Ben scrambled on top of him and started kissing his face and neck. The boy was wearing a blue vest that revealed the top of his strong arms and shoulders, and tight jeans, making it easy to see his cock, which was already erect. In imitation of his earlier client, Ben made Luis raise his arms above his head and he inhaled the sweaty aroma of Luis's armpits. He was surprised at how pleasant and arousing it was. He started to lick the area and consume the boyish fragrance. It was great and he went at it with an almost aggressive enthusiasm.

Luis squirmed beneath him, but for once Ben felt dominant and powerful, and he held the lad down with all his strength. He wanted to take his body and do what he liked to it – use Luis like he had been used by his client earlier that day.

Ben pulled the vest over the lad's head and was confronted with his smooth, muscled torso. Immediately, he started to bite at the nipples that seemed to stand out and await his lips and teeth. Luis whimpered with pleasure as he did so.

Ben moved down and kissed the boy's stomach, which was flat and hard. He could see how big and stiff his cock was, so without any further hesitation he unbuttoned the jeans and pulled them off. Luis wore tight cotton briefs and his erection was virtually falling out of them. Kneeling over him, Ben touched his penis through the material and noticed a sticky patch where the tip came to rest. He pulled the briefs down just enough to reveal the boy's swollen glans and applied his tongue to the trickle of fluid that had seeped out. It tasted sweet and he drank it down. Luis was circumcised, so the head was already totally exposed. Ben lowered the briefs a little more and took the thick length into his mouth and devoured it. It really was a huge piece of meat, and Ben was keen to take in as much of it as he could.

Next, he freed the boy's balls and removed his underwear altogether. In their sac they felt small and tight and soft to the touch. Ben played with them as he sucked on the cock, which continually leaked pre-come into his mouth.

In less than a minute, Ben could have sworn, Luis was panting furiously and trying to push his pelvis as far forwards as possible, as if he wanted his whole prick to be engulfed. Ben could not believe how easy it was to make the boy come, for Luis had already started shooting jets of semen into his mouth. Ben eagerly swallowed them. Luis's fluid was thick and salty, and seemed to flow from deep within him for ages.

When at last he finished coming, Ben was totally aroused and longed to relieve himself. He stood up and stripped, all the while keeping his eyes fixed firmly on Luis's. When he had nothing on but his boxer shorts, Ben asked, 'Can I fuck you?' The boy nodded his head, and Ben went into the pocket of his jacket that hung from an old picture hook on the wall. He pulled out a condom and a tube of KY, and laid them on the bed. 'Turn over,' he said. Luis instantly obeyed, and Ben saw his arse properly for the first time. He was keen to get stuck in. Rimming was rapidly becoming his favourite sexual act. It was the thing that seemed to come closest to a man's inside – the part that sex was surely aiming at. It was so great to go where a girl would never dare. This was something solely between men and thus created a perfect, unique pact, that at once excluded others with its dirty connotations and elevated one to a more intimate plane.

Ben leaned forwards and stroked the smooth skin on the boy's buttocks. The globes were firm and muscular. He moved Luis's leg so that it bent at the knee and automatically opened a path of vision to the area between his arse-cheeks. Ben kissed his buttocks and then parted them a little more and inhaled the musky smell that lingered there. He started to lick up and down the length of the crack, until he could not stop himself any longer from putting his tongue to the boy's tight, puckered entrance. He kissed its circumference and tried to prise it open with his tongue. It felt brilliant to be so close to Luis's perfect arsehole, and he violently French-kissed it, jabbing in his tongue as far as it would go.

Ben worked on the boy's entrance for quite some time, making it slippery with his tongue and then using his fingers – as many as he could get in – to prise it open even further. This way he could put all his energies to getting as far inside as possible. All the while, Luis wriggled about on the bed, making quiet moaning noises under his breath. He was obviously enjoying the rimming as much as Ben was, his penis stiff and leaking pre-come on to his underwear.

It was time now to fuck the lad, so Ben pulled off his shorts and unwrapped the condom. He positioned it on the top of his cock and rolled it right down over the shaft. Next, he opened the tube of lubricant and squirted some on to his fingers. Some he rubbed across the condom and the rest he put up Luis's arsehole, so that it was greasy, and thus easier to enter.

Ben knelt between the boy's parted legs and aimed his penis towards the exposed hole. He could not fathom how such a small entrance would be able to accommodate so large an object. However, he knew that it was possible, and so he put the tip of his penis against the opening and slowly pressed it in. Luis did not voice any objections, so he continued with greater assertiveness. The opening dilated a little and allowed him deeper inside, but still it was a tight squeeze. The feeling was sensational and the view even better. Soon the whole of Ben's long member was lodged right up inside the lad and Ben's balls rested between his buttocks.

Luis did not raise any objection; it was as if he was oblivious to what was happening. Ben started to move his cock in and out of the boy, each time making the movement more assertive and less like he was worried about causing pain. The feeling was supreme and sent shivers through his body. Ben used the lad as a tool to relieve himself, and now screwed him with violent thrusts of his hips. He pushed his cock deep inside and then quickly pulled it back out again, so far that it almost left Luis's body altogether. He carried on with these movements for some time, gaining momentum and using his arms and legs to help him thrust backwards and forwards.

Ben paused for a moment and decided to try fucking him another way. He asked the boy to turn on to his back. Luis followed the instructions, dislodging the sheathed member as he did so. Ben positioned himself in front and signalled for the lad to raise his legs in the air, as Eddie had once made him do. He held them there and pushed his cock back inside. This time it went in easily, the opening having already been dilated.

There was something very sexy about this position. It was like having sex with a girl. Ben was looking straight at the boy he was fucking and the boy was looking back at him. He had total control and was also able to observe every movement of his partner's face. If he pushed a little too hard he could see the wince of pain on Luis's face, and there was something terribly exciting about that. Ben realised that it was very possible to take pleasure from someone else's discomfort.

He pounded away, keeping the boy's legs in the air by gripping on to his thighs. Now he could see even more clearly his own penis as it slid in and out of the tight passage. Luis's cock was erect too. The stimulation in his arse had obviously aroused him, and a steady stream of fluid was oozing from the tip. Ben dabbed a droplet on to his finger and tasted it. He knew that his own orgasm was fast approaching, so he pushed his cock in and out as fast as he could.

Suddenly he felt himself coming. It was intense and focused on his penis, not spreading throughout his body like when you come in the open. He panted a little as it happened, and this seemed to encourage Luis to take hold of his own cock and wank it. Within seconds the other boy was coming too. A long jet of spunk shot across his chest and landed just below his chin. More followed, and Ben was thrill to see the drops of come spattered over the lad's naked body. The last few dribbles of semen ran out of the tip and Luis rested, breathless and clearly relieved.

Ben stopped coming and slowly drew his cock out. The muscles in the lad's body once again relaxed and returned to their usual state. He leaned forwards and kissed the boy with a deep closeness that had been reflected in their sex.

Ben was kept busy for the next few days with phone calls from Eddie that led to appointments with punters. It seemed as if he were the golden boy of the gang, and Eddie wanted to use him as much as possible. Some days he would do two or even three people, and yet not get a day off to make up for it. Ben didn't mind – the money was too good. He'd never had so much cash pass through his hands. And it certainly did pass through his hands. Expensive nights out on the town, dinner, drinks, perhaps a club later on: it all cost money.

At some points he thought of Paul and what he was doing. He wanted to invite him up to London; send him money, even. However, he didn't really want his friend knowing all the sordid details of what he was doing for a living, and there was no hope of covering it up. His whole lifestyle revolved around it.

On Wednesday Ben was sent to Seven Sisters, where he serviced a man who wanted to be spanked with a length of cane and masturbate himself at the same time. Ben thought this was hilarious. The easiest money he'd ever made in his life.

Later that day he'd seen an old Asian-looking man who wanted to be fucked hard with a dildo – which he provided – and afterwards, with Ben's cock. Ben had trouble keeping it up, but luckily he didn't have to look at the client's face and tried throughout to picture doing the same thing with Luis.

Thursday took Ben to Chiswick to service a very wealthy white man, who wanted him to wear a school uniform and then fuck him in it. The uniform itself was too big for him, which he thought made the sex even more ridiculous, but the punter seemed to enjoy himself and he was paying, after all.

On Friday he saw three people. The first man, it turned out, wanted only to talk, which was easy. He spoke about his wife and how he felt guilty that he was gay and couldn't tell her. He even felt too guilty to have sex, it transpired. Ben was relieved because the man was far from attractive.

The next client, a tall, sinister-looking American in his forties – who claimed to be a bit of a famous writer, though Ben had never heard of him – just wanted to rim him and nothing else. The man asked him to pretend to be dead, saying that he was into that sort of thing. Ben did as he was told, and took two hundred pounds for the job.

Finally that day he serviced a very elderly gentleman, with white hair and a faint German accent, who told him that he could get him into the porno movie business. He wanted to take some nude photographs of Ben to send off to the appropriate people, but Ben made it very clear that he didn't want to be passed around the gay community on a dirty tape. The client settled for a swift blow job and Ben coming over his face.

By the end of the week, most of the other clients had blurred into one great mass of sexual encounters. Ben had banked on having sex with someone when he came to London, but not with this many people and getting paid for it as well.

The week left him exhausted and drained of semen and sexual energy. He hoped that Eddie would give him a few days off so that he could relax and spend some time with Lee. However, it was made clear that this was not possible. Eddie needed them working all the time. Even though Ben was working really hard, the money did not go far. Eddie took a lot of it. And what was more, by the end of the week the fifty per cent cut that Eddie usually took was increased to seventy, and, as Eddie had all the contacts and made all the arrangements, there was nothing Ben could do about it.

Six

Ben stood under the shower trying to wake himself up. It'd been a late night last night and he'd smoked and drunk too much. However, he had to revitalise himself as today he'd planned to go with Lee on a day trip to Brighton.

He lathered his hands and washed himself all over, firstly under his arms and on his chest, then his shoulders and back as far as he could, and then his arse and his cock and balls. It felt good to clean his penis, and he drew back the foreskin and soaped up the head. It was so sensitive that his cock immediately stiffened and for some time he just stood under the warm water wanking himself. However, he didn't want to make himself come – he didn't need to, while he had Lee to do it for him and the clients to keep happy – so he washed off the soap and turned off the shower.

While drying himself Ben wondered what they would do in Brighton. He'd been lots of times when he was a kid but this time he'd be able to do whatever he wanted; there would be no parents telling him what to do and what not to do.

He walked back into the bedroom, where Lee was sitting on the edge of the bed already dressed and smoking a cigarette. Ben dropped the towel and started to dress himself.

'You look nice and clean,' said Lee.

'Thank you.'

'I've never really noticed what a cute bum you've got.'

'Really?' said Ben. 'You surprise me, the amount of time you spend in close proximity to it.'

'Ha, ha, very funny.' There was a moment of silence before Lee continued by saying, 'Seriously, though, shall we go back to bed for a bit?'

'A bit of what?'

'You know what I mean.'

'No,' said Ben. 'We'll never get to Brighton if we do that. It's eleven o'clock already.'

'I suppose you're right.'

Ben put his clothes on and dried his hair.

'What do we need to take?' asked Lee.

'Nothing really. Just money, keys and cigarettes. We'd better take a coat as well in case it rains or something.'

The boys got themselves ready and left the house. It was a bright morning with just the slightest rustling of a breeze in the trees above them. They walked to the bus stop and took a bus to Victoria.

It was only a fifty-minute train ride down to the Sussex coast and Ben looked out of the window for most of the journey, saying nothing, just taking in the view. Lee was reading a magazine, so Ben didn't want to interrupt him. It was so good to get away from the dirty city and all the dirty clients he'd been servicing over the past week.

They had enough money now to have a really nice time. They could eat out, go drinking, get into a club without having to worry about the cost. It was going to be a really good day.

When the train pulled into Brighton station, Ben nudged his friend.

'Are we there?'

'Yes.'

They got off and walked down the platform and out into the open air. Ben felt so relieved not to be in London. He looked across at his friend and smiled.

'So, where shall we go?' he asked.

'Don't ask me. You're the one who claims to know the place.'

'I never said that. I just said that I came here a few times when I was a kid.'

They walked through the town and into the lanes and looked in all the little shops full of overpriced trinkets. Then they went to the second-hand record stores and looked for things that they'd never been able to find before. Ben discovered a couple of albums that he'd always wanted and Lee seemed pleased with a few cheap singles he'd found.

They left the main town and walked down West Street towards the sea. From the top of the hill they could see it laid out before them like a shimmering sheet of dark blue glass just below the sky. They walked slowly down towards the front and crossed the road so that they were on the right side and then went down some steps.

The two boys stood on the concrete where the beach ended and civilisation began. It was not the most beautiful coastline in the world, but there was something about it that conjured up a nostalgic feeling. It wasn't even as if it was nostalgia for his own childhood; it was more a remembrance of generic British child-hoods past. There was such a Victorian feel to the whole scene, such a stoical blandness about it, that it made Ben feel sad.

They walked over the pebbles and down to the shoreline. Lots of people had put towels and deckchairs down on to the rough beach and were stretched out in the harsh sun or shyly dipping toes into cold water as it pushed up and down the beach at its own relaxed summer pace.

Ben sat down on the stones and looked up at his friend, who immediately sat down next to him and put his hand on his knee. They turned their attention back to the sea and watched a huge boat, that looked tiny because of its distance, slowly work its way from one side of the horizon to the other. Ben felt at ease just to be lying in the sun, watching the water and doing nothing. What was more, he had Lee beside him; and even though they weren't speaking, it didn't matter.

After a long time of just sitting on the beach, soaking up the atmosphere, the boys got up and started to walk along the front in the direction of Palace Pier. They passed all the cafes and clubs that were located under the arches of the promenade and then decided to stop in one for a beer.

Ben went in and bought the drinks and they sat on the benches outside sipping them and looking out to sea. There were lots of other people around them, but mostly couples, sometimes with children, doing the same thing that they were doing.

After they'd drunk their pints they moved on to the pier itself and walked slowly up it, looking at all the amusements they could spend their money on if they wanted to. There were loads of boys that caught Ben's eye who were either with their families or just hanging out with their friends, clearly with nothing better to do. He really would have liked to get the opportunity to seduce one of them. He glanced at Lee, who didn't seem to have noticed him looking at them.

Ben wasn't bothered about playing on any machines here, and rides only made him feel sick. Lee said that he could take it or leave it, too, so they just looked at all the other people and had a laugh at their expense.

'The only thing I *do* like is those machines where you put twopences in and try to knock money off a ledge. Do you know what I mean?'

'Yes,' said Lee.

'Can we have a go on those?'

'Of course. But let's use the ones along the front – they looked less crowded.'

Ben didn't mind waiting, so they carried on up the pier, looking at the boys and the view. It felt weird for Ben to be walking over the water. It was an odd sensation. If it wasn't for the ancient structure of the pier itself, there would have been nothing stopping him from drowning. He mused on what a funny invention it was.

When they got to all the funfair rides at the end they turned around and walked back down the other side. About halfway down, Ben noticed a lad playing a fruit machine and when they reached him Ben stopped and stood behind him, watching the game he was playing. He virtually forgot that Lee was with him, so transfixed was he by the boy's fantastic looks and sexy image.

Ben glanced over his shoulder to check that Lee was there. His friend gave him a look that told Ben he knew what was going through his mind. For some time Ben just watched the machine, sometimes glancing at the lad's face to take in his good looks, but he didn't seem to have noticed them standing behind him.

'Not having much luck, are you?' said Ben.

The lad looked around and shook his head, disappointed. There was a single second when Ben held his eye contact and then they both broke it at the same time. It was in this second that he knew that this was the one he wanted to seduce. He looked more alone and bored than the others he'd seen up the pier, and there was something very appealing about a loner you might be able to corrupt.

'Shit!' hissed the lad.

'What's the matter?' asked Ben.

'I've run out of money.'

Ben swiftly reached into his pocket and produced a ten-pence piece which he put into the machine. He had to inwardly congratulate himself for his swish handling of the moment. The lad, however, as cocky as any small-town teenager, didn't even thank Ben; he just continued playing.

Lee gestured for them to move on and Ben felt as if he could not object. They walked off and he glanced back over his shoulder just in time to catch the lad looking at him. He smiled but the lad did not smile back.

'That was generous of you,' said Lee, a note of sarcasm clearly detectable in his voice.

'I know.'

'You didn't by any chance have an ulterior motive, did you?'

'Maybe,' Ben confessed.

'Surprise, surprise.'

'He didn't seem very keen,' said Ben, a little downcast.

'Oh, I'm sure he was just playing hard to get. Boys are always up for some fun. The amount of lads I used to sleep with who claimed not to be interested or to be straight or whatever. By the time they've had a few drinks or some smoke and you've delivered a clever line or two, they're sitting in the palm of your hand, begging you for it.'

'Is that so?' said Ben.

They walked down the pier and crossed the road. There were some arcades there with lots of machines in them. Ben was sure they'd have one of his two-pence games, so he went into the first one and looked around. The place was full of lovely lads, some alone, but most in pairs or groups. It was like a gold mine of hot stuff. The games were just the bait, the boys the catch.

They wandered around staring at everything and not finding the machine they were looking for.

'Lots of nice lads here, eh?' said Lee.

Ben nodded, too amazed by the selection to say anything.

After scouting around, they decided to leave and try the next arcade along. This was a good move as they found several machines there that fitted Ben's requirements. He changed up some money into two-pence pieces and started to feed them into the machine. Sometimes he'd get the timing wrong and miss his moment; other times the coin would catch but not push any others off the trays and into the collection trough.

Ben stood playing the machine for some time, replenishing his rapidly depleting supply of coins with new ones that he won. However, soon, as with most games, more money was going in than was coming out.

'Ben,' said Lee all of a sudden, breaking the silence and making him jump.

'What?'

'You'll never guess who's over there.'

'Er . . . the lad from the pier?' Ben guessed.

'Right.'

Ben turned around and saw the lad playing another fruit machine. He looked so cute with his back to them and his head down. Ben could see the outline of his rounded buttocks through his canvas trousers and they looked really great. He wanted to go over and slide his hands down the back of them, or run his tongue down the crack and into the lad's undoubtedly tight hole.

'Shall I go over and speak to him?' asked Ben.

'If you like.'

'You're not jealous, are you?'

'No,' laughed Lee. 'But I would be if you got to do him and I didn't.'

'What shall I say?'

'I don't know. Anything. Ask him whether he wants a drink.'

'OK,' said Ben and he walked over to where the lad was standing.

'Hi again.'

The boy turned around and looked at him blankly.

'Do you remember? I gave you ten pence up the pier.'

'Right,' said the lad.

'What are you up to?'

'Just playing the games and stuff.' He had a sweet local accent that turned Ben on even more.

'Do you want to come for a drink with me and my mate?'

'I haven't got enough money.'

'That's all right, we'll pay.'

The lad nodded and followed Ben.

'Shall we go for a drink?' he asked.

'All right. What's your name?' Lee said, turning to the lad.

'Craig.'

Lee introduced them to the lad and they exchanged a smile, before leaving the arcade and walking down the front and back up West Street. Craig followed them, a downcast expression on his face.

Ben suggested a pub as they passed it and they went inside.

'What do you want to drink?' he asked the lad.

'A pint of whatever.'

'OK,' said Ben and he ordered the drinks and paid for them. They went and sat down at a table in the window and he launched into a conversation about how they lived in London and had come down for a day out to have some fun.

'What do you do?' Lee asked.

'Nothing. I'm on the dole.'

They talked on and after the second drink Craig started to

loosen up a bit. Ben was intrigued to find out about the lad, but Craig held back on lots of the facts, answering the questions with short answers and not asking any back. It was probably because he was shy or felt intimidated by two young men questioning him.

'So, have you got a girlfriend?' Ben asked.

'Not at the moment,' Craig replied.

Ben thought that this sounded more hopeful – a lad of his age not having a girlfriend must mean he'd be terribly sexually frustrated. Perhaps he'd be prepared to go with the flow and take what he could get.

'Craig?' said Ben, a little nervous.

'Yes?'

'Do you smoke dope?'

'Yeah, if it's on offer.'

'Well, we've got some, so perhaps we could have a joint somewhere.'

'Sure,' said the boy.

'Do you know where we can go? Because it's impossible in public.'

There was a silence; then Craig said, 'Well, there's this squat that me and my mates sometimes hang out in. We could go there.'

'Sounds like a good plan,' said Lee.

The boys finished their drinks and left the pub. Craig then led them through a maze of streets; all the while, Ben wondered where they were going, getting a little worried that it was all a hoax or something. They eventually found themselves climbing a hill lined with terraced houses, with other roads coming off it at various intervals. It looked like quite a poor area.

'Are we nearly there yet?' asked Ben.

'Not far,' the lad replied and carried on walking.

Eventually they turned down one of the side streets and then into another and came to a row of three houses all attached to one another that looked out on to a tiny alleyway off the main street. Craig indicated the final one of the three as their destination. They all looked in a bad state of repair but this one was the worst by far. It looked as if it had already been half pulled down.

They followed Craig down a path that led to the side of the house which was almost impassably overgrown with brambles and vines. A door that had at some point been boarded up was now smashed in at the bottom and, when Craig removed the piece of plasterboard covering the gap, they crawled in through the opening.

The inside of the house was as dilapidated as the outside. There was no furniture in it apart from lots of boxes, crates and wooden pallets used for packing and moving heavy things around. The place was covered in dust and dirt and Ben couldn't imagine it having been lived in for fifty years. The peeling wallpaper and chipped tiles were from a time long past.

Craig led the way to the back room which looked out, through a cracked patio door, on to a garden so overgrown that you might have imagined Sleeping Beauty was taking a nap somewhere in the house. The room itself had a huge fireplace in it that Ben presumed would once have been very grand and ornate. Now it was but a shadow of what it would have been in its heyday. The place was dusty and there was a huge crack in one of the walls which gave the impression that the house was not structurally sound.

Ben sat down on a tea chest and got out his dope tin. He started to prepare a joint while the other two looked out of the back window. No one said anything.

When he'd finished, he put it to his lips and lit the end. He took a few drags and then handed it to Craig. Both of them watched as the lad inhaled the smoke, held it down and then blew it out again. After a couple more drags he went to hand it to Lee, but Lee shook his head, telling him that he could finish it. The boy continued to smoke it, not wasting any. As soon as he'd exhaled smoke, the next dose would be taken in. Ben hoped that Craig would be stoned. However, just to make sure he rolled another and suggested that Craig smoke most of it.

'So, have you ever taken a blow job off a bloke before?' asked Lee.

Ben was glad that his friend had made the first move. It meant that he didn't have to say anything and probably mess it all up. Lee was much better at these things – he had a way with words and was a natural charmer when it came to seducing lads.

'No,' said Craig – a little too insistently, Ben thought.

'Not even when you were a kid?'

'Maybe,' said the lad after some hesitation. 'Why, have you?'

'Of course,' said Lee. 'When there aren't any girls around, you've got to. It makes no difference anyway. A blow job's a blow job, whoever dishes it out.'

Ben could tell that the boy was starting to wake up to the idea, and when he looked down at his crotch he saw the beginnings of an erection there. He hoped that Craig was going to let them mess about with him.

'I suppose so,' said the lad.

'Why don't you let us do it for you?'

'OK,' he said, nervously smoking the joint.

Without another word, Lee walked up close to him and dropped down to his knees, his face at the same level as Craig's dick. He reached out and started to feel it through the canvas of his trousers. Ben just stared at the lad's face, which was nervous and awkward, while his friend started to carefully undo Craig's trousers.

Within seconds they had fallen to the floor and Ben could see the skinny boy's stiff cock through his tight cotton briefs, and a sticky stain at the front where he presumed pre-come was leaking out. Lee sniffed and kissed the cock and balls without bringing them out into the open. Ben felt very jealous. He hoped he was going to get a go.

Lee paused for long enough to glance up at the boy and then across at Ben before he carefully slipped the prick out and held it tightly in his hand. He had a long, thin uncut member, and large balls that hung below it. Lee pulled back the foreskin and started to move his tongue around the swollen head with slow grace. Ben could see every movement he made and the look on Craig's face that accompanied it.

Soon Lee was taking more of the penis into his mouth, letting his lips slide down the shaft and then back up again, lingering when he reached the sticky head. Ben could see his friend slipping his tongue right into the slit at the end. He didn't even dare imagine how good the young lad's salty liquid must taste, in case he came in his pants.

Ben wanted a piece of the action, too, so he stood up and walked over to the boy. Without hesitation he reached down and took hold of Craig's balls and squeezed them tightly. The lad let out a little boyish whimper and pushed his groin further into Lee's face.

Ben stopped what he was doing and looked at Craig's arse, which was still covered with his pants. He moved himself so that he was squatting down behind the boy and gently ran his hands across the material that contained the cute bottom he had glimpsed in the arcade earlier. He never imagined that he'd actually be touching it in some squat up a back street. Craig did not object so he pulled the briefs down and let his hands travel over the smooth taut flesh. His bottom was so firm and round that Ben wanted to kiss it. He knew that it would take a lot of nerve to go that far, so for the time being he just explored it with his hands.

After a few minutes – Lee was still sucking the boy's cock deeply into his mouth – Ben started to push his hands down into the crack, separating the buttocks as he did so. It felt warm and constricted where his hand now was and he wondered what Craig's arsehole was like. With slow movements he parted the cheeks and took a look. Craig had a small, closed hole bordered with fine dark hairs, and Ben put his face close so that he could take in the aroma that was to be found there. The lad smelt of soap and sweat, and Ben could not stop himself from gently kissing the rounded cheeks.

There was nothing stopping him so he pressed on, making his mouth inch closer to the crack, and soon he was so close to the actual opening that he could smell the lad's most personal scent. He separated the cheeks even more and carefully licked the hole. It seemed to wink at him like a third eye, sensitive to his touch,

so he pushed his tongue roughly against it and heard the lad moan
with what he hoped was pleasure.

Ben had now gained enough confidence to rim with greater
vigour, so he started to work his tongue further inside, making
the passage wet with his own saliva and, at the same time, filling
his mouth with Craig's boyish taste. The lad seemed to open up,
probably as he relaxed into the feeling of what was being done to
him. His opening dilated and allowed Ben to push further in. He
stopped for a moment and inspected his good work. The boy's
crack was wet with dribble and he put a finger up to the hole
knowing that it would be simple to put it in. With great care he
twisted the digit inside until it was in to the knuckle. Craig did
not seem to object, so he drew it back out and pushed it in again,
this time with more force. The lad whimpered, but didn't stop
him. Having his cock sucked was probably so pleasant that he was
unable to make any protest.

Ben glanced around and saw his friend feasting on the erection.
Their eyes met and a smile lit up Ben's face. He wanted to have
a go at that. Perhaps they could swap.

Lee seemed to get the message without anything needing to be
said, and he let the boy's penis slide from his mouth. Lee put his
hands on Craig's hips and swivelled him around so that his arse
was now facing in his direction. Ben was confronted with a stiff
prick that stuck out and virtually hit him in the face. He took
hold of the balls that hung before him and squeezed them like a
doctor would his young patient's. Next, he angled the penis
downwards until it was at right angles to the body it was attached
to. This way it would not be so difficult to slip it into his mouth.
With his other hand he stretched back the foreskin that had
slipped forwards again. The shiny, swollen head became visible
and Ben dipped his tongue down the sticky slit at the end. The
young boy's pre-come tasted lovely, possibly the finest he'd ever
had.

Ben immediately put the whole length of Craig's prick into his
mouth and started to suck up and down it. He loved the feeling
of it hitting the back of his throat; it was as if he had the lad
completely in his power, the most sensitive part of his body at

Ben's mercy. Craig's shaft continued to leak pre-come, which Ben drank down with great enthusiasm.

He moved his hand down from the boy's balls and stretched it under him so that he was stroking his perineum. This seemed to please Craig so Ben moved it further along until he felt the tip of Lee's tongue coming into contact with his fingers. Ben thought this was fantastic. It was as if his friend was lubricating Craig's arse so that he could put his fingers in. And that's just what he did: started to ease a digit into Craig's bottom, while Lee was still licking around the outer ring, providing him with lubrication.

This went on for some time. It seemed to take quite a while for the lad to reach a climax, and Ben carried on sucking his cock and fingering him at the same time. Lee stopped what he was doing and came round to the front once again. He obviously wanted to be there for the best part.

Soon they were taking it in turns to suck Craig's cock; sometimes Ben licked the balls while his friend took the lad in his mouth, and at others Lee took a back seat and allowed Ben to do the sucking.

Obviously this became too much for the lad and he was forced to shed his load. It was Ben who had his cock when this started to happen. A jet of semen shot from Craig without warning and was swallowed down. Ben immediately gave the penis to Lee, who took the next spurt. And like this they took it in turns to swallow the warm, salty fluid fresh from his balls. Sometimes a drop escaped and trickled down the side of his hard head, but the lads were quick to lap it up. It was as if they were sharing the same meal, each drinking from the same fountain, both with a hand on the lad's cock.

Soon Craig had been drained but still the boys continued to suck as if they were trying to squeeze out another drop. The lad had not made much noise throughout the whole session, but now it was possible to hear him taking deep gulps of breath. Ben withdrew the finger that was still lodged inside Craig.

Immediately, Craig pulled up his pants and trousers and said nothing about what had just happened. Lee wiped the saliva and come from his lips and lit a cigarette, offering one to Craig at the same time. The lad took it and used his own lighter, which he produced from an inside jacket pocket.

Ben sat down again on the box he was sitting on before, trying as he did to make his hard-on not so noticeable. He too lit a cigarette and dragged deeply on it. The boy looked even more awkward now that they'd sucked him off and Ben racked his brains for something to say that would put him at ease or numb the tension in the room.

'We ought to go,' said Lee, breaking the silence.

Craig nodded and, without a word, they made their way to the door they'd entered by. They walked with the lad back to the centre of town where there was a difficult moment as to what to do next.

'I've gotta go home now,' said Craig.

'OK,' said Ben.

'Look.' The lad stared down at the ground. 'Do you want to meet later?'

'Yeah,' Ben said a little too enthusiastically. 'All right.'

'Where?' Lee asked.

'Outside the arcade at nine,' he said and was gone without waiting for an answer. The boys watched him disappear into the crowded shopping centre.

'Do you think that's a good idea?' asked Lee.

'Yes. Why not?'

'Well, you never know if he might regret what happened and stir up some trouble.'

'Don't be ridiculous. Nothing's going to happen. Anyway, there's two of us; I'm sure we can handle it.'

They walked off and aimlessly wandered around the shops, not really knowing where they were going.

'What shall we do now?' asked Ben.

'Have a drink?'

'OK, but let's go to a gay pub.'

Lee agreed and they went off in search of one.

Ben was watching two men at the bar kissing. He'd seen the whole thing from start to finish. He'd watched a young man enter alone and order himself a drink. He'd seen how he'd scanned the bar for potential talent and then, temporarily giving up, settled down to his drink and cigarette. About ten minutes later an older man entered and stood at the bar beside him, ordered himself a drink and sat down on a bar stool. The older man caught the younger's eye and they smiled at one another. When Ben turned around again they seemed engrossed in conversation. Two minutes later they were kissing.

He thought how easy it was to pick someone up in a bar. He'd never really done it, but it seemed there was nothing to it. As long as you both had the same thing on your mind – sex – then you were fine.

'Look at them,' he said.

'What?' said Lee, his mind seeming to be elsewhere.

'Nothing.'

'Sorry. I was just thinking about that lad.'

'Nice, wasn't he?'

Lee nodded and finished his drink.

'Shall we have another?' asked Ben. His friend thought this was a good idea so Ben got up and went to stand at the bar. There were two men standing next to him that he hadn't noticed before ordering drinks, so he waited for the barman's attention. He could hear the men talking to one another in hushed voices and could see them glancing across at him from time to time, but he didn't like to look back.

When Ben went to pay for the drinks one of the men spoke to him, saying that he'd pay for them. He smiled and gratefully accepted, pleased to get something for nothing. He took the pints back to his table without another word.

'The two blokes over there paid for these,' he said indicating the men.

'That's cool,' said Lee.

'Perhaps I should've invited them to join us.'

'Don't be stupid. There's only one reason people buy you a drink and that's because they want to get in your pants.'

'I suppose so,' Ben admitted.

'They'll probably be over in a minute.'

When Ben looked up he could see the two men looking across at them. They both seemed like they were in their mid- to late-thirties and neither was particularly attractive although there was something charming about the way they were staring. Ben wondered whether looks were always the deciding factor in whether you found someone attractive or not, or whether charm played an important part.

Sure enough, Lee's words came true, and the men approached their table.

'Do you mind if we join you?' one of them asked.

Ben said that they didn't mind and caught Lee's awkward glance which told him that he shouldn't have said that. However, it would have been too difficult and rude to say no, so he didn't really have a choice in the matter.

'What are your names?' said the other man.

Before Ben had a chance to answer, Lee had already spoken.

'I'm David and this is James.'

Ben was surprised that Lee had lied and done it so effortlessly that the men wouldn't have known these weren't their real names.

The men introduced themselves and continued to ask them questions about where they lived and what they did, which Lee answered sometimes with shades of the truth and sometimes with blatant lies. Ben knew that his friend was doing this more to amuse himself than to hide their true identities.

'So, are you boys a couple?' one of the men asked.

'Yes,' said Ben. 'We've been together for three years.' He wanted to have a go at making things up and there was something very entertaining about lying to complete strangers just for the sheer hell of it.

'Really?' said the man, looking shocked. 'You must have been very young when you got together.'

'Yes. I was fifteen,' Ben lied. He could tell that the men were eager to get them into bed, but he wasn't very keen on it unless they were going to pay, and this was supposed to be their day off.

After a while, everyone's glass was empty and Lee offered to get them all some more drinks.

'We'll get them,' said the older of the two men.

'That's too generous of you,' said Lee.

'No. We insist.'

'OK. You pay and we'll go to the bar.'

They agreed and Lee took a ten-pound note off them and stood up. He gestured for Ben to give him a hand, and they walked off towards the bar.

'Why are you lying?' said Ben when they were far enough away not to be heard.

'Because it's fun and, besides, I don't want them knowing all our business.'

'So, what are we going to do?'

'Just get as many drinks out of them as we can and then piss off.' Lee ordered the drinks and pocketed the change. They each carried two back to the table and sat down. The men looked pleased with themselves and Ben chuckled inwardly at the private joke that Lee and he were having. The men thought they were getting somewhere but he knew better.

After they'd drunk a few more pints, the two men started to relax into the situation and the conversation became more heated. One of them asked whether Ben and Lee had a monogamous relationship. Lee said that they did, so the man asked whether they'd consider making an exception to the rule and coming back to their flat with them.

'You wouldn't have to do anything with us,' said the man. 'We could just watch you while you made out or whatever.'

'No. I don't think so,' said Lee.

There was an awkward silence after this in which everyone just looked down at their drink or at the other people in the bar.

'We ought to go,' said Lee. 'Thanks for the drinks.' He got up and Ben followed him out of the bar and into the early evening light. They did not even look round at the two men, but Ben knew that if he had done they would not have looked happy.

For a while they just walked along the front watching the sun slowly set over the water and dusk draw across the sky and deprive them of light. Ben was very aware that it was fast approaching the hour that they said they'd meet Craig. He really wanted to see the lad again and perhaps this time get a little further with him.

He felt drunk enough now to want to have sex with someone, not caring about the consequences.

Craig was waiting for them as they approached the arcade. He had a friend with him that Ben didn't notice until he got closer. The lad looked rougher and slightly older than him. His hair was cut short and he was dressed in sports gear like lots of boys of his age.

'Who's your friend?' Lee asked.

'This is Adam.'

Ben smiled at him but the lad just stared as if he hadn't noticed.

'What shall we do?' Lee looked from Craig to his friend and then back again waiting for an answer.

'We could go to the house for a smoke.'

'OK.'

They walked off together without saying anything, Lee ahead with Craig and Ben and the other boy trailing behind. Ben searched for something to say.

'How's it going?' was his poor attempt at a question.

'All right.'

'So, what do you do?'

'Nothing much. Just sign on.'

Ben couldn't think of anything else to say, and, as Adam didn't bother to ask him any questions, they walked side by side in silence. He could hear the murmur of Lee's conversation but not what was being said, and wondered what they could find to talk about.

When they reached the deserted house for the second time that day Craig went ahead and let them inside. They followed him into the back room.

Lee sat down on a box and Ben copied him. The room was dark now; the dull light that came in through the window was not enough to properly illuminate the place. However, he could still see the boys fairly clearly, and in some respects there was something atmospheric about the semi-darkness.

'Are you going to roll a joint?' asked Craig.

'OK.' Ben got out his tin and started to stick cigarette papers together.

There was a long silence which Craig eventually broke.

'Do you want to do what we did earlier?' he said.

Ben was shocked. He had never expected the lad to just come out with it.

'All right,' said Lee – a little too nonchalantly, Ben thought. 'Adam wants to do it, too.'

Ben stopped what he was doing and looked up at the new boy, who was standing by the window. He was very attractive. Ben hoped that he would get to have a go with him.

'That's cool,' said Lee. 'I'll just have a word with Ben.' Lee came over and took him into the other room. 'Looks like we're in,' he said. 'Which one do you want?'

'Can I have Adam?'

'All right.'

They went back into the other room and Lee immediately went over to Craig and fell to his knees. Ben felt awkward and did not know how to make the first move even though the lad was clearly very keen to get his cock sucked. Adam was looking across at his friend, probably trying to take in the scene and see what was going to happen to him. Ben drew in a deep breath and beckoned the lad to come closer.

When they were standing face to face, Ben was too nervous to look him in the eye; he ran his hands down the boy's thighs and over his buttocks, which felt round and hard. His trousers were made of a shiny acrylic material and felt like satin. Ben touched Adam's crotch, feeling a little more confident, and found to his excitement the beginnings of an erection jutting out at the front.

Ben slipped to his knees and untucked the lad's football shirt. He felt the smooth, taut skin and a line of soft hair running around his navel and down towards his groin. Ben put his face closer and inhaled the smell of Adam's clean clothes. He felt the bulge and was surprised at its size, which was larger than he had imagined it to be. Slowly he pulled down the tracksuit trousers to reveal tight cotton boxer shorts and a sticky patch where the tip of his prick was resting inside them. Ben inhaled again and this time he could detect the same heavenly scent that he'd noticed about Craig's crotch. It smelt of sweat and soap and some kind of boyish musk that seemed to be the trademark of straight lads.

While he explored the area and sniffed the odour, Adam just stood completely still and let him do whatever he wanted it seemed. The boy was obviously excited and ready to be sucked, so Ben took his time over the job and let his hands take in the shape and feel of his willing body. He pulled down the trousers at the back and squeezed Adam's firm buttocks. He let his hand slide down between the cheeks and into the crack, forcing the material into the groove. He wondered what the boy's opening would look like when he eventually got to explore it.

Ben could no longer control his excitement and he gently pulled the lad's boxer shorts down an inch at a time. The head of Adam's penis came into view and he could tell immediately that it was circumcised. This pleased Ben – he liked the feel of the smooth, unprotected head with no loose skin to get in the way – and he pulled the pants down so that they completely revealed the length of the shaft and his heavy testicles. The member itself was long and thick, almost too big; however, this only added to the excitement that Ben felt as he stretched out his hand and took hold of the thing, angling it down until it was at a right angle to the lad's body and directing the tip towards Ben's open mouth.

It was huge but it glided in without too much effort; Ben's sexual excitement made the whole thing possible. He let the lad's cock slip right inside until it touched the back of his throat and he had to stop himself from heaving. It was so long that, even with the prick in as far as it would go, his lips were still not around the base.

Ben started to move up and down the shaft and at the same time he took hold of the boy's balls and squeezed them in the palm of one hand. With the other hand he pulled Adam's boxers down at the back and felt them fall to the floor. He stroked the smooth, warm flesh of Adam's arse-cheeks and then let his hand stray between them and investigate that sweaty area which was lined with fine hairs.

All the while, Adam's prick slid over Ben's lips and into his mouth, where he could taste the pre-come that was escaping from the tip in larger and larger quantities. Every time he sank right down, his nose touched Adam's pubic hairs and for a second he was able to inhale the sexy aroma of sweat and teenage musk that hung there like the school changing rooms after a rugby match.

Ben sucked with all his energy, the same view of the lad's flat stomach and line of hair always in front of him. The head of Adam's penis felt swollen and hard in his mouth, and he wondered how long it would take before the lad started to come. He allowed the hand that was exploring the lad's crack a little more freedom and it rested on the tight opening that was, in fact, so tight he could barely find it. However, when Ben did lay a finger on it, he found it virtually impossible to penetrate. Adam had obviously never been touched in that place before – not even by the doctor, Ben suspected. He was so pleased to be allowed the privilege of being the first to open up the lad's virgin hole, and, without taking another moment to think, he stopped sucking and turned the lad around.

He was instantly confronted with the wonderful sight of two firm, pert buttocks clamped together so that it looked as if he would have to bend the boy right over to be able to make them part. Ben loved it when someone's cheeks were so solid that you had to pry them apart to gain access to the soft crease between. He made Adam spread his legs as far as he could, bearing in mind the trousers and underwear around his ankles made this difficult for him. Then he angled the lad forwards slightly, so that he had to rest his hands on his knees for support. This had the effect of making his buttocks part a little so that Ben could open them even more and for the first time see Adam's crack and hole. He took a deep breath and inhaled the aroma there which smelled pungent and almost overpowering. There was something so rude about sniffing where most people would never dream of sniffing. However, the lad did not seem to object, so he went a step further and started licking and kissing the crease between Adam's buttocks, taking his time to moisten every inch with saliva and then to linger over the best place of all – Adam's tight arsehole.

Ben pushed his tongue roughly into the opening but was

102

unable to make the single closed eye dilate. Instead, he used his finger and, after wetting it, prodded the hole until he managed to squeeze the tip inside and feel the lad's warm interior. He removed the finger and, wetting it some more, replaced it as before, twisting it firmly into the gap he was creating. To Ben's great surprise, this time he managed to sink in a little deeper than before, making the path all the more accessible for next time.

He carried on like this for some time, gradually, with slow and gentle work, opening Adam up so that eventually his tongue would be able to effortlessly slide inside without the aid of fingers. This was soon achieved and Ben put his lips to the boy's anus and his tongue deeply into the passage.

He could feel the lad wriggling about and making tiny moaning noises under his breath, clearly unused to the sensation of being rimmed. Ben took a great pleasure in probably being the first to perform such a rude act on Adam. He maintained the probing movements of his tongue until he felt that Adam had been opened up enough. He didn't want to hurt or embarrass him, so he stopped and viewed his work. The boy's arse-crack was dripping wet with Ben's saliva and the hole itself was more open than when Ben had started working on it.

Ben felt satisfied and he once again turned the lad around so that Adam's cock was jutting towards his mouth. He opened wide and took the boy inside, the great sensation of having control over the huge prick giving him a thrill of pleasure. Ben gripped on to Adam's buttocks and let a finger stray back into the lad's anus while he sucked him, hoping that the combination of the two things would be enough to produce an ejaculation.

Soon enough his hopes were realised and the lad started to make low moaning noises and push his hips into Ben's face. This also caused Ben's finger to move in and out of him and a spurt of come to shoot out from the tip of Adam's prick. Ben swallowed this and the other jets of fluid that followed. He could feel how hard the head of Adam's prick had become and wondered what the sensation must be like for him. His semen was thin and watery and did not taste as salty as most of the other lads' semen Ben had swallowed.

103

Adam's prick soon dried up and Ben, after making sure there
were no droplets he had missed, let it slide from his mouth. He
then pulled his finger out of the lad's bottom and sat back on one
of the boxes, panting, an erection sticking up in his jeans. Adam,
looking flushed and guilty, swiftly pulled his trousers and pants
back up and arranged his semi-erect cock so that it was hard to
see it through the material.

Ben noticed that Lee and Craig were sitting separately, both
smoking, looking out of the window. He wondered how long
ago they'd finished and whether they had watched him sucking
Adam off.

'We ought to go,' said Lee after a short silence.

Ben nodded.

'Are you boys coming?'

'No,' said Craig. 'We'll stay here for a bit longer.'

'OK,' Lee said with a shrug, and he gestured for Ben to follow
him. They said goodbye to the lads and left the house.

It was dark outside, and when Ben looked at his watch he saw
that the time was ten-fifteen.

'Why did you want to leave so quickly?' he asked.

'It was getting late.' Lee paused and then added, 'And I didn't
want them to think about what we'd done, decide they'd been
taken advantage of by a couple of faggots and turn nasty.'

'Do you think that would have happened? I thought they
enjoyed it all as much as we did.'

'You never know how people are going to react after they've
come.'

Ben considered this and realised that his friend was right. You
may feel incredibly horny and be so desperate to get off that you
let anyone suck your dick, but when you've eventually spilled
your load and, in the cold, hard light of satisfaction, see who's
helped you get there, you usually conclude that it wasn't such a
good idea after all. Then you're just left with a kind of disgust
and a feeling of regret and, sometimes, anger.

'If we walk quickly we might be able to catch the ten-thirty
train,' said Lee.

Seven

Ben flicked through the pages of an old magazine. There was nothing in it to interest him and, besides, his mind was elsewhere. He threw it back down on to the table and looked round at the other patients. He'd already been waiting for half an hour, but it seemed like longer. Ringo had told him that you just turned up and someone saw you straight away. This must be a busy day.

The GUM Clinic men's waiting room was crowded. Ben was just one of twelve people. Some of them had been there before him and some had arrived later. A few men had been in and out of the examination rooms a couple of times, and Ben wondered what they were waiting for. Unlike the doctor's, everyone here seemed to be young. No one was over thirty and a lot of the people looked a similar age to him. He'd never been to a place like this, so he had no idea of the procedure. All he did know was that it seemed to take a very long time.

Ringo was the one who had suggested he come here. The other boys had agreed. They all claimed to visit the place more often than they visited the doctor. Sexual health in this game, Ringo had said, was of great importance. So, Ben had taken their advice, pushed his nerves to the sidelines and taken himself along.

Now he sat in the men-only waiting room, anticipating what would come next.

A man came out of what he supposed to be the doctor's surgery, and then the doctor himself followed and called Ben's name. Without hesitation Ben jumped up and went into the small room. The door was closed behind him and he sat down in a chair at the side of the desk, which faced the wall. The only things in the room were an examination couch, a trolley with medical instruments on it and a wash-basin in the far corner. The doctor himself was young and reasonably good-looking. He spoke with a cheery middle-class voice, which immediately put Ben at ease.

'What's troubling you, then?' asked the doctor.

'Nothing in particular,' said Ben. 'I just wanted to have a bit of a check-up. Make sure that there's nothing wrong with me.'

'I see.' The doctor wrote everything down on an official-looking form. 'Are you regularly at risk from venereal diseases?'

'Well, I do have a lot of sex, if that's what you mean.'

'Right. With women or with men?' he asked.

'With men,' replied Ben. The doctor made a note of this. Ben wasn't worried about telling him personal things. He knew that it would go no further, and was sure that the man must have heard it all before and far worse.

'Well, what I'm going to do is just put you through some basic tests, for syphilis, gonorrhoea, *et cetera*. Nothing too complicated. The nurse will deal with all that. But firstly I'll just take a little look at you. OK?'

Ben nodded, and his heart pounded at the thought of what would happen next.

'If you just want to stand up and drop your trousers.'

Ben stood and unbuttoned his jeans. He slipped them down to just above his knees.

'And your underwear, please.'

Ben pulled his boxer shorts down and stood quite still, lifting his shirt, so that he could be examined.

A cold hand took hold of his penis and roughly pulled back the foreskin, exposing the sensitive head. The doctor, remaining seated, used his thumb and forefinger to stretch open the hole at the end and look inside. At this point he shone a little torch at it, probably so that he could get a better look at the dark interior. Finally, he used both hands to examine Ben's balls. He held them firmly, and then slowly rolled each around, checking every part with great care.

'Can you turn round for me, please?' said the doctor, putting on a pair of gloves. 'And part your legs a little.' Ben tried to but his trousers were in the way. 'Don't worry. Just bend over.' He felt the doctor's hands part his buttocks and pry open his hole. Then a slippery finger entered him and felt around inside for a few seconds before being pulled back out again. 'That's fine,' the doctor said, and walked over to the basin and washed his hands.

Ben stood upright and pulled up his trousers and pants. The doctor dried his hands and sat back down at the desk. He made a few notes and then said, 'If you'd like to take a seat in the waiting room, the nurse will call you when she's ready.'

It was another fifteen minutes before he was called, this time into a different room, and told to sit down in a chair behind a screen. The nurse busied herself with putting on gloves and preparing instruments. She approached Ben and brought with her a small trolley that held a tray of equipment.

'We'll do the blood test first,' said the nurse. She produced a syringe and asked Ben to roll up a sleeve. After she'd found a vein and sterilised the area, she took two samples of blood. He'd been through this before and so it didn't seem too much of an ordeal.

After that was completed the nurse said, 'Now I'm going to take a couple of swabs from your penis. Stand up.' Ben stood up. 'Pull down your pants, please.' He took his trousers and underwear down once again and lifted his shirt. The nurse sat down in a seat opposite him and took hold of his cock. She drew back the foreskin and with one hand dilated the opening at the end. With the other she took a long, thin piece of wire, that looked similar to one of those plastic tea stirrers you get in cheap cafes, and inserted it down the slit and inside Ben's penis. It wasn't a very pleasant feeling, and he drew in a sharp intake of breath as it took place. The swab seemed to virtually go the whole length of his cock before the nurse pulled it back out again. She repeated the operation with a second tool. This one looked more like a long, wide cotton bud. When this too was over Ben's penis felt sore and stretched, and he pulled his trousers and boxer shorts back up.

'That's it,' said the nurse. 'If you wait outside for a moment, we'll give you your results.'

About ten minutes later Ben, who was by now thoroughly bored with the waiting room's selection of reading material, was called by the doctor back into his room and told that he was fine, that there was nothing wrong with him sexually. Ben thanked him and left.

It was Monday morning and Ben said that he'd meet Lee at Euston Station, because today was the day that Lee's brother, Joe, was arriving. Ben was quite excited about meeting the boy, who was the same age as him, and hoped they were going to get on. He could not help wondering whether something would happen between them, but tried to put the thought out of his mind. Lee was his friend and lover, so it would be wrong for Ben to fancy his little brother.

Lee was early. They met outside a fast-food restaurant and the lad said that he'd already been there for ten minutes when Ben arrived. They walked to the platform at which the train from Glasgow was expected.

'How were your tests?' Lee asked.

'OK,' said Ben. 'A bit embarrassing and uncomfortable.'

'Poor you.'

'Well, you ought to go along soon,' suggested Ben.

'No chance. No one's going to stick anything down my old man.'

'Well, don't expect me not to say "I told you so" when you're ill from too much dirty sex.'

Lee stifled a chuckle and waited at Ben's side for the train to arrive.

For once it was on time, and Lee bounded forwards when he

saw his brother among the crowd. They hugged while Ben stood a little way off, waiting to be introduced.

'This is Joe,' said Lee.

'Nice to meet you,' said Ben. 'I've heard lots about you.'

'You too,' said Joe. He was a small, slender young man, with longish blond hair that was parted in the middle and almost covered his ears. He had a similar face to his brother, with the exception of his bone structure, which was more highly defined, giving him a sensitive look. His eyes were a brilliant blue and his lips full and deep red. He looked young for his years, and Ben instantly thought him very attractive.

All three boys walked off in the direction of the underground and took a tube train to London Bridge. From there they caught an overground to New Cross Gate. Throughout the journey Lee and Joe chattered away, barely stopping for breath. Ben just listened, their matching Glaswegian accents keeping him amused and at the same time baffled as to what they were talking about. Most of it seemed to concern the family and their mutual friends.

When they got back to the house, Lee went straight into the kitchen to make his brother some tea and toast. Ben and Joe sat in the front room. Suddenly there were footsteps coming down the stairs and the door flew open and Eddie walked in.

'Hello,' he said, immediately clocking Joe. 'Who's this then? A new recruit?' He beamed brightly and sat down next to the boy.

Joe looked more than a little nervous.

'This is Joe,' said Ben, wondering why Eddie had been upstairs. 'Lee's brother.' He tried to emphasise the words in order to let Eddie know that this one was strictly out of bounds.

'Well, hello,' he said, ignoring Ben's obvious warning and leering at the boy as if he were a piece of meat.

'Hi,' said Joe.

'Have you ever considered following in your brother's footsteps?'

'How do you mean?' asked Joe, looking confused.

'By taking up a career in the sex industry.'

'I'm straight.'

'What's that got to do with it?' asked Eddie.

At that moment Lee came into the room with the tea. 'Leave him alone,' he said, obviously catching on to the situation.

'I was only talking to him,' Eddie retaliated.

'I know you. You were trying to rope him into one of your sleazy schemes.'

'I was just asking.'

'Well, don't,' said Lee. 'Anyway, what do you want?'

'My money.'

Lee went upstairs and brought down the cash that Eddie was asking for. The man counted it and then looked up. 'Is that all there is?' he asked.

'Yes. What did you expect? Half a million?'

Eddie said his goodbyes and left.

It was a warm summer's day and the boys decided to take Joe out to Greenwich. They sat on the top deck of the bus until it reached its destination, then strolled through the park and up the hill to the observatory, where they sat and looked down across south-east London, the Thames, the new Millennium Dome and the park that surrounded them.

Ben, Lee and Joe lay down on the warm grass for some time talking and absorbing the sun's heat. Ben stared upwards through the tinted transparency of his sunglasses and felt a soft breeze touch his bare chest. All three of them had taken off their shirts, and every now and then Ben sneaked a glance at Joe's torso, which was smooth and slim. He had no muscles to speak of, but there was something eminently appealing about his skinny boyish body, and Ben felt the acute desire to take him to bed and somehow look after him.

After the park, they strolled down to a pub in town and drank the rest of the afternoon away. Ben had three pints, which wasn't a huge amount for him, but in the middle of the day it always affected him more, and he felt quite drunk.

As they walked back through the crowded streets, full of shoppers and tourists, Lee and Joe talked about Glasgow and their parents. Ben got the impression that the younger of the two was not entirely disapproving of his brother's new profession. He was perhaps even a little curious as to what exactly was involved in the job. Ben wondered whether the boy was attracted by the idea of gay sex, now Lee had somehow glamorised it by his involvement.

The phone rang when they had got back to the house. It was Eddie with a job for Lee to do. He apologised to his brother for having to dash off on his first day of visiting.

'That's OK,' said Joe.

'Are you sure?'

'Of course. Ben'll look after me.' He looked over in Ben's direction and smiled.

'Do you mind?' Lee asked.

'Not at all,' said Ben.

'Thanks,' he said, picking up his keys and kissing Ben on the lips.

When Lee had gone Joe asked, 'Are you two lovers, then?'

'Kind of.' He wanted to get the boy into bed, so tried not to put him off by making out that it was serious with Lee. 'We're not going out together or anything. We're just good friends, that's all.'

'Cool,' said Joe, his eyes lighting up with what Ben hoped was excitement – perhaps at the thought of him and his brother fucking.

He searched for a plan to lure the boy to bed, and instantly remembered his friend, Paul. 'Do you want a joint?' he asked.

'Yeah,' said Joe. The look in his eyes and the excessively relaxed tone of his voice made Ben suspect that the boy didn't often get an opportunity to smoke dope and was excited at the thought of it now.

They went upstairs to the bedroom and sat down on the bed. Ben got out his tin and started to skin up. Joe watched him and spoke at the same time.

'Is this where I'll be sleeping?' he asked.

'I guess so.'

'What, with you two?'

'It *is* a double bed,' Ben pointed out. 'There's plenty of room.'

When he'd finished making the spliff, he lit it and took a few drags, then he handed it to Joe. The boy sipped smoke from it with careful naivety. Ben watched, amused and endeared.

The boy looked very beautiful with his floppy blond hair and bright blue eyes, and Ben wanted to take him to bed and show him the wonders of the sexual world he himself was still a novice in. For once he felt he was with someone who was less experienced than he, and there was something deeply exciting about that.

Joe lay back on the bed, resting his head against the pillows. Ben sat close at his side and looked into his eyes.

After the third joint, Ben suggested that they get under the covers.

'Why?' asked Joe.

'Because I'm stoned and it'd be fun.'

Joe nodded. 'I think I'm a bit stoned, too.'

Still fully dressed, they climbed into the bed and lay close together. It was now after six o'clock and the heat of the day had faded a little, making it not unpleasant to be warm under the covers.

Joe turned away from Ben and on to his side. This seemed like a gesture of encouragement and Ben gently put his arm around the boy. No movement of dissent came from him, so he gently kissed him on the back of the neck. Once again Joe allowed him this liberty.

Where his hairline ended there was smooth skin, and Ben, having started, could not stop himself continuing to move his lips over the area. The boy responded by pushing his body back towards Ben's and giving a quiet moan of sleepy pleasure.

Ben wrapped his arms tightly around the lad and smelt his hair. It was clean and fragranced with shampoo. He kissed the edges of Joe's exposed ear and let a hand stray up the front of his T-shirt. Joe did not object so Ben lifted his shirt and rubbed his soft, taut back. The lad's skin felt so lovely to his touch that he soon found himself kissing and licking it instead.

All of a sudden, Joe turned over in the bed and looked Ben straight in the eye.

Ben's first reaction was to kiss him on the mouth. 'Do you mind me doing this?' he asked.

Joe shook his head.

Ben lifted Joe's T-shirt right up at the front and started to kiss his chest. The boy was so slim and smooth that it was ecstasy to bring his mouth into contact with him. Joe stroked his hair at the back and this encouraged Ben to move further down the lad's body. Before he knew it he was kissing and running his tongue into Joe's navel, and his hands were rubbing the erection that he felt down below.

Ben undid the boy's jeans and saw that he was wearing cute striped briefs. He eased the trousers down and saw Joe's long, slim erection bulging in his pants. He moved his face in close and inhaled the musky scent that he found there. Then he slipped the boy's cock out and examined it carefully. It was smooth and of a pleasant length, but thin and rounded at the end. He was not circumcised and Ben wrapped his hand around its width and slowly stretched back the foreskin which was tight over the head. With his other hand he exposed Joe's balls. They were constricted and small and clung close to his body.

Ben licked off the droplet of pre-come that had escaped from the lad's opening and drank it down. Then he opened his mouth and with ease engulfed the swollen pinkish head. Joe let out a muffled gasp and stroked Ben's cheek.

By now Ben was totally absorbed in sucking the boy's slender prick which he took deeply into his mouth and then let slide out again. He gripped on to the tight little balls as he did so and held the foreskin down, exposing the head to the flickering of his tongue.

Within a few minutes Ben felt the head of the boy's penis harden and his balls tense up, and he knew what was coming next. Without a sound Joe started to pour out semen into Ben's mouth. Ben lapped it up and swallowed each successive squirt, hoping every time for more to follow. Soon, however, Joe's supply ran dry and Ben licked off the final traces from the still-swollen head of his prick and let it slide away from his mouth.

'Was that OK?' Ben asked.

'Brilliant.' Joe pulled his jeans and underwear up, and Ben knew that this was the signal that told him nothing further was going to happen. What had happened, however, was plenty, and Ben glowed inside with excitement at having been allowed to make the boy come. He only hoped that Lee would not find out.

Downstairs, the phone rang, and Ben raced down the stairs to answer it. As usual, Eddie's voice greeted him at the other end of the line.

'Hi,' he said.

'Ben, I want you to do a job for me.'

Ben wrote down the details, and then, rather annoyed at having his session with Joe disturbed, asked, 'Is that it?'

'No. There's one other thing. The client wants another boy to watch and possibly join in.'

'But everyone's out working at the moment.'

'I know,' said Eddie. 'I thought maybe you'd be able to find a stand-in.'

Ben thought for a moment. 'Like who?'

'I don't know. That's why I'm asking you. The money's good, though. They'd get a share of it.'

Just then he had an idea and said, 'You may be in luck, actually. I think I know someone who might help us out.'

'Really?' said Eddie. 'Who?'

'Don't worry about who it is, just be satisfied that the job'll be done.'

Ben hung up and went upstairs. Joe was still lying where he had been before on the bed. 'I've got a proposition for you,' he said.

'Oh, yeah?'

'How would you like to do what your brother does?' Ben paused, then added, 'Just as a one-off.'

Joe was silent for a moment. Ben was not sure whether he was in shock at the mere suggestion of being a rent boy, or was thinking about his decision.

'What do I have to do?' he asked.

'Probably not very much,' Ben replied. 'Maybe just watch. Or maybe the client will want you to join in a bit.'

Joe smiled and nodded. 'OK,' he said.

'Great.' Ben was pleased that the boy wanted to help out. It would make the whole thing far more enjoyable. 'There's just one thing,' he said. 'I want to keep this between ourselves.'

'Why?'

'Because I don't want Lee to know. He'd think that I was leading you astray, and I'm not, am I?'

'No. Of course not. I wouldn't do anything that I didn't want to do.'

'Good,' said Ben. 'We'd better get going soon, before your brother gets back.'

Joe nodded an agreement and put his jacket on. 'Shouldn't we leave him a note or something?'

'Yes. We'll say we got bored and went to the cinema.'

The two boys sat on the bus to Croydon where their client wanted them. It reminded Ben of the day he had run away to London and how he had passed through East Croydon station on his way to the big city. Now things were so different. He felt settled and content in his surroundings and lifestyle.

He had written to his mother a few days earlier, telling her that he was safe and happy and for her not to worry. He had not given an address or telephone number, as he wished to still remain in hiding from his past, but told her that he would call soon. He missed her and hoped that she wasn't too angry with him for running off like he had. He also hoped that she would soon be as proud of him as she would have been if he'd stayed on and taken his A levels.

They got off the bus and Ben consulted his A–Z. He led the way to the client's address and knocked at the door. A fairly attractive man in his late twenties answered and told them his name was Martin. Ben introduced himself and Joe and they went inside.

'Do you boys want anything to drink?' he asked when they were seated on the sofa in the living room.

Ben, eager to get the whole business over with quickly, declined for the both of them. Instead he said, 'Shall we get down to business?'

'Yes,' said Martin. 'Let's go into the bedroom.'

The two boys followed their client down the hall to a bedroom at the back of the house. It was large and cluttered with furniture and ornaments. There was a huge bookcase that covered most of one wall, and every shelf was filled to capacity with books. Ben wondered whether the man had read all of them.

'Do you want Joe to watch?' Ben asked.

'No,' said the client. 'I want him to join in.'

Ben looked over at the boy. 'Is that OK?' he asked.

Joe smiled and said, 'Yes.'

The client ordered them both to strip off all their clothes and they did so, Joe giggling quietly as if it were all part of some game he was playing in his head. Martin lay down on the bed and signalled for Joe to position himself above so that he could suck the lad's cock, and for Ben to kneel before Martin and do the same to him.

As he undid the man's trousers and slipped out his impressive erection, Ben saw him pulling down his new friend's pants and taking Joe's penis deeply inside his mouth. He'd certainly got the short straw, but he didn't mind. Joe was only helping him out; he shouldn't have to tackle the more unpleasant end of things.

Ben took the client's cock into his mouth and sucked on it. He had already drifted into his own usual trance, thinking about other things, especially what had happened between him and Joe earlier. The thought of this kept him interested in sucking off the client, and for once he almost enjoyed manipulating the large stiff member between his lips. He envied Martin though for getting the exciting task of making the boy come.

Ben looked up and saw Joe's cute, tight bottom moving about before him. From the angle that the lad was in he was able, every now and again, to snatch a glimpse of his puckered little arsehole as it flashed in and out of view. Ben wished he could reach forwards and use his tongue to open it up and delve inside Joe. He looked down and continued sucking his client's cock, now

116

with expert technique, giving Martin the fullest satisfaction his lips would allow him to.

When Ben raised his eyes again, he was just able to see the man inserting a finger into Joe's bottom and twisting it around. The boy let out a deep groan and Ben wished it had been his finger instead. He saw Joe arch his back and thrust his groin as far into the client's face as he could. Ben knew that the finger had been the final incentive to release his orgasm, and the boy made a high-pitched exclamation that he could not decipher, and then he knew that Joe was shooting out semen.

As if by magic, at that moment the client too began to squirt into Ben's mouth. Probably the sexual kick he'd got from Joe's orgasm had made him come in sympathy. Ben caught all the man's salty juice in his mouth and, when Martin had finally stopped ejaculating, Ben spat it out into a tissue that he had kept at the ready for this moment.

When he looked back up Martin had already taken his finger out and allowed the boy to slide from between his lips. 'Right,' he said, looking at Joe. 'That was cool. But now I want to watch you sucking him off.'

Ben was so excited when he heard the man's words. There was nothing he would have liked more. He immediately sat down on the edge of the bed and lay back, his prick rock-hard. Nothing happened for a moment so he looked up and, catching Joe's eye, said, 'Well, what are you waiting for?'

The boy knelt in front of him and took hold of his stiff cock and pulled back the foreskin. With his other hand he gripped Ben's balls and rolled them around in his palm. He opened his mouth, which seemed small, and took just the swollen head inside. It was clearly something that he wasn't used to, and he struggled to make his lips slide over it. Once inside, however, he seemed to find it easier to move his mouth back and forth, and soon he had taken even more of Ben's solid shaft.

The feeling was sublime and the view even better. Just looking down at the lad sucking away at his prick made Ben want to come. He lay back and let Joe's lips do all the work. He felt a hand on his stomach and one around his balls, and this, together with the repeated movements of the boy's gentle sucking lips, made Ben ache at the base of his prick.

'Don't let him come in your mouth,' said Martin. 'I want to see it happening.'

Ben was a little disappointed at the man's words. He had hoped to be able to shoot his load into the boy's mouth and have him drink it down. But it didn't matter, for he knew that already pre-come was seeping from the opening at the head of his cock and being accidentally drank by Joe.

The lad's lip movements were gentle and enthusiastic. He looked as if he was concentrating all his energy and skill into making Ben come, and before long Ben felt the aching in his balls becoming too intense to contain. Absorbed with excitement, he thrust his hips towards Joe's mouth in order to increase the fantastic feeling, and, without too much effort, he felt the semen rising to the surface.

'I'm going to come,' he panted. It was too late, however. Before Joe had time to let Ben's cock slide free, a jet of sticky liquid had already shot out and hit the inside of the boy's mouth. A second one left its residue on Joe's lips and face, and Ben saw him lick off the semen and swallow it, with a smile as he did so. The rest of the fluid shot out on to Joe's chest, and the masturbatory movement of Joe's hand helped it on its way.

The feeling was awesome, and Ben felt himself rapidly emptying of sperm. The boy's hand felt great clamped around his still-shooting prick, and the final trickle ran down Joe's fingers and on to his own stomach.

When he had finished coming he was surprised to see and feel the lad return his mouth to the sight of his earlier interest and start sucking at his still stiff, and now pulsating, penis. The sensation was overwhelming and Ben practically had to push the boy away. Still, it was great to see such a display of enthusiasm. He fell back on the bed, panting with exhaustion.

When he looked up again, Joe was getting dressed and Martin was counting out ten-pound notes. Ben stood up and, without a word, put his clothes back on. He took the money they were owed and immediately paid Joe his share, which the boy took with gratitude.

When they were outside, Ben asked, 'What did you think of that?'

'It was brilliant.'

'I hope you didn't mind having to give me a blow job.'

'Not at all. I can't believe you actually get paid for doing it.'

Ben felt at ease with Joe's enjoyment of the sex, and they walked back to the bus stop with a spring in their step.

'Where have you been, then?' asked Lee when they walked into the lounge.

'Didn't you read the note?' said Ben.

'Oh, yes, I read it all right.'

'Well, then, you'll know we were at the cinema.'

There was something in Lee's eye that suggested he was not convinced. Ben panicked.

'What did you go and see?'

'Erm . . . *Godzilla*,' Ben lied.

'Really?' said Lee. 'What was it like, Joe?'

'Oh, good,' he stumbled. 'Yeah. Good.'

There was a moment of silence and then Lee said, 'Why did you lie to me, Ben?'

'I didn't.'

'Oh, yes, you did. Eddie called while you were out. He told me where you'd gone, and it didn't take a genius to work out who the other person was that you took with you.'

Ben looked down at his feet with embarrassment.

'I can't believe you did something so thoughtless. He's my brother, for fuck's sake. I don't want him involved in this kind of thing. It's sordid and shameful and I wish I didn't have to stoop to it myself. But I do. And I don't want to drag Joe down with me.'

'I'm sorry,' said Ben, feeling stupid and bad.

'Don't be too hard on him, Lee,' said Joe. 'He may have suggested it, but it was me who agreed. I wasn't forced. I went along of my own accord.'

'Yes, but Ben should have known better. It makes me wonder what else he's been leading you into while I was out.'

'I can't believe you, Lee,' said Joe, sounding really angry for the first time. 'It was all right when *you* were doing the leading astray, wasn't it?'

Lee looked embarrassed and lost for words, and Ben wondered what the boy could have meant. The room was silent and Lee went out into the kitchen and the sound of the kettle boiling could shortly be heard.

Eight

'Guess what?' said Eddie's voice.

'Ooh, let me think. It couldn't be another punter to service, could it?'

'Well done. How *did* you guess?' Eddie read out the address as usual, and Ben wrote it down. 'This is very important, so I want you to be on your best behaviour.'

'OK,' said Ben. 'What's his name?'

'I don't know. He didn't say.'

'Any specified kinks?'

'He didn't mention anything, but I get the feeling he might be a bit weird.'

The row of last night had caused problems between Ben and Lee and Joe, so Ben left the house without telling them where he was going, and walked out through the front garden gate and down the street.

He took the tube to Camden and followed the directions he'd been given to a run-down back street. He walked down the road and stopped outside the appropriate house. Looking up at it, he thought the place looked like a squat. It made his own house seem like a palace in comparison. However, even squatters were allowed to hire rent boys if they wanted to and, as long as they paid the money, he was willing to do the job.

Ben went to knock at the door, but as his hand touched it the thing came open of its own accord. It had not been locked. Ben cautiously peered inside. The place looked more like a building site than a home. It was dark and bare and totally devoid of furniture. The oddest part of all was the fact that there was no noise whatsoever coming from inside. It was as if there was no one at home.

Ben stepped inside and noticed a piece of paper on the floor in front of him. It read: *Go into the first room on your right.* Ben was a little startled by this. Usually he'd turn up at a client's and they'd be waiting to let him in. This was obviously some strange sexual game that this particular punter wanted to play. Ben wasn't sure whether he liked it. However, he did as the note suggested and opened the door. The room was dark, the windows having been blacked out, and Ben could barely see anything apart from the outline of a sofa and a chair. Cautiously he ventured further inside, trying as hard as he could to see if anyone was seated on the sofa.

All of a sudden, someone grabbed him from behind and a cloth that stank of something Ben had never smelled before was clamped over his mouth and nose. He heard heavy breathing close to his ear, and then the room and the noise faded out . . .

When Ben came round, he felt sick and his head ached. He looked straight ahead of him and saw a naked light bulb dangling down at him. This brought him to the conclusion that he was lying on his back.

Slowly he tried to sit up. For a moment the room spun and then came to rest in a more orderly position. He was in a fairly large room with a concrete floor and shabby sloped plasterboard walls. There were no windows and, at first glance, no door. The only light came from the bulb above him. He looked down at himself and realised that he was only dressed in his underwear. The rest of his clothes had been removed and were nowhere to be seen.

It was at this point, as he went to rub his eyes, that Ben noticed his hands had been firmly tied behind his back. It was hard to get to his feet and, even when he had managed it, he immediately fell back down to the hard concrete floor again. His head was still so full of the drug that he'd been given to knock him out that the slightest exertion made him feel dizzy once again and he lost his balance.

There were only two pieces of furniture in the room: a single mattress on the floor and a wooden chair. There was also a bucket in one corner. Ben tried again to pull himself up and reach the bed, but he fell down. So this time he dragged himself there, which proved more successful. He clambered on to the thing and lay back, light-headed and exhausted. All the while, his heart had been pounding furiously. He could barely believe what had happened. It seemed like a horrible dream that he couldn't wake up from, or something he'd seen in the movies. Ben took deep breaths, trying to even out the pattern and calm his heart. He did not know where he was, what had happened, nor what he should do now. He surely had to do something. If only he could just find the door.

The room was cold and Ben shivered, lying on the bed in his boxer shorts. The rope that held his hands tightly together was cutting into him and he wondered whether it would ever be removed. He could not even imagine why he was being held prisoner. Was it for money, for the sheer hell of it or, worst of all, to be raped and murdered by some maniac?

Ben found it hard to tell how long he had been conscious and lying on the bed before he heard noises from below and the sound of footsteps on stairs or a ladder. All of a sudden there was a loud clanking noise and a panel in the floor slowly opened. Ben's heart was once again pounding as fast as it ever had done, and for the first time he realised why there was no door in the room – he was in an attic.

He sat up and watched as a figure appeared in the centre of the room. He was wearing paint-spattered jeans and a checked shirt, and the top half of his face, from his forehead to upper lip, was covered with a black mask. On his head he wore a grey wool hat.

Without a word the man approached Ben and stared down at

him from above. He scratched the back of his head and laughed quietly.

Ben tried to speak but he found it hard to make the words come out right. 'What . . . do you want?' he managed, in a faltering voice.

'I want to live forever,' said the man in a strange generic European-sounding voice. 'I want to learn how to fly.' Then he laughed.

'What?'

'Nothing,' he said.

'Who are you?'

'No one you know.'

'Are you going to kill me?' Ben asked, terrified.

'Not necessarily. Not unless your parents don't want to pay up.'

'So, you're holding me to ransom?'

'You're catching on fast,' said the man, with a note of sarcasm in his voice.

After a short pause Ben said, 'Can I have my clothes back, please?'

'No.'

'Why not?'

'Because you look better with them off.'

There was something about the way he said this that made Ben very afraid of what he might physically do to him. The man came closer and sat next to him on the mattress. He ran his hands over Ben's bare chest and down on to his legs, making him shudder.

'Sit in the chair,' said the man.

'Why?'

'Just do it,' he shouted, and grabbed Ben's arm. Ben was pulled to his feet and escorted to the chair. He sat down in it and the man pulled his arms behind the chair's back. From his pocket he took out some rope and secured his hands to it. He did the same with Ben's legs. 'Wait there,' he said, laughing.

Ben was terrified as he watched the man disappear from his sight and heard his footsteps echoing down the ladder. What was his kidnapper going to do to him? As long as he wasn't killed, he thought, then nothing could be that bad.

When the man returned he was carrying an all-in-one television and video player. He placed it down on the floor and went off again. When he came back for the second time he had a large cardboard box in his hands. He put the television on top of it and connected the plug to a socket in the wall. Ben watched in amazement at what he was doing. The screen lit up and the man pressed play on the video. A film that had already started became visible. It looked cheaply made and the dialogue was not in English.

'I thought you might like to watch a movie,' said the man, and with that he left the attic.

Ben just stared at the screen and watched two teenage boys in a bedroom talking about something in what sounded like German. Suddenly the conversation stopped and the boys started to kiss. Ben realised that he was watching a pornographic film. The boys, one with floppy blond hair and the other, who looked older, with short dark hair, had their hands all over each other. The dark-haired one was taking off the other's clothes and moving his lips down his naked chest.

Ben's cock began to stiffen in his underwear as he watched the figures on the screen pleasuring one another. He'd never seen one of these films before, but it certainly was exciting to watch. The fair-haired boy was now getting his cock sucked by the other one. It was a beautiful scene.

Next, the elder of the two turned the other over and started kissing his bottom. Ben hoped he knew what would happen next. He was right; the boy parted his companion's buttocks and began rimming him. The camera angle was so close up that you could see his tongue as it flickered over the tight opening and then dipped inside. It cut to a shot of the blond boy's face, distorted with put-on enjoyment.

All the while, Ben's penis ached in his pants and he longed to be able to touch it and relieve himself. However, the rope prevented him from doing almost anything – all he could do was watch and imagine. Perhaps this was some kind of torturous game his captor was playing with him – showing him such exciting scenes and yet stopping him from touching himself.

As much as he tried, he was unable to turn away from the screen. Even though it was agony not to be able to touch his prick, he could not resist watching the boys having sex. They were now in a sixty-nine position – as Ben had been with Paul – and were sucking away at each other's cocks. Ben loved the fact that the younger one was tightly gripping on to his friend's balls as he let the cock slide in and out of his delicate mouth.

The boys stopped their sucking and the dark-haired one made the blond get on all fours on the bed while he knelt over him and started to insert his penis. The whole screen was taken up with a close-up of this happening. You could see in great detail his cock pushing the lad's arsehole open and sliding inside. Then it cut to a shot of the blond boy's face, then back again to the cock thrusting in and out with violent movements.

By this point Ben could feel a sticky patch forming at the front of his boxer shorts. His cock was straining to be set free, but with his hands so firmly tied there was nothing he could do about it. The boy on the screen suddenly pulled his stiff prick out of his companion and started shooting semen over his buttocks and the small of his back.

There were once again footsteps on the ladder, and his kidnapper came into view.

'Enjoying the film?' he asked.

Ben didn't say anything.

The man looked down at Ben's crotch and said, 'Feeling horny?' Then he disappeared behind the chair and suddenly the light vanished. The man had put a thick blindfold on him, so now he was unable to see a thing. 'Just so that I can take off my mask,' he said. 'I don't want you knowing my identity, now, do I?'

Ben felt scared. What was going to happened to him? He felt a hand on his erection and then lips engulfing his nipple. Another hand took hold of the other one and pinched it between its fingers. Although he was scared, the feeling was still sublime, especially since he was feeling so turned on, the images from the film still whirling around in his head.

The hands explored his chest and the man's mouth moved down and lingered over his navel. A slippery tongue inserted itself and tickled him. The hands were now stroking his stiff penis and groping his balls through the material of his boxer shorts. Next, he felt warm breath around the tops of his legs and suddenly his prick was taken out of the slit in his underwear and the foreskin stretched back so that he could feel the head exposed. The man's mouth engulfed it, and Ben could not stop himself from taking an audible gasp of air. The lips and tongue felt so stimulating around his member that he knew sooner or later he would be forced to come. His balls were slipped from their covering and squeezed hard in rough hands; all the while, the man's mouth sucked up and down his cock.

The blindfold seemed to make the whole experience all the more exciting. Not knowing the identity or features of his seducer made the situation more dangerous and stimulating. Ben relaxed a little for the first time and allowed himself to be taken. The sensation of the man's lips working away on his erection made his balls ache with such a great intensity that he longed for his climax in order to release all the tension there.

His wishes were soon answered, as his kidnapper tightened the grasp on Ben's balls and clamped his other hand around the base of Ben's prick, making Ben arch his back as much as he could in his restricted position, and let a squirt of semen out of the tip and into the man's mouth. There was something so fantastic about coming into the moist cavity, and he relished every second of his orgasm. Spurt after spurt of liquid came out of him and with each he felt more relieved and pleasured. The man seemed to be enjoying the experience, too. His movements had become more aggressive, as if he was trying to force as much semen out as he possibly could; even after Ben had stopped coming and only dribbled a little after-fluid, he still sucked.

When the man finally released Ben's penis, Ben fell back in the chair panting for breath. The ropes had cut into his wrists and legs and had made him helpless and wholly at his captor's mercy, whom he heard panting too, as if in sympathy.

'Did you enjoy that?' asked the man.

Ben was not going to admit it, even if he did. This was the person who had kidnapped him, used the film to turn him on and then taken advantage of him while he remained trussed up in the chair.

'When are you going to let me go?' he yelled.

'When your parents pay your fifty-thousand pound ransom.'

'How do you know who my parents are?' Ben was angry.

'I know a lot of things about you.'

'At least take this blindfold off so that I can see you.' There was no reply. 'Why won't you let me see your face? Are you scared or something?'

'Now, Ben,' said the man, 'if you were going to kidnap someone and then try to get away with it, would you let your hostage know who you were?' He stopped for a moment. 'No. You wouldn't, would you? So that's why. Don't worry, as soon as I get the money you'll be let go, totally unharmed. I'm not a murderer; I just need the cash.'

There was something familiar about his tone and the words he used, but Ben couldn't believe that he actually knew the man. It was too ridiculous. No one he knew would do something like this, surely?

'Where am I supposed to piss?'

'In the bucket. I've even put some toilet paper there for you.'

'How considerate of you,' said Ben, sarcastically.

'Are you hungry?' the man asked.

'Not really,' said Ben.

'Well, I'll bring you something up later, all the same.'

Before he left, the man removed Ben's blindfold. When he blinked up into the electric light of the room, his kidnapper was once again wearing the mask he'd had on before. Ben watched him descend the ladder and saw the hatch slide back over and a bolt was snapped across on the other side.

Ben sat, still tied to the chair, not knowing what to do or even what to think. The prospect was too terrifying. He felt so sorry for his mother who would have received some horrible ransom note, probably put together with pieces of cut-up newspaper. She would surely be worried to death, and it was all his fault. He should never have run away from home in the first place. Now his mother would be out of her mind with worry. The police would probably have been informed and his photo would be in their hands.

He wondered how he would explain it all to her when, and if, he was released. If only he'd said a little more in his letter to her, revealed his address or mentioned a few names. As it was, there was nothing to go on but the south London postmark.

And what of Lee and the gang? Did they even realise he was missing? Perhaps they just thought he was out somewhere with a client or doing something else. He hoped that Eddie would be sensible enough to call the police and give the address of the person who he had sent Ben to see earlier that day. This would be the biggest clue to his whereabouts.

Time passed as Ben sat, unable to move in the chair, contemplating his fate. How much time, he did not know. It could have been minutes or it could have been hours.

Even though he had no watch and the room no windows, his body clock told him that it was night time and he needed to sleep. He wondered whether the man was going to untie him and let him sleep in some kind of peace. He tried to bang his foot on the floor by making the chair he was strapped to rock about on its legs as much as he could. This did not seem to make a lot of noise. Instead, he shouted as loud as he could, and immediately the hatch opened.

'For fuck's sake, shut up!' screamed the man. 'What do you want?'

'I want to be untied so that I can sleep. Or were you planning on leaving me tied to this chair all night?'

'I was planning on leaving you tied to the chair all night,' said the man, laughing to himself. 'But, since you asked so nicely . . .' He undid the ropes at Ben's feet and then freed his hands from the back of the chair, but he did not untie them from one another.

'Aren't you going to free my hands?'

'No,' said the man, and he watched as Ben stumbled across the room to the mattress. Ben fell down on to it and tried to make himself comfortable. 'I'll bring you some breakfast in the morning.' He disappeared and closed the hatch behind him. The light in the attic room was turned off and Ben lay quite still in absolute darkness.

He was awoken in the morning, or what he presumed must be the morning, by his kidnapper, who was standing beside him with some toast and cereal. There was a cup of tea that looked cold and had hardly any milk in it on the floor beside him. His arms ached from the position they had been in all night.

'What time is it?' he asked. 'And what day is it, for that matter?'

'It's Wednesday, and the time is –' the man looked at his watch, '– ten past nine in the morning. I brought you some breakfast, as I don't want to be accused of starving you.'

There was something more jovial in his tone of voice today, and Ben wondered what it was that was making him so cheerful. He still wore the mask and hat that he had worn the day before, and his accent still seemed too strange to be real. But why would he want to disguise his voice? Maybe to stop Ben describing it to the police or being able to identify him by it? Or maybe, Ben mused, it might be because it was someone that he knew.

The man untied his hands so that he could have breakfast, but Ben didn't feel like eating. He had barely slept for most of the night, and had only just managed to catch a few hours after his body had finally lost its ability to stay conscious. He was still so worried about what would happen to him that he felt the food might make him throw up. He nervously sipped at the lukewarm cup of tea.

Later in the day Ben once again heard footsteps on the ladder. The man came up to where he was sitting on the edge of the bed and ran his hand through Ben's hair.

'What do you want?' said Ben.

'Just a bit of fun, that's all.' The man took hold of Ben and pushed him face down on the mattress.

'Ow,' Ben yelped.

The kidnapper tied a blindfold around his face from behind.

He felt the man's hands all over his back and the backs of his legs and finally over his buttocks. The hands were replaced with lips that moved over his bare flesh, kissing and biting every exposed part of him. Ben felt scared of what the man was planning, but at the same time a little turned on by his attention.

His boxer shorts were slowly slipped down, until they rested at the base of his arse-cheeks. The man's hands travelled all over them, gently exploring their shape and their texture. Ben was surprised at how gentle the touch was, and he tried to relax a little, knowing there wasn't very much he could do about it anyway. His legs were parted slightly and the hands gently slid between his cheeks and right down into the crack. A finger stroked along the muscle that joined the base of his balls to his arsehole, while the other hand held his buttocks apart. He felt the finger rest on his hole and delicately brush against it, teasing, but not trying to enter.

Lips touched the small of his back and he felt their wetness move down on to the top of his crack, and then across his tensed cheeks and then to his thighs. The whole experience was very gentle and there were points when he almost wanted to laugh. The man was now using both hands to part his buttocks and Ben could feel his mouth getting closer and closer to the area between. A tongue suddenly shot out and started to lick up and down the length of his crack. He felt exposed and somehow violated by his kidnapper's rude liberties, although he was powerless to resist. He tried his best to take some kind of pleasure from the situation.

The man's tongue ran all around the usually hidden areas of his bottom, making them wet with saliva. It was as if he was teasing Ben, coming close to his opening and yet not actually violating it. Soon, however, the tip of his finger once again touched the ring and this was swiftly followed by his tongue, which licked around the edges and then tried to carefully pry its way inside. Ben accidentally let out a gasp which only seemed to provoke the man to use more force in his rimming.

The tongue worked its way inside him, which Ben had to admit felt pretty amazing. The man's lips had engulfed his opening, French kissing it as they did so. He could feel his hole opening up and letting the probe deeper and deeper inside.

After many minutes of intense manipulation his kidnapper replaced the tongue with a finger and slowly wedged it inside Ben, using the saliva that still lubricated the passage to help it slide in. Ben's penis was stiff and he rubbed it against the mattress. The finger inside him felt so good that he was able to get a real sexual kick out of it without doing anything himself.

The finger worked its way deep into his interior and then was twisted around, as if the man were searching for something he'd lost up there. Soon another digit was inserted next to the other and Ben felt his bottom being opened up, pulled apart, in order for the man to dip further inside him. After this the tongue was once again put in, this time with greater access to a new depth that the fingers had made possible by their movements.

Ben felt his bottom being totally invaded, explored with the expertise of a professional. The man's tongue was now able to travel right up inside him without too much difficulty. This continued for some time, and Ben was shocked at his seducer's stamina. Then, with a gentle movement, the man removed his tongue and fingers and softly caressed the ring once more before leaving the area alone. He sounded excited and out of breath.

Ben, blindfolded and trussed up, did not know what to expect next. However, he had a feeling that the man had not yet finished with him. He braced himself for the next onslaught. He felt his boxer shorts being pulled right down to his ankles and then removed. He kicked his legs in a vain protest, but the man just held them down and then parted them further. He heard a rustle of clothing and the sound of a packet or something being ripped open. Then he felt a partly clothed body on top of his own and his legs were held far apart and hands were on his buttocks and warm breath on the back of his neck. The next second he felt something cold and slippery sliding between his arse-cheeks and coming to rest against his stretched opening.

'This won't hurt a bit,' said the man with a chuckle, and Ben felt the man's cock begin to open his passage and work its way up it. At first it felt acutely painful and uncomfortable, but soon a kind of numbness overcame him and he felt his muscles relaxing around the huge intrusion. He couldn't really even tell how far the man's cock was up inside him. It was only when the man started to move it aggressively in and out that Ben realised that he had already been fully penetrated.

The man had his hands around his waist and was kissing his neck and shoulders, the stubble scratching Ben, while he pounded his thick cock into Ben's arse. When he pulled it out, it felt as if he were completely withdrawing, but then the next thrust came and the thing was back inside again. Although Ben felt violated and used, his own penis still ached with sexual tension, and he rubbed it against the mattress, trying to make the most of the ordeal.

The fucking went on for some time. The man's breathing became heavier with every movement he made and Ben could tell how close he was to coming by the noises he made. His bottom was sore and loose with the expert screwing he was getting. He could feel the cock as it went deeply into him. It touched something inside that made his own prick twitch a little and yearn to come.

The man's panting reached a climax and he thrust himself as far inside as it seemed possible, and he held his penis there. Then suddenly he pulled it out again and quickly pushed it back in. This time he did not remove it, but left it there, lying right down on Ben, virtually crushing him with his weight. He could feel the man's warm breath on his neck and there were wet patches over his shoulders where he had been kissed and bitten. The man lay there panting, clearly having ejaculated.

The whole experience left Ben totally pent up and tense. He too needed his relief, so he said, 'What about me?'

'What about you?'

'Don't I get to come, too?'

The man pulled his cock slowly out with a sigh and climbed off. There was some rustling while Ben lay still in darkness, his hard-on raging. He felt a hand helping to turn him on to his back and the cool air in the room touched his exposed cock. It felt pleasant and refreshing. Without warning, the man's hand took hold of his erection and started to pull the foreskin back and forth. Then the hand was replaced with his mouth and Ben drew in a sharp audible breath. The feeling was sublime. After having waited for this throughout the previous ordeal, he was so glad to be sucked by his captor.

The man let his penis fill the whole of his mouth. He took it back, and Ben felt the man's lips around the base of his erection. All the while a hand held his balls in a tight grip. The swollen, sensitive head of his prick was teased and caressed by the man's tongue, and even now Ben knew that pre-come must be flowing from the tip. He could tell that it would not be long before the feeling would become too much and he would be brought to a climax.

His kidnapper sucked away with as much enthusiasm as he had done the previous day, using all his resources to make Ben spill his semen. Ben ached so much at the base of his cock that he let out a moan and arched his back, as if he wanted to force more of his length into the man's mouth.

Suddenly Ben had the feeling that he could no longer hold back and he let the inevitable happen. A shot of fluid came out of him and into the man. Although he could not see, he knew that his juice was being swallowed down and not spat out, for the lips remained clamped tightly around him. More semen poured from him, and with every spurt he felt a greater sense of relief, until soon it felt as if there was none left.

Ben relaxed his hips and felt his penis slide out of the man's mouth and back into the open.

'Can you put my boxer shorts back on, please?' he said.

'What's wrong with you . . . oh, of course,' said the man, obviously remembering Ben's restricted state.

Before he left, the man removed the blindfold and Ben once again blinked into the light from the bulb, relieved, but a little sore.

Two days passed. Ben spent every waking and sleeping moment locked in the attic room. The man would bring up his food and talk for a while, and sometimes have sex with him. Ben was unable to do anything about this, so he just lay back and let it happen, sometimes tolerating it and sometimes actually enjoying himself.

At the end of the second day, when he presumed night had fallen and he should be getting some sleep, he lay down on his mattress gazing into the darkness. From down below, he could hear a telephone ringing. It sounded more like the noise a mobile phone makes than any other kind. He remained motionless, just listening. The ringing stopped and he heard a voice.

'Yes . . . two o'clock . . . no, not really . . . I'll have some of it.' The words were hard to make out, but it wasn't them that interested him. It was the voice. 'Don't worry . . . You'll get it, man,' it said. It was not the same as that of his kidnapper. Even though Ben knew that the accent was false, it was still shocking to hear the reality behind it. And there was something about it. He recognised it, like one recognises a voice shouting out in a crowd without being able to place it at first. Then in a flash it came to him.

Nine

———

At first Lee didn't remember who the boy lying next to him in bed was. He assumed that it was Ben, so he put his arms around him from behind and hugged him tightly.

'Get off,' murmured the boy.

It immediately dawned on Lee that it was his brother lying next to him and no one else.

'Sorry,' he said moving away a little. He leaned out of the bed and picked up his watch which he'd left on the floor the previous night. It was ten-thirty. He yawned and stretched and then said, 'Time to get up.'

Joe made a grunting noise and pulled the duvet higher so that it covered his shoulders and neck.

Lee got out of bed and moved around to his brother's side where he perched on the edge next to him and lit a cigarette. He was only wearing his underwear, but he didn't mind the boy seeing him in this state; they'd often been in the same position as kids when they'd shared a bed out of necessity.

'Are you still tired?' asked Lee.

Joe nodded and murmured, 'What day is it?'

'Tuesday.'

'Oh, right.'

'Did you really go along with Ben of your own accord yesterday?'

He nodded again.

'Well, I guess that's OK then.' He paused. 'Can I ask you something else?'

'What?'

'Did you have sex with him?'

Joe sat up in the bed. 'Kind of,' he said, a little sheepishly.

'What does that mean?' Lee wasn't angry; he just wanted to know what had happened between them.

'It means that we messed about a bit.'

'I thought you were supposed to be straight,' said Lee.

'I am. But that was just a bit of fun. I felt horny. You know how it is.'

'Yes, I know how it is.'

'Is he your boyfriend, then?' asked Ben.

Lee thought for a moment before saying, 'Kind of.'

'You like him though, don't you?'

'Yeah. A lot.'

'That's cool,' said Joe. 'He's cute.'

Lee smiled at his brother and said, 'Do you think so?'

Joe nodded.

'I hope he's OK on the sofa.' Lee stubbed out his cigarette and got up off the bed. He put on a T-shirt and went downstairs. When he entered the lounge there were covers on the sofa but no Ben. He went into the kitchen but he wasn't in there, either. Lee presumed that he'd gone out to the shop for something, or maybe Eddie had called with an early job – although that was a bit unlikely as it seemed far too early for work.

Lee boiled the kettle and made tea for them both. He stirred two spoonfuls of sugar into his cup and one into Joe's and took them upstairs.

'Thanks. Is Ben still asleep?' asked Joe.

'No. He's gone out.'

'Where to?'

'I don't know. I hope he's not trying to make himself scarce after last night's row,' said Lee.

'Don't worry. He'll be back later, I expect.'

This didn't put Lee's mind at rest, but he had no choice other than to accept it and see his friend when he returned. He sipped his tea and lit another cigarette. His brother was still under the covers.

'Why don't you get up?' he said.

'In a minute. Anyway, what are we going to do today?'

'I don't know. What do you want to do?' asked Lee. 'You're the guest.'

Joe looked thoughtful, while Lee wondered what he could show him or take him out to. Even though he'd been in London a while, he still didn't know the place very well. It was such a big city that he thought he'd never be able to find his way around it. The transport system still seemed so complicated and difficult and everywhere you went there were people who seemed to know what they were doing, people who seemed to have somewhere to go to in a hurry. He thought of the sights: Buckingham Palace, Big Ben, the Houses of Parliament, Covent Garden. There were lots of places, but somehow he didn't feel that his brother would be too bothered about seeing them. He knew that it was always more fun to see the side of the city that the tourists don't know about or aren't bothered with. But where were they?

'I don't know,' said Joe.

'Why don't you have a shower and we'll see how you feel after that.'

'OK.'

Joe climbed out of the bed. He was only wearing his boxer shorts and Lee looked at his smooth, slim body. His expression still looked like that of a little kid and it was hard for Lee – having seen the lad grow up a few years behind himself – to think of Joe as a fully-grown man now.

'Have you got a towel I can use?' he asked.

Lee found him one and told him how to turn on the shower and watched as he left the room. His mind flipped back to Ben. He was only Joe's age but it was different with him. He felt like he was older, less childish, someone whose age didn't matter, just the fact that they were together. He wished that Ben was more faithful to him, but then that was rather a contradiction when his profession was prostitution. But it wasn't that that Lee minded, it was him sleeping with Ringo and then his own brother – that really cut him up. He wondered who else Ben had been with that he didn't know about.

He was lying on the bed smoking a cigarette when his brother came back into the room. He was dripping wet and the towel was tied loosely round his waist.

'Nice shower?' he asked.

'Yeah, fine.'

Joe started to dry himself, letting the towel fall and Lee see him with no clothes on. He was smooth all over, with only the finest coating of fair hairs on his legs and arms. His buttocks were small and rounded and clearly defined. He was standing with his back to Lee drying his crotch and for the first time Lee realised why it was that people found the lad so attractive.

Suddenly Joe turned around so that Lee was able to look at his uncut cock and loose balls which hung down in front of him. His brother's prick was long but fairly slim and the balls clung close to his body, small and soft-looking. He just stood there drying his hair and Lee could not help but stare. It was almost as if the boy was inviting his gaze, or else just leaving him the option of whether to look or not.

After a while Joe looked up, catching his eye, and Lee turned his attention to the cigarette he was smoking, trying not to make it obvious that he'd been eyeing him. When he turned to look again the lad was pulling on a clean pair of pants and then spraying deodorant under his arms, which only had the faintest trace of hair about them.

'So, have you had any ideas?' said Joe after he'd finished putting on the rest of his clothes.

'I don't know what we should do now, but I thought we ought to go out to a club tonight.'

Joe's eyes lit up and he said, 'Really?'

'Does that sound like a good idea?'

'Definitely.'

'I know a place that's quite cool. Well, the music's good and it's kind of . . . different. The only thing is that it's really a gay

139

club, but there are some straight people that go there.' Lee hoped that his brother wouldn't object on the grounds of sexuality.

'That's OK,' said Joe. 'It doesn't really bother me.'

'Good.'

'What's it called?'

'The Back Door to Paradise,' said Lee.

'Sounds a bit sleazy.'

'No, not really.' Lee wondered what they were going to do with the rest of the day. He gave up trying to think of clever ideas and just said, 'Why don't we just go into town this afternoon? Have a look round the shops and stuff; then we can take it from there.'

'OK,' said Joe.

When his brother had finished looking in the mirror and getting his hair just right, Lee led the way downstairs and into the kitchen. He toasted some bread and spread butter and jam on it. This he gave to Joe. He made himself some cornflakes and they went into the lounge to eat.

The front door opened and someone entered the house. Lee listened carefully.

'Ben? Is that you?' he shouted out.

'No,' said Ringo as he came into the room. 'Should it be?'

'No. I was just wondering.' Lee put a spoonful of cereal into his mouth. 'He left the house really early this morning and hasn't come back yet.'

'Don't fuss so much,' said Ringo, switching on the television and lighting a cigarette that he produced from behind his ear. 'You're behaving like his mother or something.'

'I just worry about him, that's all,' said Lee, defensively.

'Ooh, it *must* be love,' he said, staring at the screen.

'Fuck off,' Lee joked, because he felt embarrassed.

'Who's your friend?'

'This is my brother, Joe.' For a moment Lee was worried that Ringo would fancy him or something, but he greeted Joe with about as much enthusiasm as he did everything else, barely looking over, the television obviously being more interesting.

Lee looked at his watch. It was just after noon.

'Shall we go out?' he said to Joe.

The lad nodded.

It was a bright summer's day so the two young men didn't need a coat; they just went out as they were: Joe dressed in loose green combat trousers and a baggy short-sleeved shirt, untucked, and Lee wearing his usual jeans and T-shirt.

They caught the train from New Cross Gate to London Bridge where they changed on to the underground and travelled to Charing Cross. They left the tube and went up into piercing sunlight. Lee led the way across the Strand and down towards Trafalgar Square. Joe looked thrilled to see Nelson's Column and the stone lions and the pigeons. He'd never been to London before, so Lee knew that his only glimpses of it had been in pictures or on the television.

After that they walked down Charing Cross Road and through Leicester Square and into Soho. Lee noticed some of the men who passed looking at his brother. This made him realise even more that the boy was a sexual object for a lot of people; that he was hot property. He felt like he needed to protect him from these dirty old men who only wanted to get their hands on him for one thing. Joe didn't seem to notice their glances, though, which Lee was pleased about.

'Shall we go into a sex shop?' asked Lee.

'No, I don't think so.'

'Why not?'

'I'd be embarrassed. They might think I was a pervert,' said Joe. 'Or desperate.'

'Lots of ordinary people go into them, not just pervs. Anyway, I only thought we could have a look and a laugh. I wasn't suggesting we should buy a dildo and wave it in the air down the street.'

Joe laughed. 'Let's go to some record shops,' he said.

They walked down Berwick Street and went into all the new and second-hand shops there, then on to Oxford Street and down to Tottenham Court Road. All the while, they went in and out of shops looking at the expensive things. Lee bought his brother a CD which he really wanted. Now he had more money it seemed easy just to go out and get what you wanted. He'd started to forget about all the poverty back home and adapt to being generous.

'Are you hungry?' Lee asked.

'Not really,' said Joe. 'But I am quite thirsty.'

They found a small cafe and ordered some cold drinks. Lee had a sandwich, but his brother insisted that he didn't need to eat anything.

'If you're worried about the cost – don't. I'll pay.'

'No, it's not that. I'm just not hungry.'

For a time no one spoke, then Lee broke the silence by asking, 'How are things back home?'

'All right.'

'Really?'

'Yeah. I just can't wait to get out, that's all.' Joe sipped his drink. 'I need my own space and you know what Mum's like. It's hard to live with her.'

'Are you still set on going to drama school?'

'Definitely. But getting the money's still a big problem. I don't know how I'm gonna save that amount.'

'Maybe I can help you out.'

'Yeah?' said Joe, an excited note in his voice.

'Well, I only mean that I'd lend it to you and you can pay me back at some point. When you're a famous actor.'

'That'd be really kind of you.'

'Yeah, I'm nice like that,' said Lee.

When they got back to the house Nathan and Alex were watching television. Joe wanted to go upstairs so that he could listen to the new CD. Lee sat down on the sofa.

'Is Ben in?' he asked.

'No,' said Alex.

'Have you seen him at all today?'

Both boys shook their heads.

Lee was concerned. It was almost six o'clock and Ben hadn't been around all day. He wondered whether Ben had gone away because of their argument, or maybe he was just with a client.

Either way, he wanted to speak to him and get things sorted out. It would be nice for them all to go out to the club tonight.

'Is anyone else in?'

'Yeah,' said Nathan. 'Ringo's in the bedroom.'

Lee left the room and walked up the stairs. He knocked at the door and then entered without waiting for an answer. Things were very relaxed in the house. No one seemed to mind you bursting in on them.

Ringo was lying on the bed in his underwear with a magazine in one hand and a joint in the other.

'What are you reading?' said Lee.

Ringo held up the magazine so that he could see the cover. It was a teenage girls' kind of thing: lots of pictures of boy bands, articles about soap stars and problem pages. Lee was a little shocked. He presumed that the lad was so indifferent to everything that he'd be the kind of person who'd laugh at such tacky publications.

'I like looking at the pictures,' he mumbled defensively. 'I like boys.' It was as if this was a dark secret; he sounded a little ashamed.

'I just wanted to know if you'd seen Ben today.'

'No.'

'I wonder where he's got to.'

'I'm sure he can look after himself,' said Ringo, turning a page.

'Well, I'm not sure he can. He's not like the rest of us. He doesn't know anything about this kind of life, about having to scrape together a living and the rest of the time having to live off your wits.'

'Then he's very lucky,' he retorted sarcastically.

'See you later,' said Lee. 'We're going out tonight.'

'Who's *we*?'

'Me and my brother, and hopefully Ben, if he turns up and wants to come.'

'You'd better call Eddie and tell him you're not going to be available.'

'OK,' said Lee as he left the room.

Down in the lounge again, he dialled the number and listened to the ringing tone before it was picked up. He explained that he was going out that night and wouldn't be able to do any punters.

'That's OK,' said Eddie.

Lee was surprised. The man was usually keen for them to work every night because that was when most people wanted a rent boy.

'I'm a bit busy at the moment. You go out and enjoy yourselves and tell that gorgeous brother of yours that if he ever needs a place to stay then my door's always open.'

'Don't be so gross,' said Lee.

There was only a short queue outside the Back Door to Paradise. They'd arrived early so that it wouldn't be too crowded, and glancing in through the door they could see that there weren't very many people inside yet.

The building stood unattached at the end of a road in Vauxhall. It was a small Victorian pub that had been turned into a club. The outside, if a little run-down, made it look traditional and decent in an old-fashioned way. On a huge blackboard on the front was written, in chalk, the name of the club and the cabaret and entertainment happening that night.

When they were at the front of the queue and the bouncer had let them in there was a small table where you paid. The door staff were very peculiar to behold. Lee hoped that his brother wouldn't be too shocked. One man was dressed in a suit and was wearing National Health glasses, and the other was kitted out like the strangest woman he'd ever seen: pop-socks, gym skirt, a towel wrapped round his head with swimming goggles on top of it. They were both caked in make-up.

Lee paid for both of them. It wasn't very expensive so he didn't mind. Their hands were stamped and they walked over to the bar which was right across the other side of the small dance-floor. He ordered them pints, paid for them and turned to look back over the club.

'Did you see the weirdos on the door?' said Joe.

'I know. They're always here. I think it's their job to look odd.' Lee sipped his drink.

'What a funny little place. It looks too small to be a club.'

The interior was painted black. Even the decorative Victorian moulding had been painted over, lending the place a cheap, sleazy quality that was almost pleasing, if you like that kind of thing. There was a small stage with antique red velvet curtains drawn in front of its proscenium. People used this stage to sit on and to rest their drinks. There were some seats on a raised area on the other side of the club with small tables where people were sitting and chatting and drinking. Near the entrance was the DJ booth, about two feet off the ground and sectioned off, where the two DJs stood sipping pints of what looked like blackcurrant and chain-smoking cigarettes. Although they were both male they wore heavy make-up and women's wigs.

'Look at them,' said Joe.

Lee led the way over to a table where they squeezed in beside a very large woman and two skinny men who were giggling in high-pitched voices. The club was starting to fill up, people arriving in dribs and drabs, and although there was never a big queue at the door, the place was looking more packed, probably because it was so small.

The music, even though not terribly loud, was somehow imposing. Lee had never heard the song that was being played before – it was almost comical in its peculiarity, not the kind of thing you'd usually hear in a club. When the track ended, it was immediately followed by something entirely different, so opposed that it clashed like ill-matching colours – some modern indie-rock.

'This one sounds good,' commented Joe, taking a big gulp from his pint glass.

Lee lit a cigarette.

'Can I have one?'

'You don't smoke.'

'Well, I just fancied it, that's all.'

Lee handed him a Camel Light and lit it for him. The lad drew in a small amount of smoke and promptly blew it back out again; Lee knew that he wasn't really inhaling it.

The soundtrack changed from song to song and Lee got them

more drinks and more cigarettes were smoked and stubbed out. People crowded into the place, smoke and chatter filling the air. Some were dancing, some leaning against the pillars that supported the ceiling, and others were trying to get noticed at the bar. There were more men than women in the club, but the women that were there were dressed well and looked glamorous and relaxed. Lee suspected that a lot of the people were on drugs while the rest were trying to get high on just alcohol.

Some of the young men who were there caught Lee's eye. There were quite a number of sexy people in the place, and the atmosphere and the drink combined to make Lee feel very horny. He wouldn't mind picking someone up and going back with them, so he kept his eyes peeled for boys he fancied.

The two brothers went to stand nearer the stage. Everywhere was so crowded that if you were sitting down then you wouldn't be able to see a thing. Lee looked at his watch; it was almost eleven o'clock. They perched their drinks on a small shelf over-crowded with empty and half empty glasses and stood near to make sure that no one pinched them. They were sandwiched between lots of groups of people; everyone seemed to know everyone else. Lee didn't recognise anyone.

'Seen anyone you fancy?' said Joe over the noise of the music.

'Yeah, a couple of people. You?'

Joe nodded.

Just then the music faded out and a woman in a slinky black nightie came through the curtains. She had a 1950s haircut and stunning make-up. Lee assumed she was the club's hostess. She greeted the crowd and read out some notices like a headmaster at assembly. Then she introduced the cabaret, which was some bizarre woman singing even more bizarre songs. After all this was over, the music started up again, a little louder than before, and a lot of people started to dance.

Lee wanted another drink so he tried to make his way to the bar. The problem was that the place was so crowded that you could hardly get past all the people, some of whom would dance into you and spill some of your drink.

When he eventually came back with their drinks, Lee found

his brother talking to a man and a woman. He handed Joe his drink and lit a cigarette.

'Who are your new friends?' he asked.

'I don't know what their names are,' Joe tried to say discreetly.

'I'm Rupert and this is my friend, Fiona.'

Lee introduced himself. The man was probably in his mid-twenties and had dark floppy hair and a slim body. His eyes were very dark too, and he was wearing a shirt with bright flowers on it with the cuffs unbuttoned. Lee thought he was very attractive.

The woman had short blonde curly hair and was wearing a long old-fashioned cocktail dress. She had immediately turned to Joe and was talking to him. Lee was left with the man who was smiling at him.

'I haven't seen you here before,' he said.

'No? Well, I've only been a couple of times. Are you a regular?'

'Yeah,' said Rupert. 'I come here most weeks.'

'It seems like everyone knows one another,' Lee commented.

'Lots of the people come here all the time. They wouldn't go anywhere else.'

'It's very different.'

'So, where do you live?' Rupert asked, sipping his drink.

'New Cross Gate.'

'Not very far away, then.'

'No,' said Lee.

'But you're from Scotland originally?'

'Yes. Glasgow.'

'What do you do?'

Lee took a sip of his drink before answering.

'I'm a courier,' he lied, too embarrassed to reveal how he really made his money.

'That's nice,' said Rupert. He went on to say that he was a photographer and lived in Streatham. He had his car parked outside so he wasn't drinking, but he said he had taken a line of speed.

Lee glanced at his brother who caught his eye and winked which suggested that he was getting in with the girl. He hoped that Joe would strike it lucky with her and that he would too, with Rupert.

They chatted about various things that didn't seem terribly important and Lee wondered what he ought to be saying to make his intentions clear. It was difficult to tell how the man felt about him.

'Would you like a drink?' asked Rupert.

'That'd be really kind.'

When the man had gone off to the bar Lee turned to talk to his brother. However, it was not easy, as the lad was busy kissing Fiona. He had his arms around her and she had hers on his arse. They were held together in this position for at least thirty seconds until someone tapped her on the shoulder and she turned around to greet a friend.

'You work fast,' Lee whispered into his brother's ear.

Joe just smiled a bashful smile and didn't say anything.

'Bit old for you, isn't she?'

'No, not really. She's only twenty-three,' retaliated Joe.

'I don't know what to do about this bloke.'

'Do you like him?'

'Yeah.'

'Well, make a pass, then.'

'He might say "no" if I do.'

'You won't find out if you don't ask,' said Joe.

'No. I suppose you're right.'

When Rupert came back with the drinks Lee asked him, 'Do you have a girlfriend or a boyfriend?'

'No,' he replied. 'I'm a single man.'

'Really?'

Rupert nodded.

'Can I kiss you?'

'Yes.'

Lee leaned forwards and kissed the man gently on the lips, then he pulled away just enough to look into his eyes before he went back for a more passionate kiss. He put his arms around Rupert and they stayed with their mouths open and together for some time.

Lee thought the man was a good kisser and enjoyed being stuck to him, their tongues entwined, tasting one another's saliva. He ran his hands slowly over Rupert's back, but felt a bit embarrassed snogging someone in full view of his brother and the rest of the club's clientele. He'd never really done it before – well, only with girls – and it seemed as if everyone was looking at him. None the less, Rupert was the first to pull away.

'That was good,' he said.

Lee did not know what to say; he just stared and smiled shyly. Then the man turned to his female friend and said something to her that he couldn't hear, then he turned back to Lee.

'Would you like to come home with me?' he asked.

Lee hesitated and then said, 'Yes, but I'm worried about Joe. He's just visiting me and I can't leave him to go back to my house alone.'

'That's not a problem because I think he wants to go back with Fiona, and we live together.'

'I see. That would work out fine,' said Lee feeling exciting about the prospect of having sex with the man. He certainly was attractive. However, he didn't feel right about being unfaithful to Ben, who would probably be waiting at home for him now, wondering where he was. Then Lee remembered about Ringo and his brother and whoever else there might have been and he didn't feel so guilty. It wasn't as if Ben was totally devoted to him, faithful to the last. He was entitled to have some fun, too.

At one o'clock they all decided to go home. Even though the club hadn't ended, Lee had had enough of it and, what was more, was dying to get Rupert into bed. His brother also seemed pleased that they'd decided to leave, his hand constantly entwined with Fiona's.

They walked out into the Vauxhall night, which was warm and clear, and followed Rupert to his car, which was parked a few streets away. It was a bright red mid-eighties Alfa Romeo. Lee got into the passenger seat while his brother and the girl sat in the back. The engine was started and they drove off into the night.

It didn't take very long to reach Streatham, the streets being clear at that time of night they were able to speed along. They pulled up outside a detached town house four stories high with a black front door. Rupert led the way up the path, into the building and up to the top floor where their flat was.

The place was spacious and minimal. The lounge had a stripped pine floor mostly covered with Oriental woven rugs. There were two long book cases filled completely with hundreds of books. Lee thought to himself that they must be heavy readers, but he couldn't believe that they'd read every book in the flat. There were also two large sofas in the room and some other furniture that he barely noticed.

Rupert put on some music then poured them all drinks and they sat down in pairs, the man putting his arm around Lee's shoulder and kissing him lightly on the lips.

'What's this music?' asked Lee.

'It's The Smiths.'

'Bit depressing, isn't it?'

'No,' said Rupert. 'Just a reflection of reality.'

Lee looked across at his brother only to see him snogging the girl.

'Shall we go to bed?' said Rupert.

'OK,' said Lee, keen to get on with things. It was good for him not to have to take any money, for once – he was doing this for the pleasure of it, not the profit.

Rupert led the way down the passage, past the kitchen and into his bedroom. A double door faced out on to a balcony and the back garden. The room was big and had a high ceiling and decorative architrave.

'Nice flat,' said Lee.

'Well, that's the advantage of living in a dreary area like Streatham – you get more for your money.'

'Do you own it?'

'No, it's just rented.'

Lee put his drink down on a desk piled high with papers and opened books and odds and ends.

'Can I smoke in here?' he asked.

'Of course.' Rupert produced an ashtray from the floor at the side of his double bed. He handed it to Lee and they held eye

150

contact while he lit a cigarette. The man turned on the stereo in his room and put a record on.

'I hope Joe's going to be OK,' said Lee.

'Oh, I'm sure. He's in very capable hands.'

When he'd finished the cigarette he stubbed it out and sat down next to Rupert on the bed. He put his hands around Rupert's neck and rubbed his hair at the back. The man leaned in close and kissed him. They both took their shoes and socks off and lay down on their sides facing one another. Rupert took hold of Lee and tipped him back so that he was lying down flat, and started to run his hands up the inside of his T-shirt. He bent down and kissed his stomach and, raising the top up even further, he bit at Lee's nipples and suckled on them.

Lee ran his hands through the man's hair and after a while pushed him away and started to undo his shirt. Rupert had a smooth, slim body which he kissed and licked all the way from the nipples down to the navel. He aggressively pushed the shirt off him and raised his arms so that he could get access to the area underneath, which firstly he smelt and then licked. He loved the aroma and taste of men's armpits. It gave him great pleasure to linger there and take in their details.

Next he moved down, and, while kissing Rupert's firm stomach, he unbuttoned his trousers and slid them down so that his tight boxer shorts were visible. He reached out and grasped the man's stiff prick and manipulated it through the fabric of his underwear, then he moved closer and pulled his pants down. The cock sprang out, long and hard and circumcised, and he immediately put it in his mouth and started sucking.

Lee felt quite drunk from all the pints he'd had at the club and he was extremely aroused, desperate to take in as much of Rupert's erection as he could. It felt so great sliding in and out of his mouth and he often stopped and just let his tongue explore the swollen head, running it along the bottom edges and then into the slit at the end where he could taste the sticky secretion that escaped there. At the same time he squeezed the man's balls which were small and warm.

Rupert stopped him and made a gesture to suggest that he turn himself around so that they were lying side by side but facing in opposite directions. Lee swivelled around and then returned to sucking the man's cock. He felt hands undoing his jeans and then pulling them and his underwear down. His cock, stiff and twitching, slid into a warm, wet mouth and was sucked with great vigour. He could tell that Rupert was taking him right back for he felt the lips slide right down to the base and then back up again.

They remained like this for a while, sucking each other at the same time. Lee was loving every minute of having the man's prick in his mouth while his own was serviced. He could feel his balls tensing and a climax starting deep down inside him. However, all of a sudden Rupert stopped what he was doing and signalled for Lee to stop, too. He pushed Lee so that he was lying on his stomach and then he parted his legs. Lee was fully exposed to the man's fingers, which rubbed across his buttocks and down into the crack.

Lee knew what was coming next. A digit pushed apart the cheeks and came into contact with his tight opening. He felt it push to get inside, but it only slid in a small way, then it was withdrawn again and replaced with Rupert's tongue. This more slippery probe made Lee feel as if he was being opened up. He relaxed all his muscles and let the man delve into him.

The tongue not only worked on his hole but also all the way up and down his crack, lingering on the base of his perineum where his balls started. It then glided back along and came once again to rest in its favourite place. He could feel the man working it inside him and then using his fingers on the slippery entrance, almost as if he were tunnelling deeply into him, excavating his inner secrets. Lee parted his legs even more so that Rupert would have unhindered access to his bottom. He was enjoying every minute of the probe.

Soon he could feel both a finger and tongue inside him which stretched him open and made his balls ache to be relieved. The man was sometimes delving so deeply that he put pressure on Lee's prostate gland which made Lee's cock twitch with excitement. He hoped that Rupert would use more than just his fingers and tongue, next – he had the overwhelming urge to be fucked.

The man squeezed another finger inside him and used the two to pry him open so that he could put his tongue between them and rim him more deeply than Lee thought possible. The ordeal lasted for more than twenty minutes and was only ended when Lee raised his head, and, looking over his shoulder, said, 'Do you want to fuck me?'

Rupert stopped rimming and looked up.

'OK,' he said and got up from the bed and started taking off his clothes. Then he reached into a drawer in the bedside cabinet and produced a condom and a sachet of lubricant. Lee remained stretched out on the bed, looking up at the man's slim body with its striking erection jutting out. He too removed his clothes and then returned to his face-down position.

Lee beckoned for Rupert to come closer, which he did so that he was standing at the foot of the bed, inches away from Lee's face. Lee took his prick deeply into his mouth and sucked on it for a moment before releasing it wet with his saliva. Rupert took this opportunity to put on the condom and rip open the sachet of lubricant. He approached Lee from behind and put some of the slippery ointment on to his hand. Lee felt a cold finger slide effortlessly into him and twist around inside. Then it was withdrawn and the man knelt over him and the tip of his slippery prick touched his arsehole and started to push its way in.

'Tell me if I'm hurting you,' said Rupert pausing for a second.

'It's all right. Do it as hard as you want.'

The man quickly pushed his cock in deeply, which made Lee draw in a sharp breath. The long probe being inserted so swiftly sent a shudder of pain through his body. He bit on to the bed sheets and closed his eyes. Rupert drew his prick slowly back out and then thrust it back in, just as hard as he had done before.

After the third or fourth jab of Rupert's penis, Lee started to loosen up. It was useful that he'd already been opened up by the man's fingers, otherwise the initial penetration would have been even more difficult. Soon, however, the shaft glided in and out of him and Lee only felt the pleasure that it sent in waves through his body. Rupert was lying on top of him, putting all his weight down on to his back, and was kissing his shoulders and neck and sometimes gently biting them. Lee turned his head so that he could see the man fucking him and they kissed for a moment before Rupert's concentration was once again taken by the act he was performing.

Lee pushed his hips up towards the man's thrusting groin, trying to get Rupert's cock into him as deeply as he could, taking pleasure from every stroke. His own prick was as hard as iron and he was trying to wank himself by rubbing it against the sheets. All the while, Rupert continued to push his penis in and out, panting for breath as he did so and clinging on to Lee's shoulders. It felt so enjoyable to have him driving deeply in with his long cock.

Soon Rupert started to pant and make low moaning noises and Lee felt him heave his dick inside for one or two more violent thrusts and then fall down on to him, totally out of breath with relief. Rupert promptly slid his penis from Lee's arse and lay down on the bed beside him. Lee's bottom still ached from the thing that had been up it, and it was almost as if he was still there inside him.

Rupert kissed him on the lips and whispered, 'Do you want me to make you come?'

Lee nodded and turned on to his back in preparation. Without any delay, the man moved his head to waist level and took a firm hold of Lee's stiff prick. He placed it to his lips and started to drink down the liquid that flowed from the tip. Lee could feel the foreskin being drawn back and Rupert's tongue going into the slit, but all he could see was the man's head moving about from above.

After this Rupert began to let the cock slide deeply into his mouth, making it wet and slippery with his saliva, at the same time wanking the shaft and thus making the loose skin slip up and down it. With his other hand he squeezed Lee's balls tightly, pulling them downwards and making them ache to produce their salty fluid.

It did not take long for Lee to reach a climax. The cock that had been in him had left its mark on his memory and on the inside of his bottom, and this, together with the man's manipulation of his penis, made the first spurt of semen travel up the shaft and out into Rupert's waiting mouth. More followed until he felt totally empty and drained.

The man let his cock go, and Lee could tell that he had swallowed his come – which Lee found a great compliment and a turn-on.

'That was great,' said Lee, meaning both the blow job and the sex in general.

Rupert simply nodded an agreement. He moved again so that he was lying beside Lee and they kissed and hugged each other for some time.

'Shall we go to bed?'

'Yes,' said Lee. 'I'm tired and pissed. Can I use the bathroom?'

'Sure. Turn right and it's the door at the end of the passage.'

'OK,' said Lee and he left the room. As he walked down the hall, another door opened and closed and there was Joe standing in front of him.

'Where are you going?' Lee asked.

'Same place as you, I expect.'

'How was it?'

'Very nice,' replied the lad. 'How about you?'

'Yeah, cool.'

'Can I go first in the toilet?' asked Joe.

'All right.'

'I'll see you in the morning,' he said closing the bathroom door behind him.

When Lee and Joe arrived back home on Wednesday morning, tired and hung over, they agreed that since it was still so early and they hadn't had enough sleep, they would go back to bed for a nap before facing the day. Lee went into the bathroom and took some paracetamol before taking the packet to the bedroom to give to his brother.

Joe was already getting undressed when he entered and once again he stared at the boy's slender body with only tiny boxer shorts covering his private parts. He handed Joe the painkillers, which he quickly swallowed before sliding beneath the covers. Lee undressed himself and climbed in beside him.

'So what was he like?' asked the boy.

'Great. Very sexy with his clothes off. Good at sex, too.'

'Did you get his phone number?'

'Yeah. But I don't know that I'll call him because I don't want it to get in the way of Ben and me.' Lee thought for a moment and then added, 'Having said that, I wonder where he is? I thought he'd still be asleep, but it didn't look like the bed had been slept in since we made it yesterday morning.'

'Oh, don't worry. He's probably just made an early start and already tidied it.'

Lee said no more about the subject, but deep down he was very concerned. There must be a logical explanation for Ben's continued absence; however, he was unable to unearth it. Lee decided it would be best to change the subject, at least until he was able to shed some light on the mystery.

'What about *your* dirty shag, then?' he asked.

'Oh, she was good. We went all the way.'

'I hope you used a condom.'

'Of course,' said Joe.

Lee thought for a moment and then said, 'So, your trip to London's been pretty exciting so far, and that was only the second day!'

'Certainly has,' agreed Joe.

'Tell me more about it when we wake up later,' he said noticing that his brother's eyelids were drooping. 'Go to sleep now.'

He watched as Joe slowly drifted into a calm sleep on the pillow next to him. However, Lee wasn't able to rest so quickly – his mind was full of Ben and where he might be. Maybe he'd gone out to see a client and never came back. It was a risky business, prostitution – being sent round to complete strangers' houses and not knowing what they might do to you. Lee vowed to phone Eddie when he woke up and see whether he knew anything. Perhaps he'd sent Ben out on a job. Lee did not even like to entertain the thought of what might have happened to him if he'd visited the wrong client.

Joe was still sleeping, so Lee left him in bed and went downstairs. When he entered the lounge, to his surprise, Eddie was there chatting to Nathan.

'Hello,' said Lee.

'Did you have a nice night?' asked Eddie.

'Yeah.' Lee was eager to get on to the subject of Ben, so he said, 'Do you know where Ben is? He's not been around for a couple of days.'

Eddie shook his head.

'When did you last send him out on a job?'

'Probably at the weekend.'

'I think he must have slept on the sofa on Monday night, then when I came down in the morning he was gone, and he hasn't been back since. Did you give him a job on Tuesday morning?'

'No,' Eddie replied.

'I wonder where he's gone to?'

'I wouldn't worry. He's young and impulsive – he's probably just gone off for a wander somewhere. He'll turn up again sooner or later.'

'Maybe we should phone the police,' suggested Lee.

'Don't be ridiculous!' exclaimed Eddie, his face filled with horror. 'He's bound to turn up. We don't want to get the pigs involved. They'd put me away for running this little business, and then where would you all be? Homeless and jobless and back on the streets where I found you.'

Lee didn't say anything but he could see that Eddie had a point. At the same time, he was worried about his friend. If he was in trouble, then the rent boy business meant nothing to him compared to Ben's safety and happiness.

'But if he doesn't come back soon, we ought to think sensibly about what we need to do next.'

'Of course,' said Eddie. 'But let's give it a few more days.'

Lee nodded an agreement.

★

Later that day, when Joe had finally got out of bed and was taking a shower, Lee went into the bedroom and found Ben's bag. He was curious as to whether anything had been taken so he took a look in it. He knew most of the boy's possessions because he had so few and he could tell, when he rummaged through the bag's contents, that nothing in the way of clothing or toiletries had been taken. The only thing that seemed to be missing was his address book, which Lee thought odd. If he was going away to visit someone, thus needing to know their address or telephone number, he would also need some clothes. It was peculiar that he should have been gone for so long without taking anything with him and without letting Lee know where he was. It wasn't like him. It was very out of character. Then it suddenly dawned on him that maybe it wasn't Ben who'd taken the address book but somebody else altogether.

A few days later, Joe was preparing to leave. They'd had a fun time together and even though it had only been brief, they'd managed to cram in a lot of things and have a laugh at the same time.

Lee took him to Euston and made sure he got on the right train.

'Don't worry about Ben too much,' said Joe.

'It's hard not to.'

'I know. Look, if he doesn't turn up soon, then I don't think anyone could blame you if you called the police.'

'If I had his address book, I could tell his mother, but I haven't.'

'Don't do anything too rash.'

'No, I won't. I just want to make sure he's safe.'

Lee hugged his brother and watched him get on board the train. When it had pulled out of the station he walked back towards the tube.

Two days later, Lee knew that he'd had enough of waiting and that now was the time to act. He felt nervous about telephoning the police – they'd probably want to come round and ask him lots of questions. He didn't know whether he could just make a phone call, then they'd find him without any detailed information.

Lee went into the lounge, which was empty, and called Eddie.

'Hi,' said the man.

'Look, Eddie, I don't want to be pushy, but it just seems like no one gives a shit about Ben. He could be kidnapped or even dead for all we know and nothing's being done.'

'Cool it, Lee. He'll turn up —'

'For Christ's sake,' Lee interrupted, 'you've been saying that for too long. It's time to do something. If you don't, then I will. I'm perfectly prepared to call the cops.'

'Don't do that,' said Eddie. 'I'll call them.'

'All right. I don't mind who does it, I just want it done.'

'Consider it so. I'll phone you back and let you know what they say.'

'OK,' said Lee, and he hung up.

Lee waited for the man to call again, and soon enough the telephone rang.

'Did you speak to them?' he asked.

'Yes,' said Eddie.

'What did they say?'

'They said that they couldn't do anything till he'd been gone for at least a week. He's not a minor so it's not of total priority.'

'What?' Lee was stunned. 'Of course it's a priority. It's a huge priority. He could be lying in some gutter with his guts cut out.'

'Look, I'm only telling you what they told me.'

When Lee put down the phone he felt angry and betrayed by the police. It seemed oddly irresponsible of them not to take this seriously. He felt like calling them himself.

Lee had nothing to do the following day and all he could think about was Ben and his whereabouts. It plagued him like a virus that he couldn't shake off. Every possible kind of danger that the lad might be in went through his mind. He wondered whether Ben had picked up a punter by himself and been kidnapped or murdered by him.

It soon became too much for Lee to bear and he could not

stop himself from telephoning the police and finding out whether they'd treat the situation more seriously.

However, when he called, they told him that no one by that name had been reported missing, and that in cases like this they would never wait a week before doing something.

Eddie had lied on both accounts. Lee couldn't understand why he would want to do that. The only explanation could be that he didn't want Ben found, that he had some part in his disappearance and wanted no one to know about it. After all his careful thought, the culprit had been right under his nose the whole time. Lee made up his mind to get to the bottom of it.

Ten

———

Ben had barely been able to sleep all night with the thought of the voice going round and round in his mind. It was, without a shadow of a doubt, Eddie's voice. Could his kidnapper really be the same person who had helped him out of trouble, given him a job – albeit a shady one – and put money in his pocket? The thought was so terrible, but it made Ben search back in his mind to try and find a clue from something Eddie had said or done that would reveal the reason why he had kidnapped him. All he remembered was that Eddie always seemed to need endless money, as if he had an extravagant lifestyle, or maybe a huge debt. Ben felt so betrayed by the person he had trusted. He could hardly bring himself to believe the truth. There was something so macabre about it all.

Before he had any more time to plan his response he heard the sound of footsteps and saw the hatch opening. The man – Eddie – came into the room, still in his mask, and he set down a tray with breakfast on it.

'Your parents are taking their time,' he said, still with the phoney accent. 'I'll have to send them your ear or something if they don't pay up soon.'

Ben thought it best not to let Eddie know that he knew his

true identity. It seemed now that since he knew who his kidnapper was, he couldn't take the situation so seriously.

'Why don't you send them my dick?' he said. 'That'd be far more appropriate.'

'We *are* cocky today, aren't we?' said Eddie. 'If you'll pardon the pun.'

There was a pause before Ben said, 'Well, I can't eat breakfast with my hands tied.'

Eddie undid the rope that held his hands behind his back. Ben felt hungry as he hadn't eaten very much over the past few days. He reached out and lifted a piece of toast to his mouth. 'Haven't you got any jam?' he asked, biting into the plain, buttered toast.

'Oh, I'm so sorry,' said Eddie. 'The jam's off today, I'm afraid. Perhaps sir would like to reorder from the breakfast menu.'

'There's no need to be sarcastic. I was only asking.' Ben sipped from the cup of tea. 'Can I go out for a walk today? I'm sick of being cooped up in here. It's not good for my health. I might pine away through lack of light and fresh air.'

'In a word – no.' Eddie went to leave the attic.

'Don't go,' Ben surprised himself by saying. 'It gets lonely, locked in here all the time.'

'What?'

'I'm bored of my own company. It's not very nice of you to do this to me.'

'You don't say,' said Eddie.

'Look, can't we make a deal?' Ben was searching for an idea. 'What say you let me go and I'll give you some money later on? I could pay you in instalments. My mother will be out of her mind with worry. It's not just me you're hurting.'

Eddie laughed. 'Look, I'd love to stand around here talking rubbish, but I have actually got things to do.'

'What like? Kidnapping other innocent people?'

'If you want to stay alive, I suggest you shut the fuck up and get on with your breakfast.' He paused and then added, 'If you want me to come up later and give you a good seeing to, that's fine by me.'

'No, it's all right,' said Ben. 'And you can take this away. I'm not hungry any more.'

Eddie retied Ben's hands, picked up the tray and left the room. As soon as the hatch was closed, Ben felt an overwhelming sense of anger come across him and he struggled with the ropes. If only he could get free then perhaps when Eddie came back up he'd be able to overpower him and escape. Ben looked around the room, trying to see something he could use to cut through the rope. There seemed to be nothing. The mattress would be useless, so would a bucket, but Ben wondered about the chair. He stood up with a lot of difficulty and walked over to it. On the surface it looked useless, but when he turned it over he noticed four long bolts that held the legs on to the seat. These bolts stuck out and had sharp edges where the metal had been roughly cut. This was the perfect tool. It might take some time but with patience and persistence Ben believed he would be able to wear away at the rope until it snapped.

He positioned himself so that his back was facing the upturned chair. He felt for the sharp bolt and started to rub the rope against it. He hoped that he would only have to cut through one piece and then the rest would become loose and he would be able to slip his hands out. It was not easy. Every time he worked the rope over the bolt, the jagged metal caught his wrist and cut him. Ben knew that it would be worth it in the end, even if he was scratched to pieces.

It took him what seemed like an hour to cut into the rope and throughout this time Ben kept his ears pricked for the sound of feet on the ladder. He was prepared at any moment to jump up and sit down in the chair or cross to the mattress. However, luckily there were no sounds of Eddie approaching.

Eventually his efforts paid off and one strand of the rope snapped. He wriggled his hands around, and with a squeeze he was able to pull one free. It felt great to be liberated. He used his free hand to pull the rest of the rope off the other. Ben stood the chair back up and hid the rope under the mattress.

He realised that the only thing he could use as a weapon against Eddie would be the chair, so it would be useful if he was sitting on the thing when the man came into the room. Then all he would have to do would be to stand up and batter Eddie over the head with it as hard as he could and get out of the room. He hoped that this would give him enough time to get down the ladder and bolt the hatch behind him. Of course, the element of surprise was everything.

Ben waited for the man to come up, but nothing happened. Eddie never seemed to visit him at any particular times, just randomly when he felt like it. He knew that he'd have to attract Eddie's attention in some way – provoke him to enter the room. Ben banged the chair on to the floor three times. He knew that Eddie would be unable to ignore it. And, sure enough, Ben soon heard the familiar footsteps on the ladder. He prepared himself: hands behind his back as if they were still tied there, perched on the edge of the chair ready to grab it and use it as a weapon. The hatch opened and Eddie stepped up into the attic room.

'What do you want?' he said.

'I've really hurt my leg badly. Come over and take a look.'

Eddie walked towards him and Ben drew all the courage he had, and when the man was standing right in front of him he swiftly raised the chair above his head. Eddie yelled, and Ben brought it crashing down with as much power as he could muster. The man crumpled to the floor and Ben dropped the chair and ran over to the hatch. However, even as he was putting his foot on the first rung of the ladder Eddie was raising himself and yelling, 'You little bastard.'

It was hard to climb down a ladder quickly, as Ben discovered. The man was already on his feet and lunging towards the opening. Ben realised that he did not have enough time to close the hatch. If he attempted to, Eddie would probably be able to reach out and grab hold of him and stop him from getting away. Ben had to use his head start to get out of the building rather than stop Eddie leaving the attic.

He raced down the ladder as fast as he could but, by the time he reached the ground the man had already started to descend, shouting angrily as he did so. Ben was terrified. He had to escape, otherwise he'd be done for. He found himself in the flat that he'd been to with Lee just after they first met. It was now confirmed who his kidnapper was.

He made a dash for the front door. However, he wasn't fast enough. Eddie had already descended and Ben turned his head just in time to see the man dive through the air towards him and grab hold of his ankles as he hit the floor. Ben lost his balance and toppled down, the door open and freedom within sight. Eddie took a firmer hold and held him there, face down on the floor.

'What a stupid thing to do,' he hissed through gritted teeth. 'You're really going to regret that.'

Ben shook with fear at how he would be punished. Now he had no chance of getting away. He would probably be trussed up even more thoroughly this time.

Eddie bent one of Ben's arms back behind him and levered him into a standing position. Then he escorted him back along the hall and towards the steps up to the attic.

'Don't try anything, just get up the ladder.'

Ben did as he was told and walked slowly up towards his attic prison. Eddie followed close behind. He didn't dare try and escape again. His only weapon had been surprise, and now that his ace had been played there was nothing left. Eddie was bigger and stronger than him – he had no chance against him physically.

Eddie tied Ben's hands behind his back even tighter than before, and when he was powerless to defend himself, he slapped him round the face with the back of his hand. Ben yelled out in pain.

'How could you do this to me, Eddie?' he cried, not caring whether the man knew that he knew his true identity. 'Why don't you just drop the phoney accent and take off that mask?'

Eddie was rendered speechless for a moment, and then slowly he removed the hat and the mask and Ben saw his face, which was twisted with anger.

'If you hadn't tried to escape, you wouldn't have known who I was.'

'Don't kid yourself,' Ben whimpered. 'I've known for some time. And after all I've done for you – renting my body out so that you could make a living. I trusted you, and this is how you repay me.'

There was a pause during which he just stared at Ben, and then he said, 'Well, I'm going to teach you a lesson for hitting me over the head. That hurt, you little prick.' Eddie disappeared down the ladder and returned with a length of cane and a huge plaster that he stuck over Ben's mouth. 'This'll sort you out,' he said, laughing, and he pushed Ben face down across the seat of the chair. Ben struggled but there was nothing he could do – he was bound and gagged. Eddie pulled down his underwear at the back, which was still the only thing Ben was wearing. Ben knew what was coming next and he braced himself. He saw the man raise the cane in the air and bring it whistling down on his bare bottom. The shock of the blow was more alarming than the pain, which Ben didn't feel at first. It was only when the next slap hit him that the pain cut through his body and made him yell inwardly, as the gag stopped him from making an audible cry.

Eddie continued to beat him, the cane whacking down repeatedly on his naked arse. Ben looked up at him, his face screwed up with pain and anger, but the man was unmoved. He let rip with all his force and Ben had soon lost count of how many strokes he had received.

When Eddie finally finished beating him, Ben's bottom was so sore that he wanted to cry, but pride kept him from letting his tears show. Eddie had a cruel smile on his face, which only made Ben more angry. How he wanted to have his revenge.

'Shouldn't have tried to escape, should you?' he said. 'And if you ever try anything like that again, I'll make that beating look like a walk in the park.' With that he left the room and locked up the hatch. Ben was left still lying across the chair, his pants round his ankles and his bottom red raw.

Ben lay on his side on the mattress. He couldn't sleep for the pain he felt in his bottom, so he lay awake, staring into the darkness. The flat was silent. He assumed Eddie had either gone out or was asleep.

As if from nowhere, there came the faintest sound, like a tiny scratching in the walls or the buzz of electricity. Ben sat up and listened more carefully. The noise was coming from below the hatch. He remained motionless, praying that Eddie had not come back to give him a second beating.

The hatch slowly slid back and a small amount of light seeped into the room. With gentle steps someone crept up the ladder and into the attic. The light suddenly came on and Ben found himself staring at his friend, Lee. He could barely believe it. It was like a miracle, something that he had never for a second imagined might happen.

Lee put a finger to his lips in order to silence Ben – although this was pointless as he couldn't talk with the gag on, anyway – and raised a hand that told him to stay where he was. Lee quietly slipped the hatch back over the opening and with delicate steps came over to where Ben was sitting. He threw his arms around him and they stayed clasped together for some moments before Lee pulled away.

'I'm so pleased to see you,' he whispered, and he carefully peeled back the plaster that covered Ben's mouth and dropped it on the floor.

'Oh, Lee, thank God. I can't believe you're real.'

'Shh . . . We don't want to wake Eddie.' Lee kissed him on the lips and their tongues met with a greater passion than Ben had felt in a very long time. He was so pleased and yet astonished to see his friend that he hardly knew what to say.

'How did you find me?'

'That's a long story,' said Lee. 'I'll tell you when we're out of danger. All that matters now is getting you away from here.'

'Can you untie my hands, please?'

Lee reached behind him and undid the rope.

'Where are your clothes?'

'Eddie took them. I've been in my pants for days.'

Lee took off his jumper and helped Ben into it. 'I don't have a spare pair of trousers, I'm afraid. I didn't expect to find you half naked.'

'Doesn't matter. Shall we go?'

Lee nodded. 'We must be very, very quiet.'

The two boys slowly crossed the attic floor and Lee opened the hatch. Ben went down first, holding on tightly to the sides of the ladder to steady himself – one noise and Eddie might hear them. Lee followed behind closing the hatch and turning off the light as he did so. When they were both downstairs, neither one moved for a moment, but just stood there in the darkness, listening. There seemed to be silence, and Lee gestured for Ben to follow him.

'Ah, Lee, how nice of you to drop in.'

Both boys spun round at the same time. Eddie was standing at the bedroom door with a gun in his hand. Ben had to stop himself from yelling out. He couldn't believe that he'd been caught again; his bottom still hurt from the beating he'd received for trying to escape the last time.

'Don't move a muscle, you little sods.' Eddie shook his head in mock disbelief. 'Let's go into the living room and catch up on old times.'

Ben and Lee sat down on the sofa side by side. Ben thought about the horrible twist his life had taken since the last time he'd sat there. It was like a macabre parody of that first innocent meeting with Eddie. If only he'd known this then, he'd never have got involved with the whole rent boy thing in the first place. It was, he knew, no use saying 'if only' and 'I shouldn't have'; things had taken their course and he had to deal with the consequences.

'You were very clever, Lee. I'm surprised you worked it out so quickly. I thought I'd have at least a week's head start on you.' Eddie sat down on the other sofa, still brandishing the gun. 'So, what gave it away?'

'At first I believed you,' said Lee, looking, Ben thought, remarkably relaxed, considering. 'Ben had waltzed off somewhere, but it was nothing to worry about. He'd be back in a couple of days. I even believed you when you said you'd reported him missing to the police. You said that they couldn't do anything about it till Ben had been gone a week. Why would I suspect you of lying? I looked through your bags,' he said, turning to Ben. 'Your address book was gone. My first thought was that you'd got bored with turning tricks or needed some time to yourself, so you'd gone off for a while and you'd send word soon. After a couple of days, I started to get more concerned. I was really worried, so I contacted the police myself. They told me that no such person had ever been reported missing.'

'Well done,' said Eddie with a dry chuckle. 'I wondered how long it'd take you.' He lit a cigarette. 'Obviously I didn't want to tell the Old Bill, but I needed to stall you all, just until I'd got the money. Then I could release Ben and no one would be any the wiser.'

'Hasn't quite worked out that way, though, has it?' said Lee, a little sarcastically, Ben thought.

'No,' Eddie retorted, 'but the show's not over yet. Remember I'm holding the gun. I'm calling the shots.'

'How do you know I haven't told the police where you are?'

'I don't. But I'm willing to take a gamble.' Eddie took a last drag on the cigarette and stubbed it out. 'Right. I want you two upstairs. I've got a really good idea for a little game I'd like to play.' With his eyes still on them, Eddie reached into a drawer in a small cabinet at the side of the sofa and produced some condoms and a tube of lubricant. He gestured for them to stand up and walk towards the attic ladder. He followed behind with the gun stretched out in front of him. They climbed the steps and waited in the room for his instructions. 'I want to watch you two fucking,' he said.

'What?' said Lee.

'You heard me. I want you to do everything that I tell you to. And remember, if you try anything stupid or disobey me, I'm perfectly willing to use this.' He indicated the gun. 'Now, Lee, take that jumper off Ben.' Lee, a grudging look on his face, did as he was told. Ben stood near the mattress in only his boxer shorts. 'Now, you undress him,' he said, looking at Ben.

Lee was wearing a short-sleeved shirt that Ben, standing in front of him and staring a little intensely into his eyes, started to unbutton and slip off. The garment fell to the floor. Ben dropped down to his knees and unlaced Lee's trainers and slid them off. These were followed by his socks. Then he stood up again and undid Lee's trousers and let them fall to the floor. The lad stepped out of them.

'Leave his pants on,' commanded Eddie.

Although there was something humiliating about being told what to do with Lee, there was also a powerful sensation of lust that he felt, having not had sex with his friend for what must have been over a week. He was looking forward to fucking with him, even if it had to be a live sex show for Eddie's entertainment.

'Touch his cock and then suck it.'

Ben dropped to his knees again and started to caress his friend's penis through the fabric of his briefs, which almost immediately became stiff against his hands. Trying to ignore Eddie's presence, he leaned in close and inhaled the fragrance of Lee's crotch. It smelt as if he'd just had a shower – so fresh and inviting, with just the slightest hint of sweat about it. Ben breathed in deeply and with trembling hands he pulled the briefs down at the front and Lee's erect cock slid instantly into view. The foreskin was still concealing the head, and Ben reached out and pulled the lad's underwear further down until it rested at the base of his prick, but still covered up his balls. Then he took hold of the thick shaft and slowly drew back the loose skin. The head of Lee's prick was purple and swollen; it glistened with pre-come that had oozed from the opening and covered the whole of the surface area and made it slippery and shiny. Ben took some of the fluid on to the tip of his finger and placed it to his lips. It tasted just like it always did.

Clasping the lad's balls through the material of his briefs, Ben let his mouth engulf the head and at the same time he ran his tongue over it, dipping it into the slit at the end every so often. His free hand alternated between stroking Lee's smooth flat stomach and slowly masturbating him. Whenever he did the latter, the lad would let out a groan and push his hips further forwards into Ben's face.

He moved his mouth up and down the length of the lad's prick for quite some time. Occasionally he would stop and lick his balls or take one into his mouth and gently suck on it. Sometimes his hand would stray behind him and he'd end up squeezing Lee's tightly clenched buttocks or working the hand between them.

'That's enough of that,' Eddie suddenly said. 'Now I want Lee on his back on the bed and you to rim him. With his legs in the air,' the man added, as if he needed to clarify the order.

Lee went and laid down on the mattress and Ben positioned himself between the lad's legs. He signalled for Lee to lift his legs, and then he pushed them even higher. Ben needed to have full access to the area in between. Lee looked so lovely laid out like this, he thought, that it was a pleasure to rim him. He lay on his front with his bottom up in the air and lifted the lad's balls. His arsehole was beautifully displayed, open before him, so he brought his face closer and inhaled the smell that lingered between Lee's cheeks. It was amazing: a hint of talc, soap and a sweet yet sweaty aroma that was solely the lad's own. Ben extended his tongue and licked at the perineum that lay before him. It was a hard strip of muscular flesh covered with soft hairs that he lapped at like a puppy. Then he moved down to Lee's tight opening. To aid him he placed a thumb either side and parted the buttocks a little more. As he did this, the hole opened up and he was able to put his tongue in and manoeuvre it about. He licked around the edges and over the soft skin at either side, and then went back in, making the ring moist with his saliva and continually working away at the anus itself.

After a while the lad began to loosen up and Ben was able to get much further inside. He introduced a finger and worked this right up. The saliva that he'd left there made its passage more smooth, and he felt his digit delve right into the unseen depths without too much difficulty. Lee was tight and well muscled inside, and there was something so fantastic about feeling his interior. The lad let out a boyish moan, which only made Ben want to probe further and he twisted the finger around, trying as he did to loosen him up and make easier access for his tongue, which he put back in once he'd slowly withdrawn the digit.

This time, Ben was able to get right inside his friend. The passage opened up and he pushed his tongue in deeply. It felt sublime to be probing such an intimate area, the lad panting all the time he was in him. He didn't understand why it was so rewarding to give someone else pleasure, but it was.

Ben pulled his tongue out and just licked around the outer rim for a while before inserting two fingers side by side into the lad's opening. These did not glide in so smoothly, but with a bit of effort and some gentle twisting he was able to gradually ease them up. Lee let out a whimper, probably a warning for him to be more gentle, but in his excitement Ben was unable to slow down, so he ignored his friend and twisted the digits around inside him, regardless of his cries. It was so fantastic that only Eddie's calling out for him to stop made him come back to his senses.

'I want you to suck each other off at the same time,' he said.

Ben looked up, giving Lee the chance to relax his legs. Eddie was now sitting in the chair, his gun still in his hand, but now pointing towards the floor. He had an erection clearly visible in his trousers and was gently stroking it through the material.

Ben took his underwear off and lay next to his friend on the mattress, but facing the opposite direction. His mind flipped back to the time he and Paul had made each other come in the tent in Paul's garden, that heavenly night before he'd given it all up and come to London looking for something better. He knew now that he hadn't found it. He'd just found a different set of constraints, a different trap to escape from.

He took hold of Lee's prick and angled it downwards, bending it back against itself so that he was able to line it up with his mouth. He opened wide and took it inside. The pre-come that had been there before had increased, and it now flowed like water from a spring, probably encouraged by the rimming. His own penis dribbled too, and he thought of how it must taste as Lee took hold of him and, with a hand on his bottom and one at the base of the shaft, guided him into his mouth. He felt the warm, soft wetness of the boy's lips as they slid over him and caressed his rock-hard head.

The lad was producing the sticky fluid so fast that Ben could feel it trickling into his mouth and seeping down his throat. He stretched back the foreskin and sucked away on the swollen head, the whole time his own cock being sucked and manipulated. It felt great to be joined together in mutual pleasure with someone so sexy. He just wished he could see what the lad looked like as he worked away on his erection.

It was easy at the angle their bodies had to be in for Ben to reach round and feel his friend's arsehole, which was so conveniently available to him. While he sucked he gently inserted two fingers once again, the passage still loose and welcoming from his first exploration. He knew that this would help the lad to come more quickly to orgasm, and immediately he saw the boy's balls tighten because of it. Out of the corner of his eye he noticed Eddie, gun still in hand, stand up and approach him from behind. He felt the weight of the man denting the mattress as he sat down, but he could not see what he was doing.

Suddenly a hand touched his buttocks and parted them slightly, then a cold, slippery finger came into contact with his opening, and, before he knew it, had slid into his bottom. Although it felt like a dirty violation, the finger twisting up inside him, there was something deeply exciting about another person's touch being added to the act that himself and Lee were performing. Furthermore, the finger made him want to come. The lad's enthusiastic lips sucking away at him, the cock pushing deeply down his throat and Eddie's anal stimulation seemed utterly overwhelming. He knew that his climax was already in the hands of others – he could do nothing to stop himself from letting it out.

Lee had started to thrust his hips into Ben's face, which forced him to suck harder and use his finger, which remained firmly embedded in the lad's bottom, as a weapon of control over his aggressive movements. He could tell from the way his own prick was being sucked that Lee was coming to a climax, but he did not realise how soon it would happen. Before he had a chance to prepare himself for it, a large squirt of semen shot out into his mouth and was automatically swallowed. In fact, he had no choice, the lad's prick being thrust so far into his mouth that the liquid had nowhere else to go. More spurts of warm fluid followed which were also drunk down. At this moment Ben too started coming, the sensation so intense that he thrust his hips into Lee's face and he felt Eddie's finger being pushed even deeper inside him.

He let the lad's penis slip from his mouth and licked off the last drops of semen that seeped out of the tip like an afterthought. He felt himself drained and the finger slide out of him. Both boys lay back on the bed panting.

'Don't think it's over yet,' said Eddie with a smirk.

'What do you want us to do now?' asked Lee, throwing a quick smile at Ben who realised that the lad was obviously looking forward to the next part.

'I want to see you rimming one another at the same time.' Eddie moved the gun, as if to make the suggestion an order.

Lee made the first move, climbing on top of Ben, who had turned on to his back, his penis hard once again at the idea of what was to happen. He raised his legs in the air with the help of the lad's hands. As he did this Lee knelt over his face, his legs spread so that Ben had his arse splayed out before him. Immediately he felt the lad's tongue dipping into his arsehole and licking him out. He continued the work that he had started earlier and used his fingers to pry open the hole as much as he could. The boy was loose now and easy to penetrate and he pushed his tongue into the opening and worked it around until it slid deeply in, then he explored the interior and made it wet with his saliva. Ben could see Eddie watching everything and stroking his cock at the same time.

'Stop now,' said the man after a while. 'Lee, I want you to fuck him.'

Ben was not prepared for this, but the idea made him excited, and he moved so that he was lying face down on the bed.

'No,' said Eddie. 'I want you facing one another.'

Ben turned on to his back and Lee positioned himself in front of him. The man threw a condom and a tube of lubricant on to the bed. Lee opened the sachet and stretched the rubber over his erection. He opened the tube and put some of the sticky ointment on to the tips of his fingers. Some of this he spread over his sheathed penis and some he slicked over and into Ben's arsehole.

The slippery fingers felt big and cold inside him as he lay there with his legs as far up in the air as he could get them.

Lee leaned forwards and took hold of his own cock at the base, angling it towards Ben's hole. He braced himself and felt the tip touch his ring and then push it open and edge inside. The first moments were painful, but after several hard shoves the lad's prick went all the way in and Ben felt a sense of relief as his muscles loosened and accommodated the intrusion. All the while, his friend stared deeply into his eyes with such an intensity that Ben almost felt as if they were in love with one another.

Lee started to move his cock in and out, slowly at first, but then with greater momentum when he'd opened the passage more. Ben, his legs far up in the air and his cock hard as iron, enjoyed watching the lad push his prick in and out of him, the movement making his balls tighten and ache.

Eddie moved from where he was sitting and leaned towards Lee. He put his hands either side of the lad's thrusting hips and steadied them so that eventually he was moderating their movement, deciding how hard and deep he pushed his cock into Ben's arse. He felt as if he was being fucked by two people. Even though it was Lee whose prick was in him, somehow Eddie was calling the shots, deciding exactly how he would be screwed.

Next, the man moved one hand away from Lee's hips and let it drift between his thrusting buttocks. He slid it into the crack and Ben could see him slowly pushing a finger up into the lad's bottom. It was now this finger that was controlling his thrusts. Lee must be feeling something similar to him – both of them having something inside them.

Ben lay back on the mattress staring up at his friend who maintained eye contact with him throughout. Eddie seemed to be making him push harder and deeper in with every movement. Ben felt the lad's cock drive deeply inside and then slide back out almost to the point where it would become completely dislodged and his anus return to its natural shape, then another heavy thrust would bring it back in, making him gasp with the sensation of discomfort.

Soon Lee was panting with the aggression of someone so

utterly captured in his own pleasure that, Ben thought, he must only be able to concentrate on his penis sliding in and out of the passage. The lad leaned forwards, smiled and then kissed him hard on the mouth. Then, without any further noise or warning, he pushed his cock in harder and further than he had done before and left it there for several seconds before pulling it back out and then immediately shoving it deeply in again. Ben could tell that Lee was coming, and he put his arms around the lad's body, holding him close, trying to share the moment with him.

Lee slowly pulled his cock out and fell down beside him on the bed. Eddie smiled at them with something of a perverse expression on his face.

'Very nice. I should have captured that on film. Would've made me a fortune.' He paused. 'Now get up and put your pants on.' The boys did as instructed. Eddie handed Ben a length of rope, the gun pointing straight ahead of him.

'Tie your friend's hands behind his back,' he said.

Ben looked at Lee, who only shrugged and turned around and put his arms behind his back. Ben tied them.

'Tightly.'

'All right,' said Ben. He pulled the rope, as if it would go no tighter, but he was only pretending. He didn't want to hurt his friend. Eddie seemed satisfied. He nodded.

'Now take this,' he said, handing over a thick piece of sticky plaster. 'Put it over his mouth.' Ben did as he was told, then watched as Eddie pushed Lee backwards on to the mattress. 'Turn round.' The man tied Ben's hands tightly behind his back and then applied a piece of plaster to his mouth. 'Now I suggest you behave yourselves. And if you try anything I'm fully prepared to kill either or both of you.' He turned away and left the room, bolting the hatch behind him.

Ben sat down on the mattress beside his friend and put his head on his shoulder. He could not believe the situation that they'd managed to get themselves into. He looked into Lee's eyes. The lad motioned with his head, but he didn't understand what he meant. Lee leaned down on the bed so that his head was behind Ben's back and his face rested against his hands. He realised immediately what the lad was doing – he wanted him to remove the plaster from his mouth. With some difficulty and some awkward movements Ben succeeded and his friend sat up again.

'Great,' he said. 'That was easy.'

'Mmm,' Ben tried to speak.

'Oh, sorry.'

Ben leaned down and Lee removed his gag.

'Excellent. Now how are we going to get ourselves out of this mess?'

'Shh,' said Lee. 'We don't want Eddie to hear us.'

'Sorry.'

'We need to be very clever if we're going to get out of this alive.'

Ben had a thought. 'Is it possible to undo each other's hands?'

'Let's try. Turn round so that we're back to back.'

The two boys turned away from one another and Lee struggled to untie the rope around Ben's wrists. After a while he stopped, panting.

'It's no good. He tied it too tight.'

'I'll try to undo yours. I tied it quite loosely.'

Ben patiently unknotted the rope that he had fastened himself, trying to remember how he had tied it. After several minutes it became loose enough for Lee to slip his hands out.

'That's better,' he said, and then he untied Ben.

'So, have you got a plan?'

'No,' said Lee. 'Not yet.'

'But what are we going to do?' Ben put his head on his friend's shoulder and kissed him there. Lee took hold of his head and raised it so that they were looking straight into one another's eyes. He kissed him on the mouth once, and then a second time more deeply.

'Look, there are two of us and our hands are no longer tied. We can overpower Eddie when he comes up in the morning. We'll be ready for him.'

'But he's got a gun,' Ben whimpered.

'That's a chance we're going to have to take. There's no

choice. All we need to do is get the gun off him, then we've got the power.'

Ben was frightened and started to sob quietly. Lee put his arm around him and pulled him close to his chest.

'Don't worry, baby. Everything's going to be OK. Just you wait and see. Trust me.' Lee stroked his hair. 'Try and rest now.'

Eleven

When Ben woke up, Lee was sitting on the edge of the mattress in the same position that he'd been in when Ben had fallen asleep. 'You OK?' Ben asked.

'Yeah. Fine.'

'Sorry, I fell asleep.' Ben stretched his arms.

'Don't be silly. You needed a rest after all you've been through.' Lee leaned forwards and kissed him on the lips.

'That's nice,' said Ben and he moved in for another kiss.

'Remember,' Lee said pulling back, 'we've got to get out of here today.'

'Didn't you tell anyone you were coming here?'

Lee looked guiltily down at the floor. 'No,' he said. 'It was only a hunch that I'd find you here. I never really thought Eddie'd stoop to kidnapping. But don't worry, we'll get out.'

'You won't do anything dangerous, will you? Eddie's got the gun and I think he knows that he's in trouble whatever happens. He may not care whether he kills us.'

'He may be stupid, Ben, but I don't think he's completely lost his grip on reality.'

'I wouldn't be so sure.'

Lee put his arms around Ben's bare shoulders and brought his head to rest on his chest.

'Look, all I'm saying is just be careful. Don't do anything dangerous.'

'I just want to get us out of this situation, that's all.'

'What's that?' said Ben. The two boys listened. Someone was moving about below them.

'Eddie, I expect. Let's put the plasters back on and hide the rope.'

They replaced the gags they'd taken off the night before and hid the rope under the mattress, putting their hands behind their backs as if they were still tied up. Soon footsteps were heard climbing the ladder. Ben caught his friend's eye and he tried to smile.

When he entered, Eddie was dressed in a suit and he held the gun down at his side.

'Still here, then? Haven't tried to escape overnight?'

Lee made a noise behind his plaster.

'What?' said Eddie. 'Got something to say?' He walked over and Ben watched his friend lean back slightly on the bed, trying to conceal the fact that he no longer had his hands tied. The man pulled off the gag. 'Better?'

'Yes. Much better,' said Lee.

Eddie walked away and sat down in the chair. 'So, what was it you wanted to say?' he asked.

'I just wondered whether you'd like a blow job.'

Ben was surprised at his words. This was the last thing he'd expected to hear. He glanced across at his friend but Lee had his eyes fixed on Eddie.

'Oh, yeah?' said the man. 'Why? What do you want?'

'Well, I won't pretend. I just thought that perhaps if I did you a favour you'd be a bit nicer to us. Especially to Ben.'

'I'm not sure whether I believe you, and I'm not sure whether I want your empty gesture, even if I do.'

'Well, take it or leave it. But don't say you weren't asked.'

Eddie was silent for a moment and then he said, 'What does little Ben think to all this?'

Ben made a low murmuring sound.

'Shall I take that as a "yes"?'

Ben nodded slowly. He knew that somehow this was all part of Lee's crazy plan to get them out of here. He just hoped his friend wasn't going to do anything dangerous.

'All right, then, I'll let you.'

'You'll need to undo my hands if you want it done properly.'

'OK.' Eddie approached the lad, the gun hanging loosely in his hand. The moment he reached forwards Lee lashed out at him, knocking the gun out of his grasp and sending it spinning across the attic floor. The lad went to hit him but Eddie put up his hand, stopping the fist in mid-air. Ben jumped up and ran towards the weapon where it lay some feet away. He knew that his friend needed his help. He had to put himself at risk, too. However, he was just not quick enough. Eddie let go of Lee and delivered a swift punch to his cheek, then turned, and with great speed flew at the gun. It was like a very short race – a race that only took a split second. As Ben fell to his knees, hands reaching out before him, trying to grab the thing, a foot pounded down on his hand and stopped it, inches away from its target. Eddie pushed him out of the way and took hold of the gun.

Lee still sat on the mattress, a hand held to his reddened face. Ben lay on the floor. Eddie was crouching down in the spot where his weapon had landed, right beside the hatch that lay open, his flat visible through the opening. If it had travelled any further it would have fallen through. The man stood up to his full height and pointed the gun firstly at Ben and then at Lee, his eyes filled with a mixture of terror and fury.

'I'm gonna kill you,' he snarled at no one in particular.

Ben looked up, trying to catch his friend's eye, but in vain. The boy was staring with hatred directly at Eddie. The thing that happened next amazed him. While it was happening he felt that he was in a dream or watching things from the outside like one watches a television. Lee slowly rose from the bed and started to move towards the man, whose fury seemed to turn to panic and, to Ben's amazement, he took a step backwards, towards the open hatch. It was as if he wanted to use the gun but couldn't. He could see Lee approaching him, challenging his power, but Eddie clearly could not muster up the determination to actually fire.

The lad took one more step closer and in sync Eddie took one more step back. Ben looked down at the man's feet, and in that second saw him lose balance, his heel coming into contact with the edge of the opening, and fall through the hatch and down on to the floor below.

For the first few seconds after Eddie had disappeared, Ben and Lee just stared at one another in silence. Then they moved to the edge of the opening and looked down. The man was lying motionless at the bottom of the ladder. He was on his back, staring up at them, but his eyes were closed. He had a cut on the side of his head, but other than this there were no noticeable injuries.

'What are we going to do?' Ben said.

'I don't know, but this is our chance to get away.' Lee picked up his clothes which were lying in a pile where Ben had taken them off him the previous day. He put them on and handed Ben the jumper he'd lent him before. 'If we can't find your clothes, we'll take something of Eddie's.'

Without saying another word, Lee started to climb down the ladder, carefully stepping over the man lying on the floor. Ben followed him.

'Shouldn't we check whether he's alive or something?' he said.

'I guess so.' Lee bent down and put a cautious hand to the man's neck. Ben held his breath, praying that he wasn't dead.

'There's a pulse,' said Lee. 'He's just knocked himself out, that's all. It's best not to move him.'

'Why's that?'

'I don't really know, but I've seen it on television.'

'Shouldn't we call an ambulance or something?'

'Do you think so?' asked Lee.

'Yeah. Look, you find my clothes, I'll make the phone call and then we'll get out of here.'

Ben went into the kitchen where he remembered the telephone was. He dialled and asked for an ambulance, telling the person at the end of the line that there'd been an accident, someone had fallen off a ladder and was unconscious. He gave the address and then hung up.

'Have you found them?' Ben called out.

'I think so.'

Lee came in carrying Ben's stuff.

'Where were they?'

'Just lying on the floor.'

Ben dressed himself quickly, and, as he did so, noticed the gun that still lay in Eddie's hand.

'Should we leave that there?'

'Yes,' Lee replied. 'We don't want to take any of the evidence.'

'That depends what we're going to do about this – whether or not we're going to tell the police.'

'What are you talking about? Of course we're going to tell them, aren't we?'

'I don't know,' said Ben. 'I don't want to get us all into trouble for being rent boys.'

'Look, we'll talk about this later. The ambulance will be here any minute.'

The two of them left the flat door open and ran down all the flights of stairs and out into the Stockwell morning. To Ben, it seemed so bright outside. It must have been almost a week since he'd been out in the fresh air, and it was only now that he realised how dependent one was on such simple things.

Lee lead the way through various streets to the nearest bus stop. He paid for them both and they went and sat at the back of the bus.

'Where are we going?' asked Ben.

'I don't know. I just wanted to get away from this area.'

After a few minutes they found themselves in Brixton. Lee signalled that they should get off. They walked aimlessly until they arrived at a pub.

'Let's go in here. We can talk and have a drink.'

Lee ordered them a pint each and they sat down at a small table in a quiet corner at the back of the pub.

'I can't believe we're free,' was all that Ben could manage to say. Tears that he was unable to control were falling down his face.

Lee touched his hand under the table. 'Everything's OK now.'

'I'm sorry about what happened with Joe,' said Ben, the memory flooding back to him as he looked up into the lad's eyes.

'It doesn't matter.'

'But I *did* lie to you. You were right.'

'That's all in the past now. It doesn't matter at all.'

'Has Joe gone home?'

'Yes,' said Lee, smiling warmly. 'But he said that he really enjoyed himself with you.'

'Oh, good,' Ben murmured. 'I'm glad.'

'He said that he'd given his full consent to everything that happened.'

Time passed; neither lad spoke. Ben just sipped at his drink while Lee went over to the cigarette machine and bought a pack of cigarettes. He offered one to Ben, who took it gratefully. Lee lit it for him.

'What now?' said Ben. 'I don't know whether to tell the police. You see, I don't want to get you lot in trouble.'

'Don't worry about that. First things first. Let your mother know that you're safe.' Lee got a ten-pence piece out of his pocket and handed it to Ben, who walked over to a payphone near the bar.

'Hi, Mum,' Ben said after dialling the number and waiting for a voice at the end of the line. 'It's your son.' He tried to tell her as little as possible, promising to call again later, and simply reassuring her that he was safe and well.

'What did she say?' asked Lee when he returned to the table.

'She was relieved.'

'Obviously. Did you tell her what really happened?'

'No. I didn't say very much at all.' Ben sipped his drink. 'I promised to call again in an hour or so.'

'Have you decided whether you're going to tell the police the real story?' Lee paused and then said, 'I think you should.'

'I don't know. I just don't want any of the boys to get into trouble.'

'Is that the only reason?'

'No, not really. It'll mean that my mother will find out everything. She'll never forgive me if she hears what I've been

184

doing for a living. She'll blame me. Because it really *is* my own fault that I got kidnapped in the first place.'

'No it's not,' said Lee.

'Yes it is. If I hadn't have got it into my head to run away from home none of this would have happened. Mum wouldn't have had to go through all this stress. The whole point was for me to get my independence and not have to bother my parents any more, and look, the entire thing has backfired on me.' Ben started to cry again.

'But don't you want Eddie to get his comeuppance? He'll get away with it, otherwise.'

'Yeah, but if I turn him in he'll probably get sent away for years.'

'So what?' argued Lee.

There was a silence and then Ben said, 'I suppose you're right. But maybe I should talk to the others about it.'

'I'm sure they'll just tell you what I've told you – to get justice.' Lee finished his pint. 'Come on,' he said. 'Let's go home.'

Ringo, Alex, Nathan and Luis were all in the lounge when they arrived back. Ringo stood up.

'Where the hell have you been?' he asked.

'That's a long story,' Lee replied.

'First Ben goes missing and then you, and then you both appear again together. Where have you been? On your bloody honeymoon?'

'If you've got a week or two I'll explain it.'

'Anyway, it's good to see you both back safe and sound,' said Ringo. 'Especially you, Ben. We were really worried.' The other boys all agreed. 'Let's have a drink to celebrate.'

'God knows, I need one,' said Ben.

Ringo disappeared and came back a few minutes later with a bottle of brandy and some glasses. He poured them all drinks and then sat down on the floor along with Nathan, making space for them to sit on the sofa.

'So, tell us what happened?'

Lee took it upon himself to do all the explaining, which was fine by Ben, who didn't want to have to go through the whole thing all over again. As the story unfolded, the lads looked more and more amazed, unable to take in all the facts and especially believe that it was Eddie behind it all.

'I can't believe he'd do something like that,' said Nathan. 'He's completely crazy.'

'Yeah,' agreed Luis. 'But why? What was his motive?'

'He needed the money, I guess,' said Ringo.

'But he had the money he gets from us, so why would he need more?'

'He must be in debt. Probably something to do with drugs.'

Lee told of their attempted escape and how they had been caught and imprisoned, and then of the fight and the struggle for the gun and Eddie falling through the hatch. Ben could hardly believe that all these things had only happened that morning. Lee made it out like they were heroes in some action movie and the gang just sat in silence, listening with their mouths gaping open.

'Have you told the police?' Alex asked after the story had been recounted.

'No,' said Ben. 'I don't know what to do.'

'They're going to want to know what happened to you. They'll want to catch the kidnapper,' added Ringo.

'I agree,' said Lee. 'It all needs to come out.'

'I know. But I don't want to get you lot into trouble.' Ben looked down at the floor. 'And what will my mother say?'

'You're a big boy now, Ben,' said Ringo. 'You're eighteen. It's up to you what you choose to do for a living. Your mum can't stop you.'

'Yeah, but I don't want to upset her.'

'Look, firstly, *we* don't mind if you go to the police. We're willing to give them a statement, aren't we, lads?' The boys were all in agreement. 'You don't want him to get away with it, do you?'

Ben shook his head.

'Then tell them everything you know. They'll be able to catch him easily. He'll probably still be in hospital.' Ringo smiled reassuringly.

'I'm just worried about my mum, really,' said Ben. 'She'll be in such a state.'

'Why don't you call her again now?' Lee said. 'You told her you would.'

Ben took the phone out into the hallway so that he could have some privacy. He dialled the number and told her everything that had happened, each step of the way trying to make her see it from his point of view, telling her not to be angry. She made him promise to come down the following day so that they could talk about it in more detail and he could be interviewed by the police. He gave her Eddie's name and told her that she could pass on the information.

After he'd hung up, Lee came out into the hallway and sat down on the floor beside him.

'Are you OK?' he asked.

'Yeah, but this is only the beginning. God knows what I'm going to have to go through with the police.'

'I heard you saying that you were going back home tomorrow.'

'I've got to,' said Ben.

'Of course. Do you want me to come with you?'

Ben thought for a moment before saying, 'I'd like you to, but I don't know whether my mum's ready for that yet. It's not that I'm ashamed of you; I just think she needs to take things one step at a time.'

The two boys sat in the hall, just looking at one another.

'Lee?'

'What?'

'Would you kiss me, please?'

Lee leaned forwards and, putting his arms firmly around Ben, he kissed him hard on the mouth, then pulled away for a moment, and then he leaned back in and kissed him more deeply, their tongues meeting and moving around in one another's mouth.

'Let's go upstairs,' said Lee.

They climbed the stairs and went into the bedroom Ben had thought he might never see again. The bed was neatly made and his things were just where he'd left them. Gently, Lee pushed him down on to the bed and, with more passion than ever before, he

187

positioned himself on top and kissed him deeply. Ben opened his mouth and took his friend's tongue inside. It felt great to be united with him in this way. He could feel the lad's hands running under his T-shirt and on to his bare flesh, touching his hard little nipples and caressing under his arms. He put his hand on Lee's arse and squeezed it. He longed to taste it once again and to suck his cock and drink down his semen.

Ben took off his top and put his hands behind his head. He wanted to make it plain what Lee should do. The lad started to kiss his stomach, softly running his lips and the tip of his tongue over Ben's smooth skin. He moved his mouth around the sides and then up towards the top, kissing the nipples when he got there and taking them one at a time into his mouth and gently biting on them. A shudder ran through Ben's body as he put a hand behind his friend's head and stroked his hair, encouraging him to stay in position, suckling on him.

When Lee had finished there he put his face to the area under Ben's arms and inhaled the scent of him. He then licked and nuzzled the fine hairs and kissed all around the muscular arms and shoulders. Ben's cock was straining hard in his trousers and a ripple of excitement passed through his body when Lee touched him there.

'Look, before we go any further, I really need to have a shower,' said Ben. 'All the time I was being held prisoner, I didn't get to wash once.'

'OK. Why don't we have one together?'

Ben thought that this was a great idea and he eagerly agreed. They left the bedroom, taking a towel with them, and went into the bathroom. Lee locked the door behind them and switched on the water in the shower. He turned to Ben and helped him take down his trousers, kissing him all the time and touching his naked body. Ben did the same in return, until they were both undressed, their cocks stiff, standing on the cold, tiled floor.

They stepped into the shower and Lee adjusted the temperature so that it wouldn't scald them. He closed the translucent glass door and they put their arms around one another and kissed, the water splashing down over their faces and bodies.

Ben let his hands explore every inch of the lad's body, taking it all in and rubbing his fingers into all the parts one would never normally see. Lee was doing the same to him, and there was something so pleasant about the feel of the water hitting him and the hands over his body. All the while, he investigated his friend they continued to kiss, Lee sometimes moving down on to his neck and gently biting him there, which sent a shiver through his body. The lad would occasionally gently lick and bite his ear, which also felt great.

Soon Ben decided that it was time to wash and he lathered up the soap and started to rub it over his chest.

'I'll do that,' interrupted Lee. So Ben stopped and the lad took the soap from him and washed him with it. He cleaned all over Ben's chest and under his arms, then he turned him around and scrubbed his back. To Ben, however, it felt more like a very slow massage than being washed. The lad's hands moved down and down until they were soaping the small of his back and then they were on his buttocks, making them slippery with soap suds. He knew that Lee would not be able to resist sliding them between his cheeks, and he was not wrong. He felt fingers travelling along the groove and brushing over his sensitive hole, and then one of them pushed its way inside. The soap made it so easy that Ben hardly felt it, just the pleasant sensation of it twisting around inside him and Lee sliding it out again. The whole process was repeated several times, while he used his other hand to either stroke Ben's arse-cheeks or to gently caress his erection which was raging out of his control. It felt so great having a soapy hand teasing his prick that in some ways it was even better than getting sucked off.

Ben turned around so that his friend could focus exclusively on his cock. The lad put more soap on his hands and then handed the bar over. Ben started to lather his own hands while Lee caressed his balls and, pulling his foreskin right back, stroked the exposed head of his penis. Ben reached down and took hold of his friend's parts as if in imitation and did the same to him.

The feeling of the lad's hands was so intense that Ben wanted to cry out; it almost tickled him, but even from that there was pleasure to be taken. All the while, he stroked Lee's prick, which felt as hard as a rock in his hands. He drew back the foreskin with every movement and then let it slide back over the head. His other hand reached between the lad's legs and rubbed along the length of his perineum. He stopped at the arsehole and pushed his slippery finger inside. The prick in his hand seemed to grow harder and he saw the boy's balls tense and cling closer to his body.

Lee moved Ben's hands away and put both of the pricks together in his own hand and massaged them side by side. It looked so sexy for them to be comparing penises, measuring them up against one another and letting them slip about and get a thrill in the process. Ben added to the moment by holding both his and the lad's balls together and rubbing them about.

After a while, Lee started to kiss him again and then took down the shower head and hosed them both off, washing away all the soap suds. He then fell to his knees, water falling freely over his head, and started to suck on Ben's cock. He stretched back the foreskin and worked on the head, moving his mouth up and down at a furious rate, which sent shudders through Ben's body.

After a few minutes of this Lee reached up for the bar of soap once again and lathered up his hands – one he used to squeeze Ben's balls, and the other he employed round the back, sliding it into Ben's crack, then teasing his hole and eventually inserting it deeply inside. He continued to suck at the same time, taking the penis right down so that his lips were around the base and the balls bounced against his chin. He then inserted a second finger alongside the first and twisted both of them around while they were right up Ben's bottom, shoved in to the knuckle.

Ben could feel that fantastic feeling that started in his balls and travelled towards the base of his penis and then across his body, when he knew that he was starting to come. He went with it, allowing the lad to take him there, the fingers working hard against his prostate and Lee's lips stimulating the head of Ben's prick with their repeated movements. He felt himself start to orgasm and then the first spurt came out and into Lee's mouth. This was followed by others, and Ben could tell that his friend was swallowing everything he produced. He carried on ejaculating until there was nothing left inside him. Lee, however, continued sucking on him, as if he was trying to draw more liquid out.

Ben pulled his cock free and stood under the warm shower water panting and empty. Lee let his fingers slide out and he stood up and kissed him on the mouth. Ben signalled for him to turn around, which he did, and he knelt down in the shower and bent his friend forwards a little and parted his legs so that his buttocks separated and he was able to get better access to the lad's bottom. He parted the cheeks further with his hands and Lee's arsehole came into view. He immediately put his lips to the area around the opening and pushed his tongue into it, trying hard to pry it open as he did so. However, it wasn't that easy, and he was only able to push a tiny way inside, the lad's hole being so tightly muscled. So Ben put the tip of his forefinger into the opening and used that to enlarge it, twisting it around and pushing it in and out, trying to loosen the boy. Then he reapplied his tongue and found that it was easier to push inside now. He continued to rim the lad, sometimes delving in with his tongue, making the passage slippery with saliva, sometimes with a soapy finger, and sometimes both going into him at the same time. When this happened Lee let out little whimpers that Ben did not know whether to interpret as whimpers of pleasure or of discomfort.

After some minutes of this, Ben left his friend's bottom alone and turned him around so that he could focus on his cock instead. He pulled back the loose skin and ran his tongue and his lips over the swollen purple head. He could detect – even with the force of the water coming down from above and washing most things away – a steady trickle of pre-come that oozed from the tip of Lee's prick. He swallowed this, which was unavoidable anyway, as he was sucking so hard on the long member. Ben's own prick returned to its erect state. He felt a hand at the back of his head and Lee pushed him down harder so that even more of the lad's penis slid into his mouth, enough to almost make him gag. However, once the shaft had slid in and out a few more times, Ben became accustomed to it going so deep and was able to take it without any difficulty. He caressed the lad's balls and let his other hand travel between his legs and a finger dip into his tight hole and press firmly against his insides.

Lee let out a groan of pleasure and all of a sudden Ben felt the head of the cock harden and a squirt of semen shoot out of it. He swallowed this and the next few emissions which were thick and tasted salty. Ben kept his finger forced up inside the lad throughout and he could feel the muscles in there contract and loosen as he orgasmed.

When he had finished releasing his liquid, Ben let his cock go and then lapped at the final dribbles of semen that came out afterwards. Both boys were relieved and relaxed and the water continued to fall down on them, warm and cleansing.

'I'm so glad that this is all over,' said Ben as he packed a bag.

'What do you mean?' Lee was laying down on the bed.

'The business with Eddie kidnapping me. What did you think I meant?'

'I thought you were talking about this house and the job . . . and me,' Lee added, a little sheepishly.

'Well, that's a point.'

'What?' Lee sat up.

'Maybe this is the end of all that.' He paused, then added, 'The house and the job I mean. Not you.'

'Phew.'

'I don't really know what I'm going to do. Just go home, get all this sorted out and then take a while to think things through.'

'Do you think you'll come back to London?' asked Lee.

'I don't know.' Ben stopped what he was doing and came over to the bed. He sat down next to Lee. 'Perhaps I ought to do my A levels.'

'I thought that was what you were running away from.'

'It was. But things change. I've changed. Anyway, we always end up running away from the place that we ran away to.'

'Very profound,' said Lee. 'But where do I fit into all this?'

'Well, that depends on what you're going to do next.'

'I guess that this house and Eddie's pimping is over now, so we'll have to find something else to do.'

'Are you going to stay on in London?' asked Ben.

'I don't know. I might go back to Glasgow for a while.'

'When things have calmed down at home, will you come and visit me?'

'Of course.' Lee kissed Ben lightly on the lips and they were silent for a while.

'I guess I could write about my adventures,' said Ben. 'It'd certainly make a gripping novel.'

'A dirty novel, more like.' Lee chuckled to himself.

'Yeah, maybe that's what I'll do – become an erotic writer.' He looked out of the window.

'No. I wouldn't bother, if I were you.'

Ben glanced back at him, puzzled. 'Why not?' he asked.

'Because I expect it's all been written before.'

Ben laughed and once again turned his eyes to the window.

Epilogue

'Morning,' said his mother as Ben entered the kitchen. 'I'm just doing you some breakfast.'

'Smells nice,' he said, opening the fridge in search of orange juice. How he'd missed the luxury of food being cooked for him and not even having to buy it himself. He got a glass, poured some of the freshly squeezed juice into it and sat down at the kitchen table.

'Did you sleep well?'

'Yes, fine.'

His mother put a plate down in front of him with scrambled eggs, bacon, mushrooms and toast on it. Ben felt ravenous and was pleased to see all his favourite breakfast things before him. He started eating straight away.

'What classes have you got today?' asked his mother.

'English and history.'

'That's nice, dear.'

'Not really. English is OK, but I hate the history tutor. He's so boring.' Ben carried on eating. He was keen to get to his sixth-form college and get the lessons over and done with as swiftly as possible because afterwards he was meeting Paul for a drink.

When his breakfast was gone and his mother had already started to wash up the plate, Ben went up to his room and sorted out his books, putting the ones he needed for the day into a bag, along with paper, pens and his Walkman. He switched his stereo on to standby and left, closing the door behind him.

Out in the street, he breathed in the cool September air and looked up at the trees, some of the leaves having already turned to gold and ready to fall. The few that lay on the pavement crunched under his feet, and Ben found something satisfying about treading on them. It was only at this moment that the kidnapping came back into his mind. A day seldom went past in which he did not think about what had happened in London, but today it had taken all this time for the thought to come to him. As usual he dismissed it, trying not to put himself through the trauma of turning old events over in his mind.

When he got to the college and went into the students' common room, the first person he saw was a boy named Michael who was in the second year, like him. The problem was that everyone in his year had got to know each other ages ago, but since he'd only just started attending and didn't need to go through the basics that you were taught in the initial year, he was finding it hard to make friends. However, Michael had been very nice and was one of the few people who seemed bothered enough to talk to him and even hang around with him between classes.

'Hi,' said Ben.

'How are you?'

'Not too bad.'

'I was just wondering, Ben, whether you wanted to go for a drink or something after college today?' asked Michael.

'I'd like to, but I've already promised to see someone else. Perhaps tomorrow.'

'Yeah, that'd be cool.'

Ben wondered whether Michael wasn't just a little too friendly. He didn't want to doubt his motives for inviting him out, but there was something that told him the kid fancied him. Ben didn't mind that – he was quite attractive and seemed really sweet, and it was always flattering to have someone after you. He had never realised that even in a small town there were still boys who liked boys and that if you had a bit of patience and looked out for the signs you'd get the rewards in the end.

When he thought about it more he rather hoped that Michael did have a crush on him. It'd be exciting to be conducting a secret affair with another boy and for no one else in the college to know about it. That had never happened at school so he could make up for it now.

'What class have you got now?' Michael asked.

'History.'

'Yeah?'

'Yeah. Boring.'

'Are you going to be in English later?' the boy asked.

'Absolutely.'

'Oh, well, I'll see you then. And we'll go out for that drink tomorrow, OK?'

'OK,' said Ben. 'It's a date.' He didn't think Michael had heard his last sentence because the lad had walked off to his class, and in a way he hoped he hadn't because it sounded a bit suggestive.

Ben gathered up his belongings and went off to his own classroom.

Michael stayed with him throughout the lesson, sitting at the same table as him and whispering comments about the tutor or some college gossip into his ear. And when it reached four o'clock and the end of the day, he followed Ben out of the room and down the corridor.

'So, who are you meeting?' he asked, adding, 'That's if you don't mind me asking.'

'It's just an old friend of mine from school. He's about to go off to university so I want to see him before he does.'

Michael nodded and there was a difficult moment where Ben knew that he wanted to pull away but it was as if the boy wanted to say something.

'So, I'll see you tomorrow?' said Michael.

'Yes.' He turned and walked down a different corridor and out into the afternoon light.

★

Paul was sitting behind a table with a half-empty pint glass in front of him. He was smoking a cigarette and looking at two women standing near the bar. Ben saw him first and paused before calling his name or going over. It was interesting just to watch him when he didn't know he was being watched. You were able to get some sense of how the person was when you weren't around and when they thought they were anonymous.

After a few seconds Ben walked over to the table and made his presence known so that Paul wouldn't think he was being spied on. He was dressed casually in combat trousers and a short-sleeved check shirt which suited him and showed off his strong shoulders and fit body.

'Hi, Ben,' he said.

'Who were you looking at?'

'Those two birds at the bar. What do you think?'

Ben glanced over at them and said, 'They're OK.'

'Do you want a drink?'

'Don't worry. I'll get it,' said Ben. 'Are you all right with what you've got?'

Paul nodded and Ben walked over to the bar and ordered himself a pint of cider which he took back to the table and sat down opposite his friend. He thought to himself how good his friend was looking. Paul's hair had been cut short at the sides and back but was still floppy on the top with a long fringe that hung down over his eyes. Ben couldn't help but look deeply into his eyes.

'I'm glad you decided to do your A levels again,' said Paul. 'It doesn't really matter. It's only a year and then you've got them out of the way and you can go on to university or whatever.'

'Yeah, I know.' He sipped his drink. 'And the college is so much better than the school sixth-form. You call the teachers by their first names and there's no uniform or rules or any of that crap.'

'Sounds cool,' said Paul.

'I can't believe you're off to uni, though. I'm really jealous.'

'Yeah, it should be good. I'm really looking forward to it, actually.'

197

The two boys talked of their futures and what they hoped to do over the next few years. Paul did not mention London or the kidnapping and Ben was glad. They'd discussed it when he came home after the ordeal, but from then on it was rather a taboo subject and Ben preferred it that way. He wanted to move on from that and put his life back together. Maybe one day he would be able to laugh about it and treat it as just another piece of history, but at the moment it was still fresh in his mind and upsetting to dwell on.

'Have you made any new friends at the college?' asked Paul.

'Yes. A couple. But it's hard when you're the new boy, isn't it?'

'I've got all that to come when I start at Bristol. Although as soon as you've met a few people, then you get to meet their friends and eventually you find that you know everyone.'

As they talked Ben couldn't help thinking about that night in the tent in Paul's garden at the beginning of the summer. It all seemed so long ago now, such a long time before all the trouble began. It had been so great doing what they did to one another, but Ben knew that it was all just the sexual attraction of a drunken moment. There was no substance to it. Paul had never mentioned it again and he knew that it was not a moot point, which was a shame because he still found the lad extremely attractive.

They agreed to meet again later in the week to say goodbye before Paul's weekend departure. He made Ben promise to come and visit him at university and said they would go out to the student union and the local bars and that it would give him an insight into what university life was like for when Ben himself decided to go away and do a degree.

'You *are* going to write to me as well, aren't you?' asked Ben.

'Of course. And I'll telephone. But you've got to promise that you'll make your visit in the first term, because I expect I'll need as much support from my old friends as I can get.'

Ben sat in the classroom looking out of the window. It was history again and he wasn't very interested in what the tutor was saying. Nineteenth-century politics wasn't very inspiring, but he knew that he wanted to pass the A level or else there wouldn't be any point in being there in the first place, so he opened his notebook and tried to write down some of the things that were being said.

He looked at his watch – only fifteen minutes until the class was over. He was supposed to meet Michael afterwards and go for a drink with him. The boy knew nothing about his past, only that he'd dropped out of school just before the exams and now he was retaking. He didn't know what to tell him because there were bound to be questions. The lad was sweet and quite sexy and he didn't want to say anything that would suggest he had somehow been involved in dodgy things. He hoped that they were going to get on well and that Michael was interested in being more than a friend, and, for once, would make the first move and make it easy for him to say yes.

When the lesson had ended he walked out of the room and in the direction of the common room where he said he'd meet Michael. However, when Ben got there he was nowhere to be seen, so he sat down in one of the comfortable chairs and watched the door.

Soon enough Michael came in looking a little flustered and hot, a pile of books and papers clasped in one hand and a can of coke in the other.

'Sorry I'm late,' he said coming right up to Ben and smiling a cute, boyish smile.

'You're not late at all. Anyway, we've got plenty of time. There's no rush.'

'I guess so.'

There was a difficult moment when neither of them spoke and then Ben laughed and suggested that they go to a quiet pub he knew of on the other side of town.

It was a bright, warm afternoon, perfect for a slow walk, and the two boys looked at the scenery and the passers-by and chatted quietly about their classes and the place where they lived and books and parents and life in general.

When finally they arrived at the pub Ben felt tired and thirsty. The pint he ordered was refreshing and he drank two big mouthfuls at the bar before he'd even paid for it. Then they found a table away from the other drinkers and sat down opposite one another.

Ben felt good about the fact that he was the older of the two. Michael, he presumed, must still only be seventeen, and he was almost nineteen now. The lad looked young for his age, so Ben bought the drinks just to make sure that the barman didn't query Michael's age and embarrass him by asking for ID.

Ben lit a cigarette and smiled across the table.

'Do you want one?' he asked.

'No. I don't really smoke.'

'Very wise. I used to think that you could never get addicted, then one day I realised that I was.'

There was a pause in the conversation and then Michael asked, 'Why did you drop out of school, if you don't mind me asking?'

'Oh, it was just that at the time I didn't think that I wanted to bother with A levels and university. Now I've changed my mind.'

'Right.'

'Do you want to go to uni?' asked Ben.

'Oh, yes. I can't wait.'

They talked more and Ben bought further drinks. It was still mid-afternoon and light outside, and as usual at that time of day it was easy to get drunk very quickly. After three pints Ben felt pleasantly intoxicated and he leaned across the table as he spoke, staring into the boy's eyes. This almost seemed to embarrass Michael who looked away and down at his drink.

When he looked at his watch again, he noticed that it was nearly seven o'clock. His mother always made dinner for about that time and he didn't like to be late. Ben explained this to his new friend, who looked disappointed but seemed to understand.

They finished their drinks and left the pub. Michael walked part of the way with him and they stopped when they came to the turning Ben had to take but the other boy didn't.

'I really enjoyed that,' said Michael.

'So did I.'

'I wish you could've stayed out later.'

'Sorry,' said Ben, as a poor apology.

'We ought to do it again soon.'

'Yes. How about the weekend?'

Michael eagerly agreed and Ben jotted down his phone number so that even if they didn't see one another at college he'd still be able to get in touch with him. They said their goodbyes and parted, Ben walking quickly in the direction of his house.

After dinner, the telephone rang and Ben let his mother answer it.

'It's for you,' she called out.

Ben went into the hall and put the receiver to his ear.

'Hello,' he said.

'Hi,' said Lee's voice at the end of the line.

'I haven't spoken to you in ages.'

'I know. How's it going?'

'Fine,' said Ben. 'I've started at the sixth-form college, which is great, and it's only one year and then I take the exams, so it's not like I'm going back over loads of stuff or anything.'

'Cool,' said Lee.

'Where are you calling from?'

'London.'

'So, you didn't go back home in the end?' asked Ben.

'No. I've managed to get a flat with Ringo. It's a bit of a dump, but at least it's our *own* dump. And I've got a job in an office, of all places.'

'I didn't think that was your style,' joked Ben.

'Neither did I. But you never do know until you try something. It's OK – pays well. I can stick at it for a while until something more interesting comes along.'

'Sounds like you're really getting it together.'

'Yeah. It's all right.' There was a pause and then he said, 'I miss *you*, though.'

'I miss you, too.' Ben said this without thinking, but he really did miss Lee. They'd had some brilliant times together and it was sad to think that they were apart now. All the others had only been also-rans for his affection. Lee was special. However, there was no way he was going to go back and live in London and he

201

somehow didn't think his mother would take kindly to putting the lad up in her house, so they had to live apart. Perhaps in a few years' time things would change and there'd be the chance for them to be geographically close and then maybe something would start up again. But for the time being Ben had to get on with his study and try to carve out a future for himself.

'Are you going to come down and see me?' He hadn't seen Lee since he'd left London almost two months ago. He hoped that the lad would come down and see his life, his friends and the way he lived.

'Of course. It was difficult before, but now I've got this job it means that I've got some more money and I can jump on a train. It's not very far, is it?'

'No,' said Ben.

'We'll arrange something soon.' There was silence for a second and then Lee asked, 'Are you seeing anyone at the moment?'

'No.'

'No one on the scene?'

'Well,' said Ben, 'maybe.'

'What's his name?'

'Michael. But it's nothing serious. I just think he's got a bit of a crush on me, that's all.'

'And do you like him?' Lee asked.

'He's OK . . . Well, he's really quite cute.' Ben felt guilty about saying this to Lee. It was as if he was being unfaithful to him or going behind his back. 'Do you mind?'

'No. You've got to do whatever you want. You've got to do whatever makes you happiest.'

'I guess so,' said Ben.

IDOL NEW BOOKS

HOT ON THE TRAIL
Published in January Lukas Scott

The Midwest, 1849. *Hot on the Trail* is the story of the original American dream, where freedom is driven by wild passion. And when farmboy Brett skips town and encounters dangerous outlaw Luke Mitchell, sparks are bound to fly in this raunchy tale of hard cowboys, butch outlaws, dirty adventure and true grit.

£7.99/$10.95   ISBN 0 352 33461 4

STREET LIFE
Published in March Rupert Thomas

Ben is eighteen and tired of living in the suburbs. As there's little sexual adventure to be found there, he decides to run away from both A-levels and his comfortable home – to a new life in London. There, he's befriended by Lee, a homeless Scottish lad who offers him a friendly ear and the comfort of his sleeping bag.

£7.99/$10.95   ISBN 0 352 33374 X

MAESTRO
Published in May Peter Slater

A young Spanish cello player, Ramon, journeys to the castle of master cellist Ernesto Cavallo in the hope for masterclasses from the great musician. Ramon's own music is technically perfect, but his playing lacks a certain essence – and so, Maestro Cavallo arranges for Ramon to undergo a number of sexual trials in this darkly erotic, extremely well-written novel.

£8.99/$10.95   ISBN 0 352 33511 4

Also published:

CHAINS OF DECEIT
Paul C. Alexander

Journalist Nathan Dexter's life is turned around when he meets a young student called Scott – someone who offers him the relationship for which he's been searching. Then Nathan's best friend goes missing, and Nathan uncovers evidence that he has become the victim of a slavery ring which is rumoured to be operating out of London's leather scene.

£6.99/$9.95   ISBN 0 352 33206 9

DARK RIDER
Jack Gordon

While the rulers of a remote Scottish island play bizarre games of sexual dominance with the Argentinian Angelo, his friend Robert – consumed with jealous longing for his coffee-skinned companion – assuages his desires with the willing locals.

£6.99/$9.95   ISBN 0 352 33243 3

CONQUISTADOR
Jeff Hunter

It is the dying days of the Aztec empire. Axaten and Quetzel are members of the Stable, servants of the Sun Prince chosen for their bravery and beauty. But it is not just an honour and a duty to join this society, it is also the ultimate sexual achievement. Until the arrival of Juan, a young Spanish conquistador, sets the men of the Stable on an adventure of bondage, lust and deception.

£6.99/$9.95   ISBN 0 352 33244 1

TO SERVE TWO MASTERS
Gordon Neale

In the isolated land of Ilyria men are bought and sold as slaves. Rock, brought up to expect to be treated as mere 'livestock', yearns to be sold to the beautiful youth Dorian. But Dorian's brother is as cruel as he is handsome, and if Rock is bought by one brother he will be owned by both.

£6.99/$9.95   ISBN 0 352 33245 X

CUSTOMS OF THE COUNTRY
Rupert Thomas

James Cardell has left school and is looking forward to going to Oxford. That summer of 1924, however, he will spend with his cousins in a tiny village in rural Kent. There he finds he can pursue his love of painting – and begin to explore his obsession with the male physique.

£6.99/$9.95   ISBN 0 352 33246 8

DOCTOR REYNARD'S EXPERIMENT
Robert Black

A dark world of secret brothels, dungeons and sexual cabarets exists behind the respectable facade of Victorian London. The degenerate Lord Spearman introduces Dr Richard Reynard, dashing bachelor, to this hidden world.

£6.99/$9.95   ISBN 0 352 33252 2

CODE OF SUBMISSION
Paul C. Alexander

Having uncovered and defeated a slave ring operating in London's leather scene, journalist Nathan Dexter had hoped to enjoy a peaceful life with his boyfriend Scott. But when it becomes clear that the perverted slave trade has started again, Nathan has no choice but to travel across Europe and America in his bid to stop it. Second in the trilogy.

£6.99/$9.95   ISBN 0 352 33272 7

SLAVES OF TARNE
Gordon Neale

Pascal willingly follows the mysterious and alluring Casper to Tarne, a community of men enslaved to men. Tarne is everything that Pascal has ever fantasised about, but he begins to sense a sinister aspect to Casper's magnetism. Pascal has to choose between the pleasures of submission and acting to save the people he loves.

£6.99/$9.95   ISBN 0 352 33273 5

ROUGH WITH THE SMOOTH
Dominic Arrow

Amid the crime, violence and unemployment of North London, the young men who attend Jonathan Carey's drop-in centre have few choices. One of the young men, Stewart, finds himself torn between the increasingly intimate horseplay of his fellows and the perverse allure of the criminal underworld. Can Jonathan save Stewart from the bullies on the streets and behind bars?

£6.99/$9.95   ISBN 0 352 33292 1

CONVICT CHAINS
Philip Markham

Peter Warren, printer's apprentice in the London of the 1830s, discovers his sexuality and taste for submission at the hands of Richard Barkworth. Thus begins a downward spiral of degradation, of which transportation to the Australian colonies is only the beginning.

£6.99/$9.95   ISBN 0 352 33300 6

SHAME
Raydon Pelham

On holiday in West Hollywood, Briton Martyn Townsend meets and falls in love with the daredevil Scott. When Scott is murdered, Martyn's hunt for the truth and for the mysterious Peter, Scott's ex-lover, leads him to the clubs of London and Ibiza.

£6.99/$9.95   ISBN 0 352 33302 2

HMS SUBMISSION
Jack Gordon

Under the command of Josiah Rock, a man of cruel passions, HMS *Impregnable* sails to the colonies. Christopher, Viscount Fitzgibbons, is a reluctant officer; Mick Savage part of the wretched cargo. They are on a voyage to a shared destiny.

£6.99/$9.95   ISBN 0 352 33301 4

THE FINAL RESTRAINT
Paul C. Alexander

The trilogy that began with *Chains of Deceit* and continued in *Code of Submission* concludes in this powerfully erotic novel. From the dungeons and saunas of London to the deepest jungles of South America, Nathan Dexter is forced to play the ultimate chess game with evil Adrian Delancey – with people as sexual pawns.

£6.99/$9.95   ISBN 0 352 33303 0

MORE AND HARDER
Morgan

This is the erotic autobiography of Mark, a submissive English sadomasochist: an 'SM sub' or 'slave'. Rarely has a writer been so explicitly hot or so forthcoming in the arousingly strict details of military and disciplinary life.

£7.99/$10.95   ISBN 0 352 33437 1

BOOTY BOYS
Jay Russell

Hard-bodied black British detective Alton Davies can't believe his eyes or his luck when he finds muscular African-American gangsta rapper Banji-B lounging in his office early one morning. Alton's disbelief – and his excitement – mounts as Banji-B asks him to track down a stolen videotape of a post-gig orgy.

£7.99/$10.95   ISBN 0 352 33446 0

EASY MONEY
Bob Condron

One day an ad appears in the popular music press. Its aim: to enlist members for a new boyband. Young, working-class Mitch starts out as a raw recruit, but soon he becomes embroiled in the sexual tension that threatens to engulf the entire group. As the band soars meteorically to pop success, the atmosphere is quickly reaching fever pitch.

£7.99/$10.95   ISBN 0 352 33442 8

SUREFORCE
Published in November   ### Phil Votel

Not knowing what to do with his life once he's been thrown out of the army, Matt takes a job with the security firm Sureforce. Little does he know that the job is the ultimate mix of business and pleasure, and it's not long before Matt's hanging with the beefiest, meanest, hardest lads in town.

£7.99/$10.95   ISBN 0 352 33444 4

THE FAIR COP
Published in December   ### Philip Markham

The second world war is over and America is getting back to business as usual. In 1950s New York, that means dirty business. Hanson's a detective who's been dealt a lousy hand, but the Sullivan case is his big chance. How many junior detectives get handed blackmail, murder and perverted sex all in one day?

£7.99/$10.95   ISBN 0 352 33445 2

–––––––––✂––––––––––––––––––––

Please send me the books I have ticked above.

Name ....

Address ....

....

....

.... Post Code ....

Send to: **Cash Sales, Idol Books, Thames Wharf Studios, Rainville Road, London W6 9HA.**

US customers: for prices and details of how to order books for delivery by mail, call 1-800-805-1083.

Please enclose a cheque or postal order, made payable to **Virgin Publishing Ltd**, to the value of the books you have ordered plus postage and packing costs as follows:

UK and BFPO – £1.00 for the first book, 50p for each subsequent book.

Overseas (including Republic of Ireland) – £2.00 for the first book, £1.00 for each subsequent book.

We accept all major credit cards, including VISA, ACCESS/MASTER-CARD, DINERS CLUB, AMEX and SWITCH.

Please write your card number and expiry date here:

....

Please allow up to 28 days for delivery.

Signature ....

–––––––––✂––––––––––––––––––––

WE NEED YOUR HELP . . .

to plan the future of Idol books –

Yours are the only opinions that matter. Idol is a new and exciting venture: the first British series of books devoted to homoerotic fiction for men.

We're going to do our best to provide the sexiest, best-written books you can buy. And we'd like you to help in these early stages. Tell us what you want to read. There's a freepost address for your filled-in questionnaires, so you won't even need to buy a stamp.

THE IDOL QUESTIONNAIRE

SECTION ONE: ABOUT YOU

1.1 Sex (*we presume you are male, but just in case*)
     Are you?
     Male   ☐
     Female   ☐

1.2 Age
     under 21   ☐   21–30   ☐
     31–40   ☐   41–50   ☐
     51–60   ☐   over 60   ☐

1.3 At what age did you leave full-time education?
     still in education   ☐   16 or younger   ☐
     17–19   ☐   20 or older   ☐

1.4 Occupation _____

1.5 Annual household income _____

1.6 We are perfectly happy for you to remain anonymous; but if you would like us to send you a free booklist of Idol books, please insert your name and address

_____

_____

_____

_____

SECTION TWO: ABOUT BUYING IDOL BOOKS

2.1 Where did you get this copy of *Street Life*?
    Bought at chain book shop ☐
    Bought at independent book shop ☐
    Bought at supermarket ☐
    Bought at book exchange or used book shop ☐
    I borrowed it/found it ☐
    My partner bought it ☐

2.2 How did you find out about Idol books?
    I saw them in a shop ☐
    I saw them advertised in a magazine ☐
    I read about them in _____
    Other _____

2.3 Please tick the following statements you agree with:
    I would be less embarrassed about buying Idol
    books if the cover pictures were less explicit ☐
    I think that in general the pictures on Idol
    books are about right ☐
    I think Idol cover pictures should be as
    explicit as possible ☐

2.4 Would you read an Idol book in a public place – on a train for instance?
    Yes ☐   No ☐

SECTION THREE: ABOUT THIS IDOL BOOK

3.1 Do you think the sex content in this book is:
    Too much ☐   About right ☐
    Not enough ☐

3.2 Do you think the writing style in this book is:

       Too unreal/escapist ☐   About right ☐

       Too down to earth ☐

3.3 Do you think the story in this book is:

       Too complicated ☐   About right ☐

       Too boring/simple ☐

3.4 Do you think the cover of this book is:

       Too explicit ☐   About right ☐

       Not explicit enough ☐

Here's a space for any other comments:

SECTION FOUR: ABOUT OTHER IDOL BOOKS

4.1 How many Idol books have you read?

4.2 If more than one, which one did you prefer?

     _____

4.3 Why?

SECTION FIVE: ABOUT YOUR IDEAL EROTIC NOVEL

We want to publish the books you want to read – so this is your chance to tell us exactly what your ideal erotic novel would be like.

5.1 Using a scale of 1 to 5 (1 = no interest at all, 5 = your ideal), please rate the following possible settings for an erotic novel:

       Roman / Ancient World   ☐

       Medieval / barbarian / sword 'n' sorcery   ☐

       Renaissance / Elizabethan / Restoration   ☐

       Victorian / Edwardian   ☐

       1920s & 1930s   ☐

       Present day   ☐

       Future / Science Fiction   ☐

5.2 Using the same scale of 1 to 5, please rate the following themes you may find in an erotic novel:

Bondage / fetishism ☐
Romantic love ☐
SM / corporal punishment ☐
Bisexuality ☐
Group sex ☐
Watersports ☐
Rent / sex for money ☐

5.3 Using the same scale of 1 to 5, please rate the following styles in which an erotic novel could be written:

Gritty realism, down to earth ☐
Set in real life but ignoring its more unpleasant aspects ☐
Escapist fantasy, but just about believable ☐
Complete escapism, totally unrealistic ☐

5.4 In a book that features power differentials or sexual initiation, would you prefer the writing to be from the viewpoint of the dominant / experienced or submissive / inexperienced characters?

Dominant / Experienced ☐
Submissive / Inexperienced ☐
Both ☐

5.5 We'd like to include characters close to your ideal lover. What characteristics would your ideal lover have? Tick as many as you want:

Dominant	☐	Caring	☐
Slim	☐	Rugged	☐
Extroverted	☐	Romantic	☐
Bisexual	☐	Old	☐
Working Class	☐	Intellectual	☐
Introverted	☐	Professional	☐
Submissive	☐	Pervy	☐
Cruel	☐	Ordinary	☐
Young	☐	Muscular	☐
Naïve	☐		

Anything else? _____

5.6 Is there one particular setting or subject matter that your ideal erotic novel would contain?

_____

5.7 As you'll have seen, we include safe-sex guidelines in every book. However, while our policy is always to show safe sex in stories with contemporary settings, we don't insist on safe-sex practices in stories with historical settings because it would be anachronistic. What, if anything, would you change about this policy?

_____

_____

SECTION SIX: LAST WORDS

6.1 What do you like best about Idol books?

_____

6.2 What do you most dislike about Idol books?

_____

6.3 In what way, if any, would you like to change Idol covers?

_____

6.4 Here's a space for any other comments:

_____

_____

_____

_____

Thanks for completing this questionnaire. Now either tear it out, or photocopy it, then put it in an envelope and send it to:

Idol
FREEPOST
London
W10 5BR

You don't need a stamp if you're in the UK, but you'll need one if you're posting from overseas.